About 'Roads to Down'

Every day at First Base we see young people who are slowly but surely destroying their lives with a variety of drugs. Many of these young people have taken the Road to Down and reached the place where nothing seems worth living for any more: the place where the sanctuary of suicide seems preferable to the grinding misery of carrying on with life. Several of these young people are only with us today due to the absolute excellence of the Dumfries and Galloway emergency services.

The headlines in the media say that we are the fourth richest country on planet Earth. We have an abundance of food, unprecedented opportunities and, thanks to our grandparents who slammed the door in Hitler's face, the freedom to vote for who we like and say what we think. No generation has had more going for it and yet no generation has ever been so depressed. 'Roads to Down' is about how drugs play a part in sending so many young lives into darkness. The stories don't come from New York or London or Amsterdam. They come from here. Scotland 2006. The characters are made up, but what happens is only too real.

Life is all about Choices. Read 'Roads to Down' and you'll find out a little about the stuff that the global drugs industry likes to keep under wraps. Check out the downside. And then if you choose to spend your cash on these products, at least do so with your eyes open. We see too many young people who have sleepwalked into a life of utter misery without really having a clue of the risks they are taking.

To find out more:
log on to **www.first-base.org**
or call **01387 279 680**

1 – 9 Copies	**£1.75**
10 – 99 Copies	**£1.50**
100 – 999 Copies	**£1.25**
1000⁺ Copies	**£1.00**

A Glenmill Publication

First published in 2006

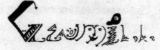

Glenmill Publishing

Dumfries

Scotland

DG2 8PX

tel: 01387 270 861

http://www.thecull.com

British Library Cataloguing in Publication Data.
A catalogue record of this book
is available from the British Library.

ISBN 0 9551057 2 2

Glenmill logo: Andrew Carroll AKA 'Gizmo'

Printed and bound in Great Britain

The First Base Agency and Gretna Football Club

The First Base Agency is a charity based in Dumfries. We advise and support families who are affected by the drug, alcohol or gambling problems of a loved one. We also offer information and advice on these issues to the community at large. A big part of this work involves our going into primary and high schools across the region giving awareness workshops to pupils, parents and teachers.

Over the last few years the Gretna Football Club 'Football in the Community Programme' has grown dramatically. Their team of coaches is now working with over a hundred schools as well as numerous community groups. The goal of the programme is to use football as a positive influence in the lives of the community from where the club draws its support – especially the young people.

In the autumn of 2005 we agreed to work together. Now the First Base Agency carries out drug and alcohol awareness work in the schools working with the 'Football in the Community Programme.'

Class sets of 'Stoppage Time' are available to all of these schools

About the Author

'Stoppage Time' is Mark Frankland's tenth novel and since 1999 he has sold over fifty thousand novels. His 2001 book, 'The Cull', took him deep into the heroin nightmare that has gripped Dumfries and Galloway for several years. After the success of 'The Cull', Mark and his partner, Carol, opened The First Base Agency in Dumfries which is an information, advice and support centre. The First Base Agency offers help to people who are affected by someone else's drug, alcohol or gambling problem, as well as being widely involved in providing the community with education and information.

To find out more about The First Base Agency,
log on to **www.first-base.org**

and to find out more about Mark and his books
log onto **www.thecull.com**

An introduction
from Brooks Mileson

MANAGING DIRECTOR, GRETNA FOOTBALL CLUB

Having grown up on a North-East council estate myself, I have seen with my own eyes the devastating affects drug and alcohol abuse can have on children and their families. From when I first became involved with Gretna Football Club, one of my main objectives was to evolve Gretna FC into a community club in every sense of the word. Not just in football coaching, but with education to children of all ages. I believe that it is the moral responsibility off EVERY football club to be actively involved in the community and that sport honestly makes a difference.

We at Gretna teamed up with The First Base Agency about 18 months ago. Mark Frankland and his staff are doing a remarkable job going into schools and educating children about drugs as well as providing advice and support from their office in Dumfries.

Mark approached me last year about the idea of writing a book chronicling the life of a young boy who gets mixed up with drugs and who is eventually redeemed through football. The book is not only an enthralling read but sends out a powerful message on the problems of drug and alcohol abuse in our society and that football can make a real difference if the club cares and is willing to tackle the problem in a constructive and positive fashion.

Brooks Mileson

Contents

PART ONE

Jimmy Doyle hated February. He had always hated February for as long as he could remember because somehow it was the only month of the year that seemed to have absolutely nothing going for it.

He parked up his car and took in the view around him with a slight grimace. It wasn't the kind of scene that the advertising firms hired in by the Scottish Tourist Board would ever choose to lure visitors to the land of lochs and glens. The adverts were all about vivid green and gold and sunshine sparkling on the dawn waters of misty lakes. Out of the car window the world was all over grey. A grey sky. Grey pebbledash walls. Grey hills all but invisible through the curtain of mean rain that had leaked down for the best part of a week.

Sunnybank Estate wasn't the kind of place that they showed on the Visit Scotland websites. Sunnybank didn't do salmon fishing and mountain bike hire. The shops didn't sell post-cards and boxes of souvenir fudge. There was no tourist information board. No brown signs guiding visitors to attractions with tea shops.

Not a chance.

Sunnybank Estate was the wrong side of the Dumfries tracks and had been that way since it had been built half a century earlier. Sunnybank was the place where a person with no housing points would be offered a flat. It was home to eight thousand people and hardly any jobs. The government was forever banging on about Britain having the fourth largest economy in the world. House prices were sky-rocketing. Employment levels had never been higher. Apparently the nation was basking in a golden era of lots of jobs and loads of money.

Yeah right.

As Jimmy stared out past the doleful sweep of the windscreen wipers there was little sign of the wonderful world of the thirty-second sound bite. In some ways Sunnybank was indeed booming. It was big on unemployment and teenage mums and heroin. Statistics proved it to be a less favoured area in need of social improvement. Men in suits were forever announcing action plans to make Sunnybank a better place to live. It always sounded great and nothing ever happened. Announcements and initiatives. Promises. Lots and lots of promises. Broken promises.

The promises of local government were right up there with February as far as Jimmy was concerned. For five years he had been in charge of the Sunnybank Rovers youth team and for five years they had been playing their games on a miserable rutted pitch with no pavilion. A pitch that wasn't fit to graze a goat let alone play football on. Every time he switched on the TV to see a smug-faced politician preaching on about how young people should play more sport and take more exercise he felt like putting a brick through the screen. Words, words, words. Young people are getting obese. Young people are addicted to their Playstations. Young people are taking too many drugs. Young people are behaving anti-socially. Young people should learn some proper respect and get out there and give up their seat on the bus for a pensioner and kick a football around and take on board a few cubic litres of fresh air.

Words, words, words.

For five years he had been trying to argue that the young people of Sunnybank needed something better than the lousy expanse of grass that lay beyond the windscreen wipers. There had been lots of earnest men in M&S suits with receding hair and cloying after shave. They lived in offices where you had to sign in and be given a name badge like you were paying a visit to CIA headquarters in Langley, Virginia. They would welcome him in with forced smiles and offer coffee and sometimes biscuits. Then they would proceed to talk in a language that meant about as much to him as Mongolian. They would rattle on about corporate strategies at the interface of local provision and the assessed needs of local service users. They would emphasise that they were non-judgemental and all their decisions would be made with a proper sympathy for minority groups. They always looked very grave and quite agreed that Sunnybank was an a area that faced community challenges and was in need of measures to enhance its levels of social inclusion in line with all relevant strategies and interfaces and protocols. How they loved to hide behind their jargon and miserable desks. But of course none of them lived in Sunnybank. Most of them avoided the place like a plague. They wouldn't send their kids within a mile of Sunnybank High School and they would probably have preferred to have their teeth pulled with rusty pliers rather than park their treasured Mondeos in any of the Closes.

Over the years Jimmy had tried every tactic he could think of to try and get them to agree to come up with a better pitch with new goalposts and some drainage and changing rooms with showers. He had tried being polite and dressing up in a suit himself. He had bought a briefcase and taken lessons from his son Jamie on how to create impressive-looking documents on the PC. He had tried stomping about offices in a tracksuit and getting mad and thumping their treasured desks. He had written endless letters and emails to councillors and MPs and MSPs. Hour after hour and day after day and month after month.

And year after year.

And here he was on a miserable wet Saturday morning in godforsaken February and still the under 16's would be playing on the same sorry excuse of a pitch that they had played on for the last thirty years. The radio had moved on to the weather forecast and some woman from South Wales seemed to find the find the fact that it was going to chuck it down for at least another three days the funniest thing she had ever heard. Her chipper, isn't life just fab voice was more than he could stand and he snapped the radio off and reached for the anorak on the back seat. Time to crack on.

He stepped out of the relative warmth of his steamed-up car into the damp misery of the outside world. The rain hung from the sky in sheets and a thin wind pushed it into his eyes.

Bloody marvellous. The joys of grass roots football. It all seemed an awfully long way away from the Persil adverts where beaming kids played in front of lots of cheering parents on pitches that were as flat as pancakes surrounded by green trees with branches filled with chirping nightingales.

Yeah right.

He gave an angry shake of his head, aware that he was being a miserable old git. It wasn't as if anyone was forcing him to look after the Sunnybank under 16s. It was his choice and his alone. It had been so for five years and he could chuck it in any time he liked so it was pretty stupid moping about. He pulled on a wool hat and popped the boot to dig for his thick rubber gloves and dog poop kit. As he bent into the boot a sudden gust of wind sent cold water down the back of his neck and made him jump in surprise. The jump thumped his head into the boot.

Grass roots football on a wet weekend when the rest of the sane world was indoors reading newspapers and eating toast. And suddenly the whole thing was bad enough to make him smile. After all, when all was said and done it was still a red letter day. It didn't really matter that it was wet and cold and that Sunnybank looked like some place on an Amnesty International poster because for the very first time in their mediocre history the Sunnybank Under 16's had made it through to the semi finals of the Rotary Cup and victory over Redhill United would carry them into the final.

When Jimmy had taken on the job five years earlier such a thing would have made flying pigs seem like a regular sight. In the early days his main task had been to somehow find a way of getting eleven bodies onto the pitch at all, let alone thinking of semi finals. In those early days it had been a result if defeats could be contained to single figures. His second game at the helm had seen six Sunnybankers sink to a seventeen-nil defeat and it would have been a whole lot worse if the ref hadn't taken pity and cut the game short by twenty minutes.

For many years Sunnybank had propped up every local league they had played in. They were more or less a laughing stock with their woeful pitch and tatty kit and their inability to find enough players for a full team. Coaches came and went but mainly went. There would have been no chance in a million years that Jimmy would have taken on the task without the nagging of his son. At eleven Jamie Doyle was an unusually tall boy who was the rock at the heart of his primary school team's defence. His ease on the ball and sureness in the tackle had earned him a successful trial with the Borough. He could have played in any of the local teams and one or two had actively tried to recruit him but all of his mates played for Sunnybank so he wanted to play for Sunnybank. Jimmy had told him that he was nuts and that he

CHAPTER ONE

should sign on for one of the teams with a flat pitch and proper coaches and decent kit: one of the teams who could manage to put eleven men on the pitch as well as a couple of substitutes. One of the teams where there were always plenty of volunteer parents to do the taxi work for away fixtures. One of the teams who were organised enough to have a Sportsman's dinner once a year to raise some cash. Not Sunnybank because Sunnybank was a joke and always would be.

Jimmy had assumed that his words of parental wisdom would be taken on board and it had been the first time that he had come to know the rebellious streak in his son. Jamie had told him that sticking by mates was loads more important than going somewhere just because they had some decent kit. The whole thing had developed into quite a row which had ended with Jamie being packed off to his room and told to mind his lip if he didn't want a proper hiding. His son's bitter words had been clear in his ears despite being shouted from behind a closed door.

"What do you have to do with it anyway? You won't have nothing to do with football. You're always saying so. Not even on the tele. Why don't you just leave me alone?"

This was true enough. Jimmy had made his vow not to have any truck with football in any way, shape or form thirteen years earlier at the age of twenty-one. It had been on the day which had started off as the best of his life and finished as the worst. Like his son, at eleven Jimmy Doyle had been a shoe-in for the Borough team and it had stayed that way all through his junior career. He was a right winger who had a natural engine which worked for ninety minutes every time. He had pace, good feet and a football brain that showed him how to find space and make a pass. He made his debut for Queen of the South at seventeen and two years later he was transferred to Kilmarnock in the first division. At twenty-one he was an ever present and the papers were making noises about him being one of Scotland's brightest young prospects. Everything had seemed possible. There had been talk of a move to one of the Glasgow giants or even a trip south of the border to England. The local paper spotted an ex-Celtic player at two home games and some modest research revealed that the man in question was working as a scout. All of this made his first trip to play at Parkhead the biggest day of his young career. He was finally about to step out onto the biggest stage in Scotland and ahead the road to glory lay open. As he walked out into the shadows of the huge stands of the famous old ground he had felt a sense of destiny. All the training and the games on rutted Sunday morning pitches had brought him to this culminating moment. He had arrived.

Ten minutes later he was being carried from the pitch on a stretcher with a white hot pain in his leg that was worse than any pain he had ever known in his life. The next day a doctor had spent some time looking at X-Rays pinned on a lightbox and had shaken his head. He had said that he was sorry. Really sorry. Everyone was. It was the cruciate ligament and it was the worst he had ever seen. The club had sought a second opinion. And a third. And a fourth. But every opinion had been the same. Career ended. Finished. Wrapped up. Done and dusted. Jimmy Doyle's football life was frozen in time like a mammoth under the Siberian ice. His name would slowly but surely be forgotten. Remember that Jimmy Doyle? Young lad. Played on the wing in the early eighties. Got a couple of caps for the Under 21s. Got crocked up at Celtic. After five years he was forgotten, a ghost face in sticker annuals from the 1985 season gathering dust in the bottom of bedroom cupboards.

For a while his anger at what had happened had been as white hot as the pain that had signalled the end of his dreams. He had lived out a couple of months at the bottom of a bottle, fighting anyone he could and spending a couple of nights in the cells. Then his dad had driven up to Ayrshire and dragged him back to Dumfries to dry out and calm down. It had been on a cold, wet February morning that he had taken a long walk in the rain and vowed to have nothing to do with football ever again. Not on the TV. Not on the radio. Not anywhere. Football had waved the dream in front of his eyes and pulled it away just at the moment when he seemed to have reached it. It was the only way that he could make any sense of anything.

A mate managed to get him a start as a postman and slowly but surely he came to terms with a much different life to the one that had for a while seemed possible. Every day he was up and about early and walking the empty streets delivering small town mail sharing a few words with morning dog walkers. He avoided the billboards outside newsagents shops which announced football headlines. At break times the other lads would devour the back pages and the same banter as working men shared all over the world. Who was up for a transfer.

CHAPTER ONE

Who was up for the sack. Who would stay up. Who would go down. And they would try to draw him in because he had been a part of it and he was expected to have an inside track, but he would just shake his head and focus on the crossword.

Slowly but surely the mental and physical wounds healed. Jock Stein died of a heart attack in Cardiff as Scotland made it to the World Cup finals in Mexico where Archie Gemmill scored the goal of a million re-runs. Maradona dumped England out care of 'The hand of God' and the people of Scotland laughed their collective socks off. On cold mornings his leg was stiff and sore, but after a couple of years it was only when he was asleep that the football career that never was came to haunt him. He had a recurring dream where he saw the Celtic left back closing the space between them in grinding slow motion. Every instinct told him what was about to happen and no matter what he did, he couldn't drag his leg clear of the full set of studs that was bearing in on the inside of his knee. And then at the moment that the deadly steel touched his leg he would jump awake in a sweat and he would relive the memory for a while in the dead hours of the night before going back to sleep.

In 1987 he married his long time girlfriend Helen and a year later they bought a property on the edge of Sunnybank. Jamie arrived in 1989 by which time he was well and truly in the habit of ignoring football completely. It never crossed his mind to watch Match of the Day or to listen out for any results at quarter-to-five on a Saturday. But as the twentieth century drew to a close, it started to become more difficult. At parents' evenings Jamie's teachers told him that the lad was coming on a treat at his football. It was like father like son, but the son could never understand why his dad would never come along to watch. This became the core of many a row with Helen. What had his stupid leg got to do with their son? How did he think it made Jamie feel when he never turned up and most of the other dads did? She dug his Under 21 caps out from the attic one day and Jamie put them up on his wall along with old newspaper cuttings charting the prospects of the Kilmarnock right winger who was an outside bet to make the plane for Mexico. Jimmy had gone ballistic when he saw them and had been about to tear them down only to be stopped by his son's tears.

It had been a turning point. The following Saturday he had broken his vow and turned up to watch Jamie in the Soccer Sevens and had been impressed with the boy's poise and time on the ball. Soon they were kicking a ball in Sunnybank's excuse for a park where father refused to allow son to use his right foot in order to strengthen the left. Soon mates started to appear to join in the kickabouts, drawn by the sight of the Under 21 caps on the bedroom wall and the press cuttings which confirmed that their local postman with the limp had once been on the brink of making it big. This had been the time of the row about Jamie finding a better club than Sunnybank which in the end had led to an even greater turning point for Jimmy Doyle.

Sunnybank FC faced many problems, but the greatest of these was that for years they had never had any kind of proper coach. Dads would give it a go for a week or two only to get fed up with the lack of players. The ones who did turn out never seemed to be able to come up with the £1.50 sub money. Without a proper coach involved, there was never anyone to get anything organised which of course meant that the club was in a permanent state of chaos.

Jimmy realised that he suddenly had a choice to make. He could continue to argue with his son and hassle him to find a well-run club well away from the streets where they had both grown up. Yes he could do that. Just like every other dad on Sunnybank. After all, life was difficult enough. Who needed wet weekend mornings when seven turned up with empty pockets to get a proper stuffing by clubs with a full eleven in sponsored kits. It was hardly anyone's idea of a dream ticket. That was the easy choice. The sensible choice. And the more he thought about it he realised that it was also the cop out choice.

He had been taking cop out choices for years. From the very second he had felt his ligaments ripping under the challenge at Park Head he had been in a dark sulk with the world in general and his own life in particular. It suddenly hit him that he was well into his thirties and spending his life in neutral, pushing mail through letterboxes and wondering how things might have been but for a mistimed tackle. At the rate he was going his life would drift along like an unnoticed plastic bottle floating down the river Nith. One day he would get out of bed and it would be the day that his mates would give him a clock for the mantelpiece and that would be that. A whole life frittered away in a forty-five year sulk. So, sure. He could do that. It was the easy option. The soft option. And as he stared at the TV it hit him that when the clock day came he would have to come to terms with what a waste it had all been, and dealing with that would be a whole lot harder than dealing with the loss of his career. Worse still, he would be an old man and his life would all be behind him and there wouldn't be much road left in front.

It meant that the choice was whether or not it was time to leave the comfort zone. Time to stick his neck out again and try and do something worthwhile. He wasn't about to hitch a ride down to sub Saharan Africa to solve the Aids crisis. Neither was he going to hop a plane to Jerusalem and bring peace to Palestine. But taking on Sunnybank Football Club was something that he could do. Later he was amazed at how quickly he had made his mind up. His vow never to have anything to do with football had lasted nearly fifteen years. He made the decision to dump it in less than fifteen minutes. With a small nod of the head he rose from his chair and made his way upstairs to Jamie's door.

"OK then. If you insist on playing for Sunnybank I suppose you lot will need a proper coach. You can tell the lads Wednesday night. Five o clock. And there's going to be no pratting about."

He liked to think that there was no other reason for his mid-life U-turn other than a realisation that it was time to do the right thing for his son and the area he had grown up in. But in his heart of hearts he knew it wasn't entirely true. He had been along to watch Jamie in the soccer sevens three times and he had been duly impressed with the way the lad had shaped. He had potential. No doubting that. If he kept on growing and stayed keen, then there was every chance he could get somewhere. Maybe even Queen of the South. It was impossible to say if it would be any further than that. His son was a decent player, no doubt about it. But being merely a decent player wasn't remotely enough. He knew the game well enough to be realistic. Any lad who was destined for the Premier leagues of either Scotland or England needed to stand out like a beacon at the age of eleven. As a rule of thumb, the ones who made it to the top were easy to spot. They were the strikers who scored five every match. The midfielders who were never off the ball. The defenders who tackled everything that moved. Jamie stood out as a proper decent player. But he wasn't exceptional. Which of course was fair enough.

A big part of Jimmy wasn't remotely unhappy that it was not all that likely that his son would make it into pro football. More than most, he was well aware of what a brutal career choice it could be. Jamie had always shaped up pretty well in school and it would probably be much better that he focused on collecting a few decent exams and went on to do something a whole lot less risky.

But there had been one player who had stood out on the morning of the soccer seconds and from where Jimmy Doyle had been standing it had seemed like he stood out like a giraffe in a pen full of guinea pigs.

Danny McCann.

Which actually made Jimmy feel semi-spooked because in a way it was like watching history repeat itself. When Jimmy had played for the borough at eleven years old, so had his best friend Bill McCann. In those days it had been Jimmy who had always been the stand out player. The one who caught every watching eye with his pace and poise. Bill had always been Mr Solid. The thoughtful centre back who made up for a lack of pace with a natural sense for position. By the time Jimmy was turning out for Queens' reserves, Bill had more or less packed up football as he discovered the joys of Friday nights out on the town. But their friendship had stood fast as Jimmy moved up to Kilmarnock whilst Bill stayed on in Sunnybank and got himself a job with the Post Office. It had been Bill who had swung Jimmy his start as a postman when he had come back home to Dumfries with a messed up leg in 1985. Then in the late nineties they had slowly drifted apart. Bill's world had been blown into a million pieces one afternoon, when he had returned home from work to find a note on the kitchen table from his wife letting him know that she had left town with a neighbour and that she wouldn't be coming back. Three months later a postcard landed from Australia confirming that the new state of affairs was very much permanent. Bill had no more seen it coming than Jimmy had seen how his life would be flipped on its head by one fateful tackle.

Bill had tried his best to manage the task of holding down his job, keeping house and bringing up Danny on his own. For a few months it seemed as if he might have been up to the job but things slowly unravelled. He started to take solace at the bar of the local pub after work, where he could wash away the nightmare of his life with pint after pint of Tennants washed down by whisky chasers. He started being late for work, and when he arrived his eyes were bleary-red and his brain was slower than an overloaded coal wagon. Complaints about misdelivered letters were inevitably tracked back to his beat and, although his supervisor was sympathetic with his situation, the day of his sacking was always going to arrive. With no job, Bill's slide down the slippery slope accelerated. Once a fortnight he would blow his Giro in one manic night in the pub and for the next thirteen days he would barely leave the house. Jimmy had called round as much as he could with bags of groceries and a shoulder for his old friend to cry on, but their relationship became increasingly strained. Bill's life may have fallen to bits but his pride was still intact. He told Jimmy he didn't need sympathy. He told him to get stuffed and not to come back. He told him to leave him be. For a while Jimmy ignored the abuse, but in the end he had decided that enough was enough and he left Bill to sort out his demons on his own.

As his dad sank lower and lower, Danny started to run wild. Sunnybank had always been a place of rumours and by the time the new Millennium arrived, young Danny McCann was often at the centre of many a conversation in the Spar or the Chip Shop or the Post Office. It was generally agreed that the boy was turning into a proper wrong un. Trouble he was. And it was only going to get worse. All down to his dad, so it was. Of course it was a tough break that his cow of a wife had hopped it to Australia, but even so. He was allowing that Danny to turn into a proper little swine. As Danny grew older, the gossip-mongers were never short of material. The wardens pulled him for spraying that phone box, so they did. The coppers took him in for throwing stones from the bridge over the by pass. Elsie Tompkins caught him trying nick a bottle of wine in the off licence. There were tales of vandalism and fighting and foul language and bullying. More and more parents issued solemn instructions to their kids that it was a one hundred percent grounding offence if they were caught playing with that Danny McCann. It was as if the lad had had his name changed by deed poll. He was seldom just Danny McCann any more. He was almost always referred to as 'that' Danny McCann.

By the time he reached P6 at Sunnybank Primary School he was seldom to be found in any of its classrooms. When he wasn't excluded he was playing truant. Social Workers and Youth Justice workers became a regular sight at the door where they would be met with abuse by Bill with his hair all over the place and a roll up hanging from his lips. Jimmy and Helen had been the very last couple to stop Danny from coming round to the house. They had tried for as long as they could stand it, but one day a twenty-pound note had disappeared from Helen's handbag and they had decided that enough was enough. The boy was all but unmanageable.

One day when Danny was eleven the Social Workers had arrived along with a police car and the boy was taken from the house kicking and screaming and cursing with an array of swear words that would have done any soldier proud. It had seemed like all the wheels had finally fallen off the McCann wagon. They had taken the slide all the way down to the place from where there was no way back. There was lots of talk about it being a bloody shame, and about how that rotten cow should be ashamed of herself, legging it to Australia like the jumped-up tart that she was. Danny was spotted one day out with foster parents in Stranraer by a neighbour who drove a van for the council. The word was that there was no way that he would be coming back to Sunnybank. That was him away. Not many tears were shed. Everyone assumed that Bill would complete the journey all the way down to the bottom of the gutter. It was a shame, but it wasn't exactly a rare story on Sunnybank. Families broke up almost every day, and when they did it was only too common for one of the partners to turn to drink or drugs or both, whilst social workers and health visitors tried to pick up the pieces.

However Bill McCann surprised everyone. The nightmare of watching the police and social workers drag his son from the house was enough to snap him out of self-destruct mode. He stopped drinking, washed his clothes, cleaned the house and eventually got himself a job on the bins. His key workers were suitably impressed and Danny was returned to his care in time to enrol as an S1 at Sunnybank High School on the first day of term.

It soon became apparent that it hadn't only been McCann senior who had changed. Danny's Stranraer interlude had made a single huge change in his life.

Football.

The foster family had a son of the same age who was football daft so it had been only natural for Danny to go along to training with him. At first Danny had hated the idea. Training meant coaches and being told what to do and getting in bother when he didn't do it. Football

CHAPTER ONE

was all right. He had played a bit in the playground at primary school, but once every parent in the area warned their kids off playing with him, there had been very few occasions that he had been involved in anything approaching a real game. He went along to the first night of Stranraer training with a solid determination to do nothing and thereby get out of having to go again. The whole foster family thing was a shock to the system, and it was a full time job keeping up an attitude that would make sure that his temporary family would soon get sick of him and have him returned to Sunnybank. He found their patience confusing. When he did things that would have been guaranteed to send his dad into a complete tantrum, his foster parents would sit him down instead and suggest that they all talked things through. No matter what he did he couldn't manage to break through their quiet reasonable voices. He generally resorted to stomping off to his room at the top of the house, but as the days went by he was beginning to feel a little foolish.

When he had arrived at the pitch a cheery coach had tossed him a yellow bib and asked what his position was. Danny had shrugged and stared down at the grass. The coach had suggested he give it a go up front and had introduced him to his team mates.

All of a sudden it hit Danny that not a single one of boys had been told by their parents not to play with him. In fact, none of them had ever heard of him. As far as they were all concerned he was just Danny. Not Danny McCann. Certainly not 'that' Danny McCann. And for the first time in years he was part of a group who were quite happy to have him with them. And he thought why the hell not. What was the problem? A game of football would do no harm.

Half an hour later he had scored nine goals and a rather stunned coach was asking if he was up for playing for the sevens on Sunday morning. And an equally shocked Danny had said sure why not. He was still struggling to make sense of what had happened. He hadn't had the first idea that he was any good at football. The way that his new team mates had reacted to him made it abundantly clear that he was. Not just fairly good. But dead good. Seriously good. And all of a sudden he was part of a team and everyone was happy about it and no parents would be having a word with the coach and saying that they didn't think it a very good idea if 'that' Danny McCann was allowed to play. Because in Stranraer he wasn't 'that' Danny McCann.

He was just Danny and for the very first time since his mum had walked out whilst he was at school, being Danny didn't feel all that bad. That night he stayed down and watched a DVD and cleaned his teeth before bed.

Over the next few months both McCanns started to turn things around. In Sunnybank father dried himself out and after his first day at work he told his neighbour that it made a change to be collecting junk rather than delivering it. The only time he went to the pub was to watch the football on the large screen TV and when he ordered himself a Diet Coke there were small nods from other drinkers who had watched him take the slide. Seventy miles to the west, Danny's football career was taking off. His first showcase was the Sunday morning Soccer Sevens where he averaged four goals a game. It wasn't long before he was turning out for the Borough team and still the goals flowed. Those who watched him shared the opinion that he could be one of the rare ones who had what was needed to make it all the way. He was naturally fit and seemed never noticed it when he was kicked. He had the balance of a lad from a circus and it never seemed to make any difference which foot he chose to use. In front of goal he was casually deadly, generally choosing to pass the ball into the corner rather than belting it.

But the thing which really stood out for those with a trained eye was the time he always seemed to have. In the wild chaos of the small pitch games, it was almost as if he had a force field around him. When Danny was on the ball everything seemed to slow down. The second hand on the watch halved its speed. He was always able to control the ball without thinking about it and find the time to take a look around him and knock away a pass or a shot.

When Bill had at last persuaded the children's panel that he was ready to resume care of his son, Danny was fast-tracked straight into the Dumfries Borough eleven and the coach of the Sunnybank High School S1 eleven could hardly wait to work with him. When he came home he was still 'that' Danny McCann. But it was a rather different 'that' Danny McCann now. It wasn't often that wee Danny McCann who should be locked away somewhere. It was that Danny McCann who might just be good enough to make it to the Premier league one day. Did you hear that Danny McCann got four for the Borough last week? That Danny McCann's training up at Queens now? Looks like that Danny McCann's sorted himself out at last. Just like his dad.

Danny could have had the pick of any team in the district but he had chosen Sunnybank because it was where most of his mates from the school team played. It was the first real team he had ever really felt a part of and he wasn't about to break ranks just because somewhere else they had a better pitch and changing rooms. Danny's presence meant that Sunnybank started to win a few games which was something new, but they were never about to set the world on fire without a proper coach.

Jimmy Doyle of course was one of the ones who knew what he was watching when he first clapped eyes on young Danny on his first morning watching the sevens. He had felt mixed emotions that Sunday. On the one hand he was amazed at the depth of the lad's natural talent. One the other hand there was guilt because he had been one of the parents who had said that Danny McCann wasn't welcome at his home any more. He had slammed the door in his face and left him to roam the streets and get into bother just like the rest of Sunnybank. That evening he had taken a few deep breaths and gone round to see his old friend Bill for the first time in years. The Bill McCann who opened the door was a far cry from the chaotic Bill who had taken the slide to the gutter. His hair was once again cut and combed and his clothes were freshly washed and pressed. When he saw Jimmy his eyes had frozen over.

"Alright Bill."

"Jimmy."

"Long time I suppose."

No answer. Just cold eyes not blinking.

"Going to invite me in then?"

"No."

Jimmy had shuffled uncomfortably. This wasn't how it had been supposed to be.

"Like that then is it?"

"Aye Jimmy. It's like that."

And still the eyes didn't blink. Instead they seemed to burrow into Jimmy. Sharp. Piercing. Accusing. Unforgiving. Eyes that would not forget betrayal. Jimmy was desperate for something to say but in his heart he realised there was no point. Bill had been there for him when he had hit skid row. He'd met him off the train from Ayrshire and got him a start as a postman. He'd seen him right. Jimmy had tried for a while when the boot was on the other foot but he'd quit. And he had slammed the door in young Danny's face when it had been the last door in Sunnybank that was still open. It obviously wasn't a thing that Bill McCann was about to let ride.

Jimmy shrugged. "Fair enough. I'll be seeing you Bill."

"Don't hold your breath."

Jimmy had been about to try something else but the door was already closed in his face. The cold contempt of his old friend had bothered him for weeks and so it had been that on the night that he had decided to take on the job of coaching Sunnybank he had got up from his chair and thrown on his coat. Helen had glanced at the clock and seemed surprised.

"Where you off to love?"

"Mission impossible I expect. But you've got to try haven't you."

The small smile on her lips suggested that she had guessed where he was headed.

"I dare say you do. Best of luck."

Outside it had been a wet night with a thin biting wind lancing up and down the mean streets of grey houses. Jimmy pulled up his collar and strode along as fast as his leg would allow. Five minutes later he knocked Bill's door and waited with his shoulders hunched against the cold and his hands as far into his pockets as they would go. The eyes had lost none of their ice when the door opened.

"You again. Maybe I never made myself clear last time Jimmy."

"You were clear enough Bill."

"Good. Off you go then."

Jimmy stuck out the foot of his good leg and stopped the door when it was six inched short of slamming in his face again.

"I'm going to be coaching Sunnybank Bill."

Bill took a look down at the foot in his doorway and stiffened with anger.

"What do you want me to do about it? Give you a bloody merit badge or something. Move your foot Jimmy."

"I'll move it when I'm ready. I don't want a merit badge. I want some help. Both our lads play for them Bill. Come along and give me a lift."

Now there was astonishment as well as ice on Bill's face.

"Are you tapped or something? You just don't get the message do you?"

"Yeah Bill, I get the message. Loud and clear pal. You're mad as hell and you hate my guts. So what are you going to do then? Stay angry and sulk for the rest of your life. I know about that Bill. Did it, didn't I? Did it for years and bloody years. Or are you going to put all this stuff behind you and come along and do a bit of coaching? It's Wednesday at five o'clock. Up to you Bill."

Jimmy caught sight of Danny's face watching from the lounge door. "Alright Danny."

"Hello Mr Doyle."

Bloody hell. Hello Mr Doyle. Jimmy wondered what they put in the water in Stranraer. He would have never expected a hello Mr Doyle from Danny. Things were obviously changing.

"You going to be coaching us then Mr Doyle?"

"Aye. That's right enough son."

"What about you dad? You coming along as well."

Bill's eyes never left Jimmy's and it seemed as it the ice might not have been quite as thick.

"Wednesday you say?"

"Aye."

"I'll think about it."

And he had thought about it. And when the first training session of the new regime kicked off the following Wednesday night Bill had shown up with Danny and started the process of putting their friendship back on the rails.

That had been five years ago and in the intervening period the fortunes of Sunnybank Football Club had slowly but surely moved steadily forward. Jimmy oversaw all of the age groups and managed to cajole a further three coaches into getting involved. Bill took on the year group that included their two sons and the semi final against Redhill United was the culmination of all their efforts. Danny's progress had continued to be spectacular and everybody involved was waiting for the phone to ring with the news that he had made the squad for the Scottish Under 16 side. He had scored a hat trick in the last trial match at the end of January and so it seemed that it was more than likely that good news was on the way. Jimmy had done his best to keep expectations as low as possible. He had been involved in the national youth squads when he was a boy and was well enough aware that it was doubly hard for any lad from outside the central belt to get a break. One thing he knew for certain was that if Danny's name wasn't on the squad list there would be some pretty fiery phone calls headed the way of the Scottish FA. The issue of playing for Sunnybank was a burning one for Danny just as it had been for Jamie five years earlier. Just about every team from the Premier league had been to town to try to sign him onto their feeder squads but he had turned them all down. Bill had tried to get him to see some sense and even Jimmy had done his bit feeling that it was only fair, though deep down he dreaded the thought of losing his star man. This feeling was made all the stronger because of his own son's decision to knock football on the head. When Jamie had turned fourteen he had started wearing an array of mainly black clothing that was generally covered in safety pins. He had dyed his hair jet black and spent impressive amounts of time in front of the bathroom mirror gelling and arranging spikes.

Jimmy had been on the verge of an outburst for months but had been ordered to hold his tongue by Helen who had pointed out that Jamie was young and young people were different to middle-aged postmen whose hair was getting a bit thin on top. He had even held his tongue when Jamie had emerged from his bedroom one Friday night en route to the Ice Bowl disco with a ring dangling from his bottom lip. Father and son had stared each other down until Helen had called him to the kitchen to help peel some potatoes. When the front door banged closed he could hold his tongue no more.

"Bloody hell, did you see that?"

"What?"

"That thing. In his lip."

"The ring?"

"Yes. Of course the bloody ring."

"And your point is?"

He rolled his eyes. "What do you think my point is! Jamie's gone out with a bloody ring on his gob! That's what my point is."

"Oh for goodness sake Jimmy lighten up. If he wants to wear a ring in his lip it hardly makes him an axe murderer. He's at an age where he needs to search for his personality."

Now he rolled his eyes so far round the sockets that they almost got stuck. "You're just as bloody bad. Search for his personality!

That's the sort of stuff that comes from too much of that American trash on the tele. Hell, if I'd gone out looking like that I'd have been a laughing stock."

"No doubt you would. But might I remind you that the world has moved on a little. Mandela isn't in prison any more and the Berlin wall is all knocked down, and Jamie and his mates haven't even heard of Maggie Thatcher. I'm afraid you're sounding like a dinosaur darling. Now get on with those spuds or we'll be having them for breakfast."

The lip ring was obviously viewed rather differently once Jamie arrived at the Ice Bowl disco, particularly by a young gothette called Sin who sported a similar jet black spiked look to Jamie and had a lip ring that could have been a metallic twin to his. Sin was in fact a working on her real name which was Cindy and a name that she considered far too girly to be any kind of appropriate mantle for a Goth. A few weeks later the pair of them emerged from his bedroom on their way to a fifteenth birthday party across town, both wearing expressions that were a mixture of defiance and trepidation. As Jamie approached down the stairs Jimmy squinted to make sure that his eyes weren't playing tricks on him. By the time his son reached the bottom stair his father realised with a sinking feeling that his eyes were indeed working just fine.

Jamie was wearing eye shadow.

His son. At fifteen years old.

And he was wearing eye shadow.

Unbelievable.

Once again Helen was on hand to whisk him away before he threw a tantrum and the black clad pair were able to escape through the front door and into the night leaving a memory of half-buried sniggering. Eye shadow was the final straw. The ring had been bad enough, but eye shadow . . . no way. No bloody way. What would the lads say if they saw him? It didn't bear thinking about. No. Enough was enough. No son of his was about to go mincing about Sunnybank done up like a girl's blouse and that was final. Helen fell out with him completely and when he asked her what was for tea she told him to get lost and buy a bag of chips because she wasn't in the mood to cook for a middle-aged sod like him. And to make matters worse she had even said that it would do Jamie no harm to make an effort to get in touch with his own feminine side. That had been the final straw and he had slammed the door on all such suggestions and all but choked on his chips. Too much American TV. Far too much. Get in touch with his feminine side. Where the hell did she think they were living? San Fransisco? Greenwich Village? Didn't the woman realise they lived on Sunnybank? Get in touch with his feminine side. As if.

The next day he ignored her stony silence and told Jamie that it was time for them to sit down for a talk. He had given the "no son of mine is poncing about the place in make up speech" and he had felt that he had made a pretty decent job of it. Jamie had slammed off and hibernated in his room, which was no more than Jimmy had expected. It was time the lad got a dose of the real world. After all he was fifteen and when Jimmy was fifteen he had been a sub for Queens' reserves. Make up and a lip ring. His son. No way. It was time to let everyone in the house know who was in charge. There wasn't much he could do to stop his wife turning out Tofu salad night after night whilst she played CDs of dolphins to stabilise her karma. Crazy, crazy. What a dolphin could possibly have to do with stabilising mental karma was way beyond him. What he did know was that Tofu seemed to be cardboard's cousin, and even if it meant he would live to a hundred-and-eighty-nine, he would still rather have a steak pie and chips.

When Jamie had emerged from his bedroom the following weekend both he and the spiked up Sin had worn expressions of extreme resentment. Well, fair enough. He hadn't expected anything different. What mattered was that his expression of extreme resentment was worn on a face that was devoid of any trace of make up. So it was a result.

"Hey and make sure you don't make it too late. Big game tomorrow."

Jamie didn't bother to turn around when he replied.

"Not playing."

"What do you mean?"

Now the boy turned and his eyes blazing.

"You heard. I'm not playing and you can't force me."

Unbelievable. "Please don't tell me that this has anything to do with me not letting you ponce about in make up Jamie. Please tell me that."

For a moment Jamie just stared him whilst Sin sucked at her teeth to create a sound used by teenagers the world over to register utter disgust at the naffness of the adult world. When Jamie eventually did speak there was a triumphant smirk on his lips.

"Like I said dad. I'm not playing. Not tomorrow. Not ever. There's more to life than football in case you hadn't noticed."

Exit front door. Slam. And Jimmy had just stood there with the look of a man who had just had a bucket full of iced water tipped over his head. At first he had been pretty sure that it would just be a passing tantrum. Helen painstakingly explained that the boy was beginning to assert himself. It was something that was entirely natural, especially now that he had a girlfriend to impress. But weeks had turned into months and months slipped into years. Sin moved on to pastures new when she took a shine to a lad from the rugby club who had a new Ford Fiesta, and she straightened her hair out in a hurry and put the lip ring away at the back of a drawer. But the departure of his gothette made not a jot of difference to Jamie's decision not to play football again. What only made it worse for Jimmy was that whenever he started out on a good old moan about the situation, Helen would never fail to remind him that the whole thing was a case of like father, like son. After all hadn't Jimmy taken a similar sort of vow himself after the tackle up at Parkhead. And when he thought about it Jimmy had to admit that she had a point although it would have choked him to admit it.

Once the wound had healed a little Jimmy began to see the funny side. Surely there couldn't be many coaches in Scotland who had lost the rock at the centre of their defensive plans as a result of an argument over make up. Maybe it might even have been a first.

The make up drama had been played out two years earlier and without Jamie the team had been built to revolve entirely around the talent of Danny. When the team had first come together as under 13s it hadn't taken Jimmy and Bill long to end the days when only seven or eight would turn up to play for Sunnybank. By the end of the season they were picking from a squad of at least twenty-five and they always had the luxury of three substitutes. But as the boys had got older the problem of enough bodies once again began to rear its ugly head. Some like Jamie simply got fed up with football and moved on to girls and going out. Others went for girls and going out but still wanted to play football, only they often couldn't get themselves out of bed in time for the match. Others missed matches due to last minute problems like getting picked up by the wardens for a variety of anti-social activity. Some days they would have eleven and a couple of subs. Other days they might only have eight or nine. But even with eight or nine they still managed to win more often than not so long as one of the eight or nine was Danny McCann.

Danny was Mr Ever-Present and had been so for five years. The days of being that Danny McCann were now far behind him. He had barely been in an ounce of bother at Sunnybank High School. The reason was very simple: football. Being in bother meant not playing for the school team and was a price far too high to pay. Once he was out of school Danny found that he had less and less spare time on his hands as he kept up with the demands of football. All of this kept him firmly on the straight and narrow and ensured that when it was time to leave the house for a Sunnybank fixture with his dad he was always up and ready.

"Morning Jimmy."

He hadn't heard Bill approaching as he had been distracted by walloping his head on the boot of the car. He turned round rubbing at the sore spot. Bill McCann grinned.

"Wee tip for you Jimmy. Banging your nut on an open boot tends to hurt a bit. Maybe you should bear that in mind in the future."

"Thanks for that little gem Bill. Alright Danny. Fit I hope."

Danny was trying not to snigger openly. "Aye. Nae bad Jimmy. Fitter than you I reckon."

Jimmy tossed them both a pair of rubber gloves and they lined up on the nearest goal line and started to walk slowly down the pitch. It was the Sunnybank pre match routine. The needle hunt. It was a thing that Jimmy could never get his head around. If someone got themselves addicted to heroin then so be it. Lord alone knew, there were enough residents of Sunnybank who had. It was like a twenty-first century plague. But why would anyone toss a used needle on a kids football pitch. It wasn't just careless. It was almost criminal. He had been told that nine out of ten injecting addicts were carrying the Hepatitis C virus which made the dumped needles potentially lethal. The thought that a young lad could be infected with such a horrible disease whilst out playing football made Jimmy almost sick with anger. In fact he felt that way about just about everything to do with heroin which had come to infect every corner of Sunnybank like a cancer.

To his left he heard a tutting sound. Bill stooped and gingerly

CHAPTER ONE

picked up their first syringe of the morning and dropped it into the old ice cream tub that they used to stow their pickings. The line of three moved up and down the pitch six times and found another two needles as the wind picked up a notch and sent the rain hard into their chilled faces. Once the needles were clear the next job was hanging the nets and then putting in the corner flags.

With the last flag in place Jimmy checked his watch. No problem. All done and dusted and half-an-hour in hand. A small figure approached him on a mountain bike that looked to be at least three sizes too big for him. It wasn't until the cyclist had closed to thirty yards that Jimmy realised that the boy under the hood was Sammy Phillips and his heart began to sink. Sammy Philips was little brother to Les Philips and Les Philips was their goalie. There was a small chance that Sammy was merely out for a Saturday morning ride on his bike but Jimmy didn't think so. The only thing that would have prized Sammy clear of his PS2 to ride a half-mile in the downpour was to bring bad news.

Here we go. He had hoped that since it was the semi final surely this would have been one of the rare mornings when they got a full eleven and a couple of subs. He had even tried open bribery after the last training session by promising a win bonus of a full McDonalds meal for the squad after the game.

"Morning Sammy."

"Aye. Morning Mr Doyle. Our Les says to say sorry, ken."

"And for what he is sorry Sammy."

"Him and Dave Fenton smashed a windi up at that old printing place on the industrial estate. They never thought there wasn't nobody watching like."

"But there was."

"Aye. One of the wardens, ken?"

"And?"

"He called the coppers like. And they came and took our Les and Dave to the station and they had to ring our dad and he was raging ken coz he was due to play darts and he had to ring and cancel and they couldn't get a reserve in time so when our dad brought Les home he proper planted him like." The sheer heroic length of the sentence, which had been delivered with but a single breath, made Sammy's eyes bulge. He took a huge gulp of air before finishing the epic tale.

"I mean proper battered him Mr Doyle."

"I see. I gather that all of this means that he isn't going to be available for selection this morning."

"Nah. He's grounded. Big time grounded."

"OK. Well thanks for telling me Sammy."

Losing a player at the last minute wasn't exactly a surprise. It was something that happened every week. However this particular loss would take rather more sorting out than normal. Both of his subs were smaller boys who weren't remotely suited to taking up a position between the posts, which meant there would need to be a re-shuffle. He pulled the dog-eared team sheet out of his pocket and considered it whilst walking over to Bill. It took them a couple of minutes to decide to move their right back into the goals and to drop the right side midfield back into defence and to replace him with one of the subs. Making the tactical change was relatively straight forward. Putting it into practice was anything but. The right back wasn't at all happy at the prospect of being put in goal and he was ready to pack up his stuff and head back home to watch the tele until Jimmy told him that if he did he would be dropped from the squad to play in the final.

Once he had resolved the goalkeeping crisis Jimmy did a head count which came to seven. Twenty minutes to go and six more to come. OK. Not bad. No need to panic just yet. He checked out the road and saw three figures making slow progress in his direction. And that made nine and two of the remaining three would be brought along by reliable dads which meant that things were looking pretty good.

His phone trilled in his pocket and he answered it.

"That you Jimmy?"

"Aye."

"It's Wallie Gregson."

"Alright Wallie. You OK?"

"Aye. Nae bad, but our Stuart's in a right state I'm afraid."

Jimmy mentally crossed off one of the players due to be delivered by a reliable parent.

"How's that."

He sensed an embarrassed pause at the other end of the line. "He went out last night with Sam Kelly and John Campbell. Silly sods went and got ratted didn't they."

Jimmy's spirits started to sink again.

CHAPTER ONE

"Ratted."

"Aye. They got a couple of bottles of Buckie. I've no idea how. I got a call just back of ten from a mate from work. He told me they were wandering down the middle of the road singing and flicking V-signs at passing cars. I went and got them home. Stuart's been sick as a dog all night. Serves the little sod right. Maybe it'll learn him. But that's him grounded I'm afraid Jimmy. Not that he could have played anyway. It's all he can manage to get himself into the bathroom to chuck up."

"I see."

"Look I'm sorry Jimmy. I ken it's the semi final and that. All the best with it. You've got subs?"

"Aye. I've got subs."

"Well, I'll see you then."

"Sure. Thanks for calling Wally."

He pulled the team sheet out again. OK. So now he was down to eleven and the first choice centre forward was sick as a dog in his bed. The last sub would have to make a fist of playing up front although he wasn't all that likely to do a Ronaldo. So long as he kept chasing the ball down it wouldn't be that bad. He shouted Bill over and they agreed the latest tactical change. Bill wasn't too downcast with it all.

"Could be worse. At least we've got eleven."

But Jimmy was growing less upbeat with every passing second as he watched the approach of the three in the street. They had paused now. One was bent over a wall whilst another was sitting with head in hands. The third stood with body language that suggested a screwed up face and wrinkled nose.

The one bent over the wall was Sam Kelly. The one sitting on the wall was John Campbell. It seemed that both had managed to handle their night on the Buckfast a little better than Stuart Gregson. At least they had managed to get out of bed and make the walk to the pitch but Jimmy had a pretty solid inkling that they would not be good for a great deal more. Sam was in the process of throwing up his breakfast and from the way that John was sitting it seemed more than likely that he would be joining in pretty soon. He tapped Bill on the shoulder and pointed to the scene of misery being played out down the street. Bill groaned.

"Bloody marvellous."

"My thoughts entirely. They'll have to play though. We've no choice."

Bill thrust a piece of gum into his mouth and chewed angrily. Once again the two of them worked at their strategy which was now completely in tatters. Sam Kelly was the team's engine in the heart of the midfield. He was Sunnybank's main ball winner who was obviously in no state to tackle a wet paper bag. They decided to stick him out on the left side of midfield where he would do least damage. John Campbell was the second striker who would be providing little more than decoration as opposed to any kind of offensive threat. Things looked bleak. They were going to have to line up with a keeper who would have rather been back home than on the pitch. The right back was a striker who wasn't over keen on tackling. The new right side midfielder was a tiny lad with lots of enthusiasm but little ability. The left side of midfield would be wide open as Sam focused on not throwing up. And the attack? The attack was non existent. One miniature sub and one full of Buckfast.

They both looked over to where Danny was knocking a ball around with other fit members of the team. Jimmy came up with a rueful grin.

"So much for intricate planning eh Bill. It's back to the old system. Give the thing to Danny and hope for the best."

"Looks that way."

A minibus was making their way towards them. Bold red lettering emblazoned back, front and sides announcing to the watching world that here was the official transport of Redhill United FC Their left back's dad owned a coach company and he had donated the minibus three years earlier as well as home and away kit, tracksuits and a variety of paraphernalia that had earned Redhill a similar reputation in Dumfries junior football to the one that Chelsea enjoyed south of the border in the English Premier League. A few of the passengers had spotted Sam dispatching his Cornflakes over the wall as they had driven by and once they started to dismount they gathered in a jeering group until their coach ordered them to the pitch to warm up. Jimmy looked on with a feeling of mild resentment as the coach opened up the side compartment and took out brand spanking new bags filled with balls and plastic cones for practice drills. Even the kit bags were branded with the club name. Christ. Who the hell did they think they were?

Once their coach Mark Thornton had passed the players on to his junior to start a series of vigorous warm up moves, he walked over to

CHAPTER ONE

Jimmy and Bill.

"Morning lads. How's the fettle?"

"Aye. Nae bad. I see the bus trade must still be booming."

The coach zipped up his logo covered padded jacket and Jimmy noticed that it even had his initials on it. For goodness sake.

"A bit of backing never does ever harm Jimmy. Grass roots football needs all it can get. You should'nae knock it."

"I didn't realise I was knocking it. I was merely commenting on the state of the transport industry. I was genuinely concerned, what with the price of diesel and the ongoing crisis in the Middle East and all that. I mean would I want some Muslim fanatics to blow up a pipeline or something and stop you lads getting the next set of tracksuits."

"Ah give it a rest will you Jimmy. I still don't understand why you wouldn't agree to switch venues. I mean look at the state of this pitch. The council should be ashamed of themselves. Ours is like a billiard table since we had it re-seeded in the spring."

"Home advantage Mark. Home advantage. You cannae put a value on it. Once that crowd gets behind you it's like a twelfth man pal."

Thornton took a doubtful look around the empty acres of muddy grass. There was one heavily wrapped up dog walker a hundred yards away. Otherwise there seemed no sign of human activity.

"If you say so Jimmy. All your lot here then? Are we good for getting going at eleven?"

"Aye. We're good. I think that's the ref just pitching up the now."

The ref was locking his rather stately Ford Fiesta which dated back to a time when Clinton had still been in the White House. He was clearly a man who was somewhat unconvinced about the merits of doing his bit for grass roots football on a morning like this. Jimmy gave his watch a check as he saw the last reliable father park up and deliver the second centre half. That made it eleven. He wondered if the man would get out himself and therefore provide the crowd. No. The car pulled away from the kerb and moved away to toast and marmalade and the weekly trip to push a trolley round Tesco.

"Lads! Come on. Over here."

One by one they gathered round in kit that had been picked up from a company in liquidation a few years earlier. It now shared the same kind of veteran status as the ref's Fiesta, and despite all the efforts of the management team, the area on the chest remained stubbornly clear of a sponsor's logo. He was about to start up on his team speech when a surprising sound broke the wet hush of the morning.

Voices. Young female voices.

"We love you Sunnybank . . . We do

We love you Sunnybank . . . We do.

Oh Sunnybank we love you."

The shock arrival of the crowd brought a groan from the centre half.

"I dunnae believe it. It's our Sally."

The sight of 'his' Sally with two friends brought immediate interest from both the eleven men of Sunnybank and the fifteen men of Redhill. His Sally and her mates certainly brought a splash of colour to the scene as they picked their way through the mud in the kind of heels that would have make walking pretty tough on the polished floor of a ballroom in a country mansion. Their attire was dramatically multicoloured and two rather flimsy looking umbrellas offered rather pathetic protection from the driving rain. Although their clothes were big on colour they were decidedly light on substance. Jimmy was wrapped up in a jumper, scarf, wool hat and anorak and still he could feel the damp cold easing into his bones. There was more of the girls uncovered than there was covered and the very sight of them made him feel cold. It certainly made it hard to drag the attention of his players away from the girls and back onto taking on board a tactical solution to beating Redhill.

The master plan had been changed several times as Jimmy and Bill saw their squad slowly fall apart. Now that kick off was less than five minutes away, the only answer was simplicity. The first issue was the condition of the Buckfast boys.

"You lads first. How bad are you?"

Sam and John shared green-tinged faces and they both looked like they were minutes away from death. The best they could come up with was a shrug.

"Bloody idiots. The pair of you. But I suppose you made it which has to say something. OK. You'll both have to play at full back and do as little running as you can. Do not, and I repeat, do not go past the half way line because if you do you'll not make it back again. One of us will take a run to the shop and get in some bottles of Lucozade. Every time the play stops you take a swig. Got that? Good. With luck you might just be worth a light for the second half. OK . . . ."

He spent a couple of minutes re-arranging his depleted forces. The strategy was straightforward. Sit deep. Forget offside. Smother them as much as they could and give the ball to Danny at every opportunity. As they jogged out to take up their unaccustomed positions he called Danny back.

"Danny. I need you to sit right in front of the back two. Make sure you don't get pulled right or left OK. When you get the ball don't think too much about the pass. There really isn't anyone up top worth passing it to. Just take off. You never know, if you get past a couple you might make it all the way. OK?"

"OK Jimmy. Dunnae worry. We'll have 'em."

Jimmy waved over the crowd who picked their way across to where he stood.

"Morning Jimmy."

"That what you call it Sally? Warm enough are you?"

"Aye course we are."

"Bloody tapped. That's what you are. Anyway you've come, so I best not be ungrateful. Now you're here you can make yourselves useful."

A pouty sort of look jumped onto Sally's face. Making herself useful wasn't the sort of thing she did.

"Like what?"

"First off you can borrow some tracksuits. You're no use to me dead of hypothermia. Sally was about to make a speech about how she wasn't about to be seen in any skaffy tracksuit but her two friends were already rummaging through the pile and covering up limbs that were close to frostbite. Maybe it wasn't such a bad idea after all. She would never have admitted to a living soul that she was in fact pretty well frozen to the bone, but the fact was that her arms and legs felt ready to drop off. Once the crowd was better clad Jimmy issued his instructions. "That's better. OK I want you lasses to stand on the line over there. You know Sam Kelly?".

They nodded.

"Right. Well him and John Campbell took a maddy on the Buckfast last night and I'm not sure that either of them will live to see half time. So here's where you lot come in. Every time there's a break in play stick a bottle of Lucozade in his gob and make him drink. Just think of it like feeding a baby and don't worry about being all that gentle."

The quick exchange of glances followed by instant giggles woke him up to the lack of wisdom in the baby analogy.

"Yeah, yeah. Feeding a baby with a bottle I should have said."

By the time the referee had made his way to the middle and managed to locate the centre circle after something of a search, the touchline medical crew were in place looking altogether warmer in their borrowed tracksuits. Sam gave his coach a long begging sort of look and his coach returned it with a grin that said that if you're daft enough to hit the Buckie this is the kind of price you're going to have to pay. Bill took on the role of Lucozade man on the opposite touchline.

The referee's whistle set the game off into predictable frantic activity as the ball was chased about with more energy than art. By the time ten minutes had passed the game had started to take shape. Sunnybank fell deeper and deeper into their own half as they were pressed back by a more organised Redhill. The visitors' attacks seldom made it close to the danger zone thanks to constant biting tackles from Danny McCann who patrolled the ground in front of his defenders like a vengeful predator. Twenty minutes and the deadlock was only deepening. Both Sunnybank full backs had thrown up most of the Lucozade that they had been forced to drink, but neither had shirked the task of shutting the side doors on the Redhill wingers. Every home tackle was met with screaming approval from the female crowd who urged their team on with constructive advice along the lines of "Kill the posh git, Danny."

Thirty-one minutes. Yet another attack. Yet another flying challenge. Corner. Jimmy stiffened as the wind was blowing hard behind the ball. A fast-paced cross. The reluctant keeper reached for the ball. Caught the ball. Dropped the ball.

One-nil Redhill.

The smart shirts with the logos on the chest mobbed the striker who had poked the ball in from three yards. The well-worn shirts from the liquidator turned on their keeper and told him he was useless and the keeper stood his ground and pointed out that he hadn't wanted to be keeper anyway and why didn't someone else have a go if they thought it was so easy. Jimmy snapped them out of it with a bellow and they shaped up ready for play to resume.

Another car was parking up. The door opened and a lone figure climbed out and pulled a thick coat from the back seat and wandered over to the touchline twenty yards down from Jimmy. There was something familiar as the man rooted in his pockets for a cigarette and lit up. He knew the face. He was sure of it. Then it came. The face had been there on the fateful day when his ligaments had snapped and his dreams had been flushed down the toilet. Billy Laurence. Airdrie, Dundee Utd and Celtic. Left side midfielder. Two-hundred-and-forty-eight games for the Celts and thirty-three goals. Eleven caps for Scotland. And now here he was on a wet Saturday morning on the touchline of Sunnybank's famously awful pitch.

Interesting.

Very interesting indeed.

Jimmy took a stroll.

"Alright Billy."

The familiar face turned to him, mildly annoyed to have been clocked so soon by an autograph seeker. Then his expression was one of distant recognition slowly turning to definite recognition.

"Bloody hell. Jimmy. Jimmy Doyle. How the hell are you pal?"

"Nae bad. Long way from home Billy, unless you've migrated south and I never heard about it."

A smile. "You know me. I'm a Glasgow boy. Always will be. Too much countryside makes me anxious." His eyes slid down to Jimmy's leg. "How is it?"

Jimmy shrugged. "Stiff on mornings like this. Otherwise it doesn't bother me much. The price we pay isn't it?"

"Aye but some of us pay it younger than others. You ever speak to Pat? You know, after it happened."

Pat Delaney. The full back who had wrecked his life. A-hundred-and-thirty five appearances for Celtic and three goals. Forty-eight caps for Northern Ireland.

"No. Can't say I did."

The old Celt took his cigarette down to the butt and then flicked it away into the wind. The smoke wandered back out of his nose and was whisked away on the breeze.

"You ought to call him one day. He was always cut up about what happened. It was never deliberate you ken. Pat was never that kind of player. He has a chippy in Bishopriggs now. It's easy found. On the High Street opposite WH Smiths. Call in one day Jimmy. Have a pint with him."

Jimmy shook his head and smiled. "Got yourself a job with the United Nations have you Billy?"

This brought the kind of throaty chuckle that only a thirty a day habit could create.

"Aye. I'm on the first plane out to Jerusalem tomorrow."

Throughout the banter Billy's eyes had been locked onto the play.

"That him Jimmy?"

Danny had just bitten into his fourth tackle in less than two minutes.

"Who?"

"Come on Jimmy. You ken who. Or did you think I'd treated myself to a nice ride out for the day. McCann. Danny McCann."

"Aye that's Danny. How did you get on to him?"

"It wasn't rocket science. I always watch the Under 16's trials. The lad stood out for me. Got three and made a couple. Bit of time and plenty of heart. Why the hell have you got him sat all the way back there?"

"Squad problems. Two grounded and two still half-smashed from hitting the Buckie last night."

"Ah. I was wondering about the Lucozade. The joys of Scottish football eh Jimmy? You'd never see Dutch kids on the Buckie the night before a game. I suppose it's just the way we are. What's the score?"

"One nil to them."

"Big game is it?"

"Semi final. First time we've ever made it this far."

Lawrence nodded and lit up another and grimaced as the left back lurched off the field and dry retched whilst a Redhill player trotted to collect the ball which had been belted out for a throw in.

"Come on Sam. Down the neck . . ."

Sam only just managed to speak between retches of bile.

"Get . . . Stuffed . . . Sally . . . ."

Sally did anything but. Instead she took a handful of his hair and yanked his head back whilst one of her colleagues thrust the bottle of liquid energy into the full back's mouth.

Billy Lawrence winced.

"Your back room team are they?"

CHAPTER ONE

"Aye."

"Christ, you wouldn't want to meet those three on a dark night."

"That you wouldn't."

Redhill were getting much more confident now as they had realised that the Sunnybank strike force was more or less toothless. They were in the process of rolling the ball along the back four when Danny struck with a tackle that floored the centre half who was a good five inches taller than him. He was back on his feet instantly and clear away with the ball and bearing down on the Redhill goal. The keeper raced out and bought Danny's dummy; hook, line and sinker. Danny rolled the ball home without any ceremony and jogged back to meet his ecstatic team mates. The back room staff leaped up and broke into song.

"Danny, Danny, Danny McCann . . .

Danneeeeeee . . . Danny McCann."

The man from Glasgow allowed a small smile. Maybe. Just maybe. Every Saturday morning he got out of his bed early to drive the length and breadth of Scotland in the hope of spotting the next Jimmy Johnstone on some puddled up pitch surrounded by low rise housing coated in grey pebble dash. These were the places where all the jobs had drained away. Places of Giros and teenage mums. Drugs and pensioners scared to go out to the corner shop. Places from where the great Scottish footballers had always emerged. Mining towns and ports. Places where once they had built ships and spun cotton. But the factories had closed down and the conveyor belt of talent had jammed. Every weekend he stood out in the rain and waited whilst Poles and Bulgarians took the field at Parkhead. And now here was a maybe, just maybe. Pace. Measured in front of goal. Fearless in the tackle. An engine like a Mercedes. And heart. Lots and lots of heart.

Maybe.

A few minutes later the referee blew his whistle for half time and the two teams went to their coaches. Jimmy gathered the lads round and told them more of the same. He then reached into his phone and embarked on a diplomatic initiative. He clicked call register, selected the most recently received call and hit dial.

"Hello"

"That you Wallie."

"Aye."

"It's Jimmy again. Can I have a word?"

"Course. Fire away."

"Wallie, I've got eleven lads here who have just run themselves into the ground and we've held it to one each. I reckon we can manage to keep them out but we've not a thing up front. I hate to interfere and that, but can you bring your Stuart along for the last half hour. Hell, if he suffers anything like the other two it'll be the worst punishment you could give him. Half an hour Wallie. For the sake of the rest of the lads."

"Having a rough time are they? John and Sam?"

"They must have chucked up four times each and we've got a volunteer back room staff force feeding them Lucozade."

"Who's that then?"

"Sally Stamper and a couple of her mates."

Wallie gave out an ooof kind of a sound which perfectly described how it would be to have Sally Stamper and two of her mates force feed him Lucozade when he had the mother of all hangovers. "That must be worse than six months in Guantanamo Bay. You best watch out Jimmy, you'll have Amnesty International on your back. OK. Give me ten minutes. I'll bring the little sod down."

The game continued along the same lines for ten minutes, but slowly and surely the restorative powers of Lucozade started to show. The two Buckfast veterans started to show more and more signs of life and Jimmy was able to shuffle his pack. He withdrew his first sub back to full back and moved John Campbell up to his accustomed position at centre forward. With twenty-eight minutes left on the clock a car pulled up and delivered a decidedly green-looking Stuart Gregson to his coach.

"Morning Stuart. Feeling fit?"

The boy stared down at the grass and made a grunting sort of a noise.

"OK pal. Here's how it goes. You go and stand with Sally and the lasses for five minutes and get as much Lucozade as you can down the neck. Then you give me twenty minutes. I don't care if you drop dead after twenty-one minutes so long as you give me twenty. Got that?"

With another grunt the boy jogged miserably round to the medical team who immediately started their forced fluid routine. He was throwing up after less than ninety seconds which brought zero sympathy and more fluid. On the field the rhythm of the game was changing slightly. Everything Sunnybank did still revolved around Danny who was roaming the centre of the pitch and hammering into tackle after tackle. Now he had an outlet when he won the ball and at last more of the game was being played in the visitors' half. As the clock moved past seventy minutes Jimmy removed his sub and sent a relieved Stuart Gregson on to join John Campbell up front. Stuart looked like a man who had been released from one of Saddam Hussein's jails when he was set free of the Lucozade girls. As the game moved into the last ten minutes the momentum was with Sunnybank as Redhill fell further and further back on their penalty box.

The moment came in the eighty-fourth minute when Danny collected the ball forty yards out and surged past three defenders to reach the bye line and cut the ball back for John Campbell to belt it home high into the top corner. He had been hoping for such a moment all week and had gone so far as to work on an appropriate celebration routine. This took him to the corner flag with the rest of the team in hot pursuit. Once he arrived at the flag he was just about to start up the kind of performance he watched every Saturday night on Match of the Day when his stomach once again rebelled and half a pint of Lucozade exploded out of him.

The goal broke the spirit of Redhill who had started to argue amongst themselves despite the commands from their coach that they shut their traps and get focused. As the game moved into stoppage time Danny once again crashed through the defensive lines and was about to put the icing on the cake when he was scythed to the floor.

It was a stone-cold penalty which the ref duly awarded. Danny picked himself up and placed the ball on the spot. On the far side of the field a couple of crows were being tossed about on the wind and the traffic hummed along the by-pass in the distance. Everything was as normal as it could ever be. But as he casually clipped the ball into the corner and sent the keeper sprawling in the opposite direction, everything was anything but normal. Sunnybank were in the final. Sunnybank the joke, with their horrible pitch and raggy kit. Sunnybank who had never come close to winning a thing from as far back as anyone could remember.

Jimmy shook hands with the Redhill coach who looked like a man who had just stuck his face in a bucket of worms.

"Good game Jimmy. All the best for the final."

"Cheers Mark."

Thornton shook hands with the Celtic scout and his eyes flickered with recognition.

"Are you Billy Lawrence?"

"Aye."

"Down to watch Danny McCann?"

"Aye."

"Worth the trip was it?"

"Aye, it was worth the trip."

The man in question was in the middle of a scrum of celebrating Sunnybank players who had defied both the odds and the effects of Buckfast to make it through to the club's first ever Rotary Cup Final. The all of a sudden he was thrown into utter confusion as the tracksuited figure of Sally Stamper was all of a sudden wrapped all around him. Not only that. Kissing him too. When she was done she pulled back and grinned at his look of blind panic.

"I reckon you deserved that."

He couldn't think of a thing to say so he just stared with a dumb kind of look. Some of the other lads had noticed by this stage and there was nudging and smirks. The attention threw the blood into Danny's cheeks. Sally was quite unconcerned.

"Come over here. I want a word with you in private."

She took his hand possessively and marched him clear of his sniggering team mates. She only spoke when they were well clear.

"So. You going to ask me out then?"

"What?"

"Not that hard. You just say do you want to go out Sally."

"Well I don't know . . ."

"Course you do. There's a disco on at St Mary's tonight. I think you should take me. Escort me."

Her eyes were drilling into his and all the control he had felt sitting in the hole in front of his back four suddenly seemed a very long way away.

"Cannae. Got no money."

"Not good enough. I've got lots."

"Aye well . . ."

"Not good enough."

"My dad might . . . ."

"Your dad nothing. You're fifteen and old enough to take a lass to a dance. Your dad will be fine."

"Aye but . . ."

"So that's arranged. You can call and collect me at seven."

"But . . ."

"See you later Danny. Seven sharp."

She marched away whilst he worked his mouth like a fish washed up on a beach. Jimmy and Bill stood on her route back to her friends who were peeling off the borrowed tracksuits ready to depart.

"What have you been doing to my star man then?" Jimmy couldn't help a smile.

"Nothing Mr Doyle. In fact Danny's just asked me out."

"Really. You know I could have sworn that it looked like it was the other way around."

This brought on a shocked look. "Come on Mr Doyle, It would'nae be right for a lassie to ask a lad out, now would it?"

Jimmy just shook his head. Once she was clear he noticed that Bill was looking less than happy with the situation. One minute all had been well with the world. The team had made the final. Danny had played out of his skin. And to cap it all a Celtic coach had been there to watch. But now his sense of complete well being had been torn up and tossed into the damp breeze that swept through Sunnybank. All of a sudden he was in a horrible situation and he knew it.

In one respect he was no different to any dad who lived on the estate. The idea of his lad going out on a date with the daughter of Les Stamper was little short of a nightmare. The Stamper family had maintained a reign of terror over Sunnybank for a similar period of time that Saddam had done much the same in Iraq. But no F16 fighters and Abrams tanks had come to Dumfries and there was no sign that the rule of the Stamper clan was going to weaken any time soon.

They had come south to Dumfries and Galloway from Paisley in 1975. The pioneer had been Terry Stamper who had migrated from the Central Belt with a family of nine made up of himself, a wife, five boys and two girls. Les was the oldest and he had been eleven when the family had arrived. Terry had been a man who liked a drink and a fight. It wasn't long before he became the stuff of legend as he embarked on series of closing time brawls from which he invariably emerged victorious. Sometimes he would be caught and prosecuted and packed off to prison for a few months whilst the family was left to fend for themselves. Over the years the family had grown and thrived as one by one the children had grown up and become parents themselves. By the time the bells rang in the new Millenium, Terry's seven children had given him a total of seventeen grandchildren who ranged in age from three to Les's oldest who was twenty. It made the family something of a mini army and they worked on a Three Musketeerish principle of all for one, one for all. If anyone was daft enough to cross any member of the Stamper clan they would have the whole lot to deal with and that would have needed at least a platoon of paratroopers. The Stampers were not known for holding back when handling grievances. They sorted out business with knives and baseball bats and those who crossed them generally disappeared into the infirmary for months at a time.

For twenty years the family grew but didn't prosper. They made ends meet by cashing their Giros and attempting a wide variety of petty crime. For years they could have been held up as a decent example of crime not paying. Most of their collective energy was spent on maintaining the family's fearsome reputation. What they never managed to discover was a way of turning their reputation into cold, hard cash. Then things changed dramatically when Les returned from a four-month stay up in Barlinnie for an assault charge.

His cell-mate had been serving six months for possession of Class A substances with an intent to supply the good folk of Motherwell. The two men hit it off during the long hours of the night when the lights were switched off and the old Victorian prison slowly faded down into silence. An agreement was hatched. A partnership was forged and when Les returned to Sunnybank he had telephone numbers for places in Glasgow and Liverpool where he could buy drugs at a wholesale rate.

The Stampers soon found that here was the way to turn their reputation into the kind of cold, hard cash they had always yearned for. The key to making a success in the world of selling drugs wasn't all that difficult to learn. Number one, they needed to know where to buy the stuff and Les came home from Bar L with plenty of numbers. Number two, they needed a secure base to operate from where neighbours would think once, twice and a-hundred-and-ninety-three times before picking up the phone and passing information on to the police. Sunnybank was perfect and between them the family now had seven houses dotted across the estate. Third, a reputation for unthinking violence was a must not only to collect owed money but also for discouraging any other wannabe dealers from setting up and having a go themselves.

It didn't take long for the Stampers to clear away all competition The memory of this period lived on in several scarred faces and lifelong limps. They sent out a very clear message. No way. Not now. Not ever. Not unless you are willing to take the cut or the snap of the legs. And the message was heard loud and clear. By the late nineties the Stampers owned the Sunnybank drug trade; hook, line and sinker and the money poured in by the thousand. They could have moved out of town and lived in a sprawling mansion in the country. They could have bought flats in Edinburgh. They could have chosen studio apartments in New York.

But they didn't. They stayed exactly where they were because Sunnybank was theirs and there was no way that it would ever be otherwise.

So, not surprisingly every instinct in Bill McCann's body told him to do everything in his power to keep Danny clear of having anything to do with that family. But that was where he had a second problem. It was the fact that he caught himself thinking of *that* Stamper family. Not *the* Stamper family. *That* Stamper family. That Sally Stamper. As in don't have anything to do with that Stamper family. Keep away from that Sally Stamper. She's trouble. Bad news. Dangerous. Same with all of them. Scum of the earth. They were the subject of constant gossip in the Post Office and the Spar shop and the bookies and the newsagents and the Social club on a Friday night and the church on a Sunday morning. It was never loud gossip because loud gossip could be overhead and being overheard could mean a brick through the front window at best or a sliced up cheek at worst. It was whispered gossip. Gossip that would only start when all parties had carefully checked that there was no way that any of the clan was listening.

Bill could remember only too well when he had been *that* Bill McCann and his son had been *that* Danny McCann. There had been no invitations to birthday parties or days out to the beach. No calls asking if his Danny wanted to come round for tea. No Sunday afternoons round at a friend's house to play the Playstation. The Sunnybank word had been that it was a good idea to stay well clear. Because that Danny McCann was a little toe-rag. That Danny McCann was bad news. A wrong one. A bad apple. Same with the dad who never went ten minutes sober. A disgrace. That's what they were. A disgrace.

And now that Sally Stamper had made a beeline for his son and he would have to make his mind up what to do. He didn't know a thing about Sally. As far as he could see she was a sparky thing. Pretty, no doubt about that. There was plenty of spirit about her. Had she had any other surname he would have been chuffed to bits for his son. But she didn't have another surname. Her surname was Stamper and would be until she walked up the aisle to take on somebody else's. So was he to be like all the others? Was he going to judge her simply because of the name she had been unlucky enough to be born with?

And suddenly he knew that there was no way he was about to do that. Not after the way he and Danny had been treated. He said nothing to Danny when the two of them started the walk back home after the team had consumed their victory bonus McDonalds. They talked through the game and the prospect of the final and how the coach from Glasgow had seemed to be impressed. It was only when they got in and Danny emerged from the shower that he found the nerve to tell his dad.

"I'm going out tonight dad."

"Oh aye. Where's that then?"

"St Mary's. There's a disco on."

"That with the lads then?"

"Not really. Maybe some of them will be there."

By now Danny was studying a six-inch square of the lounge carpet with every bit of concentration he could muster. Bill pretended ignorance.

"Who're you going with then?"

"Sally Stamper." It came out almost as a whisper.

"Ah. The leader of the Lucozade crew. Has this been coming for a while or is it sort of sudden?"

"Sort of sudden I suppose."

Bill felt it only right to put the lad out of his misery. "Well she's a bonny lass, a right handful mind."

Danny looked up with surprised eyes. "So you don't mind then?"

"Look. Sit down a second."

They both sat and Bill arranged his thoughts with a swig from his mug of tea. "OK. There's no point pretending that the Stampers are a family of angels. I know that. You know that. Everyone in Sunnybank knows that. But just because her dad is a scum of the earth drug dealer doesn't mean I'm about to tar his daughter with the same brush. She's fifteen and it will be up to her which road she decides to walk. Just like it's up to you to decide which road you want to walk. You're not little kids any more. Either of you. If I start banging the table and ban you from seeing her you'll probably go off on some hair brained Romeo and Juliet thing and I'm not that daft. So, no. I don't mind. I merely expect you to keep your eyes open and make the right decisions. Fair enough?"

"Aye. Fair enough. I won't be stupid. Promise."

"That'll do then."

By the time it was time to leave Danny's stomach was a twisted up knot of nerves. It had been getting steadily worse all afternoon and from five o'clock onwards it had become little short of a nightmare. The whole thing had been so out of the blue that he found it really hard to get his head around the situation. One minute he had been celebrating making it to the final and the next minute Sally Stamper had been wrapped around him. Just like that. No warning. No preamble. And as his brain replayed those few seconds over and over the real problem was that it was almost impossible to decide which feeling was the better. He knew that he had been completely railroaded in the most public way possible. Was she taking the mick? Probably, and if she was taking the mick he was staring down the barrel at a pig of a week at school. The thing was that there really was nothing to be done. He had said yes. Sure Sally. Of course Sally. Seven o'clock sharp Sally.

And now it was twenty-to-seven and it was time to go. His dad looked up from his chair with a look of mild amusement at his son's obviously nervous state.

"Normally I'd say don't worry she won't bite, but with that one I wouldn't be so sure. Go on. Get lost. Behave yourself."

Three minutes to seven and the nerves were at breaking point. Now it wasn't just a case of being nervous about what he was going to say to Sally. Now there was more. Now there was the sudden reality of the fact that he was about to knock on the front door of the house where Les Stamper lived. Never in a million, zillion years would he have imagined he would have ever made his way up the street past the shiny Range Rover and Porsche 911 that were such a constant source of gossip. Past the cars. Through the gate. Up the path towards the bland eye of the camera over the door which was another constant topic of local debate. He rang the bell and noticed that his hand was shaking so he quickly pushed it deep into his pocket.

Five seconds. Ten seconds. Fifteen seconds. And the door was opening. He took a gulp of air when he saw it was Les Stamper.

"Danny I suppose?"

"Aye."

"Well come on in then."

Stamper stood back to let him by before closing the heavy door with the kind of sharp click that spoke of several locks. It wasn't the sort of door that was normal on Sunnybank. It was a specially designed door with a panel of steel through the middle which would stave off the sledge hammers of a five in the morning police raid.

"That way. The lounge. Grab a pew."

There were two other men in the front room sprawled on a black leather suite cradling tumblers of light brown whisky.

"Danny, this is my dad Terry. And this is my brother Eric. Go on. Don't stand there like a bloody plank. Sit will you. Want a beer?"

Danny wasn't even close to being capable of speech so he just shook his head and sat. The other two seemed to have already forgotten his existence and were focused on the biggest TV he had ever seen in his life which was showing the second half of the Sky 5.15 game between Arsenal and Newcastle. Les flopped down into his armchair, lit up, and collected his glass from the coffee table. It was the first time Danny had ever been within fifty yards of the big man and he seemed much more ordinary than he would have expected. Les Stamper wasn't all that tall, an inch or two under six foot. He wasn't particularly broad either. He wore a short-sleeved shirt which showed arms which were covered in tattoos. They weren't all that muscled. Strong, but not iron-pumped. The fact was that Les Stamper didn't look all that different from a hundred men on the estate. He could have been a builder or a van driver or a bin man. And yet his was a name that was spoken in hushed tones. The schoolyard had always been filled with tales of Les Stamper and what he had done. Who he had cut. Which legs he had snapped. What top end car he had bought.

"You sure you don't want a beer then?"

"No thanks Mr Stamper."

Les took a sip from his glass. "Yeah, well dunnae think you're getting any of this. It would be wasted on you. Any idea what this is have you, Danny?"

"No Mr Stamper."

"It's the real deal Danny. Forty years old and three hundred quid a bottle. The Beatles would have been number one when they put the lid on this. Think about that."

Danny nodded not quite sure what it was that he was expected to think about.

"You don't drink then Danny?"

"No Mr Stamper."

"No. I don't suppose you would. Because you're an athlete aren't you Danny?"

Nod.

"I hear there was a Celtic coach down this afternoon. Our Sally says he was well impressed. Not bad Danny. Not bad at all. It would be quite a thing to see a Sunnybank lad run out at Parkhead. Quite a thing. I don't think it's happened before."

"Our coach played there once. Jimmy. Jimmy Doyle."

For a moment a flicker of annoyance slipped across Les's eyes. He didn't like it when people contradicted him.

"Aye. That's true enough. But that was for Kilmarnock wasn't it? The day he got crocked. Poor old Jimmy. They say he could have gone all the way so they do. And then . . . Poof. Tough old world Danny. Always has been. Always will be. But Kilmarnock isn't really what I meant. I meant running onto the pitch wearing those hoops. That's what I meant Danny. The hoops."

"Yes Mr Stamper."

One of five mobile phones on the coffee table started to ring as Thierry Henri flashed a shot a few inches past the Geordie post. Les snapped it open and listened with a slight frown. At last he answered whoever was on the other end of the line.

"OK. You can lay him on another twenty. 'Til Wednesday. Tell him that's it. Explain the consequences."

He tossed the phone back down and stubbed his cigarette.

"So Danny. Like I was saying. You're an athlete."

What was all this about? Danny was feeling more uncomfortable by the second. Where the hell was Sally?

"Yes Mr Stamper."

Les Stamper half turned in his chair so that he was able to stare hard and square into Danny's face.

"Well I think it's a good idea to get something clear Danny. Very clear. You don't want to be thinking about getting athletic with our Sally. Because if you do, I might just have to get a bit athletic with you. And if I get athletic with you, Danny, you'll never be athletic again. You'll be about as athletic as poor old Jimmy Doyle. You get where I'm coming from Danny?"

"Yes Mr Stamper."

Stamper held him in a stare for a few moments longer and then broke the look. "That's good then isn't it. It's good when people understand each other. It avoids conflict. Avoids nastiness. Better that way. Now sit back and watch the match. She'll be out in a minute."

Danny felt almost frozen and tried to focus his attention on the Arsenal players weaving their familiar patterns across a rather frantic black and white defensive line. There was no escaping the fact that he had just been threatened. Not just any kind of threatened. Threatened in person, to his face, by Les Stamper and it was all he could do to stop his limbs shaking like tree branches in a force nine gale.

Les's prediction that his daughter would be along in a minute turned out to be wildly optimistic. By the time Sally at last flounced into the front room, Thierry Henri had scored twice and Les had fielded another seven calls on four different mobiles. Each time he would issue his instructions using few words in a low muttered voice, and then toss the phone back to the coffee table.

"Sorry for being so long Danny, you know how it is with us lasses."

Terry Stamper's watery old eyes took in his granddaughter's skimpy outfit with disapproval.

"Jesus Les, she looks like a hooker."

Les followed his father's gaze and gave a sort of grimace as he blew smoke out of his nose.

"They all do dad. The whole lot of them. So what am I supposed to do about it? What she wears is her mum's lookout."

Terry let out a short mocking laugh. "Well her mum was no better herself was she?"

"Leave it out Dad."

"Or what Les? Or what . . . ?"

Danny could sense Les Stamper tense up and he wished he could turn himself into something liquid and disappear down under the cushion of his chair and hide away with the fifty pences. Slowly the tension drained out of Les Stamper and he pulled a wad of notes from his pocket and peeled off a twenty, which he passed to his under-dressed daughter.

"Go on. Get lost. You know the drill."

Danny eased himself to his feet and hoped it wasn't too obvious how desperate he was to get out of the room. Les reached out and blocked his way and gave him yet another of his stares.

"And you know the drill too, don't you Danny?"

"Yes Mr Stamper."

"Good Danny. Very good."

Outside it was a dreary night and Sally pulled a small umbrella from her bag to stave off the thin rain that had swept in from the west since morning. Danny had a thick hooded top on and a decent pair of training pants and he felt half frozen by the time they were a few yards down the street. He reckoned Sally had to be in danger of frostbite.

"You not freezing?"

"Course I'm freezing. What do you think I am, an Eskimo or something?"

She had pushed an arm through his and he could feel her shivering.

"Maybe you should go back for a coat then. It's a good couple of miles to St Mary's."

She chuckled. "We're not walking you daft sod. Here. Our ride."

As they turned the corner he saw a Peugeot 206 was waiting with the engine running. The fumes from the extra large exhaust were drifted away on the wind and up into the dark skies above. There were blue strips of light fixed to the chassis and the throb of base from the stereo could be heard clearly from fifty yards. She quickened her step toward shelter from the rain and the warmth of the heater.

"Our Baz. He's giving us a lift."

Her Baz was the second oldest of Les Stamper's three boys at seventeen and he had left Sunnybank High School a year earlier to join the family business. Officially he was unemployed and eking out an existence of £40 a week which was only paid when he attended the right number of sessions at his training provider which meant that it wasn't paid very often. Logically, his complete lack of either employment or income made it hard to explain the brand new car with the fancy sound system and the head to toe Nike that he wore. But his second name was Stamper and that meant that his benefits were topped up generously with other earnings.

Sally swung open the back door and jumped into the warmth with relief. Baz was banging the steering wheel enthusiastically to the rhythm of the music, which thundered out of a cluster of bouncing speakers. He had his baseball cap pulled back to front and a glowing joint clamped between his teeth. As Danny followed Sally into the back, his senses were hit from all angles. His skin glowed with a blast of heat. His ears flinched at the hammering music and his nose wrinkled at the fog of cannabis.

"Alright Sal. Good to see you're all wrapped up hen."

"Yeah, yeah. Very funny. Come on Danny. Shut the door will you."

Danny did so and the music seemed to rear up from the floor and wrap itself round his head like a great blanket. Baz was speaking to him but he couldn't hear a word, he just saw a pair of moving lips. Sally had to almost scream to be understood through the noise.

"Switch it down will you Baz!"

He did so and tried again with Danny.

"You alright Danny boy!"

Baz had been two years ahead of Danny through school and it was the first time he had ever spoken his name.

"Aye Baz. Nae bad."

Sally thrust an arm forward that was nearly blue with cold. "Here. Give me some of that."

She relieved her brother of the joint and took a long pull. And then another. And then she pushed it at Danny whilst Baz engaged first gear and pulled away from the kerb.

"Heard good things about today Danny boy. Oh yeah. Big, big, big my man. A man down from Celtic they say. Get some of that." It seemed to Danny that Baz had been watching altogether too much TV. He merely answered with a noncommittal "Aye Baz."

CHAPTER ONE

Of much greater concern was the joint, which he suddenly found himself holding. A couple of years earlier he had got into the way of smoking two or three cigarettes a day with the other lads on the way home from school but he had knocked it on the head as his football career had started to take off. But this wasn't a cigarette. This was a joint and he had promised himself time and again that there was no way in a million years that he was about to take that particular road.

He tried a smile and made to pass the joint back to Baz. But unlike all the passes he had sprayed around the pitch that morning, this one was unsuccessful. Sally intercepted and gave him a rather stern look.

Sally wasn't having it.

"You're not going to be boring are you Danny? Because if you're going to be boring it might be best if you just get out and go home for an early night."

He flushed. "I'm not being boring, it's just . . ."

She rolled her eyes theatrically and imitated him in a mincing sort of voice. " . . . it's just I'm a sportsman Sally. I daren't risk my fitness Sally . . . don't be so soft. It isn't forty fags a day. It's a joint. You're legs aren't going to drop off are they?"

Danny knew that he had been boxed off into a corner. He caught Baz watching his face in the mirror with a big grin. Sally had him fixed with a look that said her interest in him was on the verge of evaporating in the next thirty seconds. And even with the volume down a bit, the music was still hammering into his skull. It was a case of either stop the car and take the walk home for a night in front of the TV with his dad, or stay on the back seat with Sally Stamper. Suddenly it wasn't much of a contest. With a shrug he put the joint to his lips and crossed the line.

Three pulls later the music seemed to turn into a living thing and his feet were banging out the beat on the floor. To his side, Sally was laughing and outside the last of Sunnybank was slipping away into the night. Soon they were climbing away from the orange lights of the town and into a million acres of dark countryside. Baz had his foot down hard now and through the window the hedges and trees blurred by faster and faster. The joint did another round and this time he took and smoked without a second's hesitation. The road through the front windscreen was like something on a Playstation. Corners jumped at him and then vanished as the small car flew through the night. The music seemed to hit a new level and now it was if it was playing somewhere deep in his chest.

At last they reached the brow of a hill and Baz pulled up so that they could look out at the spread of street lamps far below. It was an exposed place and the wind rocked the car slightly. Now Baz reached down and produced three bottles of WKD which he opened and passed round. It was nectar. Sweet and cold and fantastic all the way down his throat and into his stomach. He had never tasted anything quite like it.

It was if they had ridden a million miles clear of Sunnybank and all its rain and graffiti and gutters filled with litter blown by the cold wet wind. And now they were in their own private dreamland where the music filled every corner of his senses and the chilled sweetness of the drink caressed his throat. And all of a sudden Sally had pulled him to her and was kissing him and the dreamland was complete.

For a few minutes he was gone and lost and when he looked up again they were moving again. Fast. Climbing up higher and higher with pine trees either side of the road. Sally tapped him. In her palm were two white pills stamped with some sort of cartoons that he couldn't make out in the dark of the car. She took one with her thumb and forefinger and swallowed it. Then she took the second and eased towards his mouth. And somewhere far below where the orange lights glowed in the night a very small voice was trying to shout to him. No Danny. Don't Danny. Remember what you always said. Remember . . . .

But the voice was lost on the wind as they shot through the forest. It wasn't the right voice for dreamland. All wrong. It wasn't a time for that voice. It was a time for the music and the sweet liquid in his throat and the blur of the trees outside and Sally Stamper. The pill offered a promise of more. Another level. The lift all the way to the top. And he was way past even thinking of saying no to it. Not a chance in a million years. He opened his lips and took the offered pill and swallowed and once again she was kissing him.

Later he was to understand that the magic of the next few hours was all to do with a mix of chemicals. The cannabis swung open his senses to the music and the speeding car and Sally. And once all the senses were open the ecstasy poured in a sense of ultimate well being that he had never dreamed possible. The few hours that followed seemed to fuse and merge into complete magic. Everything was perfect. Completely perfect. Like being in a film. The world had become widescreen and Technicolor and quite unlike anywhere he had ever been. Sharper. Crisper. Extraordinary. They hurtled back down from the hills and parked up a couple of streets away from the St Mary's disco. He had been to the disco a few times before but it never ever been like it was with Sally that night. Before it had seemed boring. Before the old church hall had seemed rather threadbare and in need of a lick of paint. Before he had never wanted to join the crowd on the dance floor and had hung out with the lads from the team instead. Before he had always been happy enough to walk home early to catch Match of the Day on the TV. But this time it was different. The peeling walls were masked by the blaze of the lights, which seemed to explode all through his head like the greatest firework display ever. The music poured through him and he danced until he was drenched in sweat. And more than everything else, he was filled with a sense that absolutely everything in the world was right.

Completely right. So right that it couldn't possibly be better. And as he danced others tapped him on the shoulder and shouted congratulations about getting to the final. And about the coach who had come down from Glasgow to watch him. And he wanted it all to last forever. For the rest of his life and about a million years beyond. His life in fact had suddenly become a thing that was perfect. More than perfect.

And then Baz was shaking them by the shoulder and saying it was time to go which seemed crazy to Danny because it would never be time to go. Never. Outside the rain didn't seem to matter any more. The car again. The music again. The streets outside like the backdrop of a film again.

But not for long. Only a few minutes until they arrived at the close where Sally lived and she kissed him and climbed out. It was hard for him to get his head around the idea that the evening was over. What time was it? The clock on the dashboard said midnight. Too early surely. It was a night that needed to last all the way to the break of dawn. For a moment he felt a little off balance as he watched Sally dart through the front door and into the house. What now? Walk home? He was about to open the door when Baz leaned over the front seat.

"No problem my man. Your cab is prepaid. I'll run you. Didn't Sally explain?"

Danny wasn't sure that Sally was supposed to have explained anything. He wasn't sure what day it was. But it wasn't a problem. Nothing in the world was a problem. Nothing could be. He clicked the door back closed and shrugged. Baz slipped the gears and pulled away.

"Cinderella. That's what our Sally is. The Cinderella girl. If she's gets in after midnight Dad goes off on a big one. And I mean a big one. Know what I mean?"

Danny nodded. Not that he really did know what Baz meant, but somewhere in the dim and distant memories of the night he could recall the look on Les Stamper's face when he had warned about athletics with his daughter. So he could imagine that when Les went off on a big one it wouldn't be all that great.

"Want to go home or do you want another spliff Danny boy?"

He wasn't ready for home. Not even nearly. All he wanted was for the magic to go on and on until the rest of his life. He voted for the spliff and clambered into the front seat as Baz once again left the wet pavements of Sunnybank behind and sped away into the countryside.

They listened to more music and smoked in a deserted Forestry Commission track and the minutes glided by like high clouds on a breezy day in Spring. At last they arrived back at Danny's road end and Baz reached into his pocket and pulled out a card and passed it over.

"There you go Danny boy. Open 24/7. Just like Tesco."

Danny studied the card, which was blank other than a mobile number. He looked up with an expression of not understanding. Baz grinned.

"I'm your man Danny. Weed, eckies, base, Charlie, whatever. It's all just a phone call away. Tell your mates. OK?"

Danny pocketed the card and nodded that it was OK. Of course it was OK. Everything was OK. He was about to close the door when Baz's expression sharpened. "You don't mention any of this to my Dad, OK? Like nothing. This is my private sideline, ken what I mean?"

Danny nodded his head.

"That we're cool my man. You going to be taking our Sally out again then?"

"Don't know."

This was amusing. "Don't know much do you Danny boy? We'll see I suppose."

CHAPTER ONE

And he was gone, booming exhaust and blue lights reflecting on the wet tarmac. Danny watched him away round the corner and then headed for home. Inside his dad was asleep in the chair and a film about vampires was playing on anyway. It seemed best to leave him be, so Danny raided the kitchen for a couple of bags of crisps and a handful of biscuits and tiptoed to his room. For a while he thought about going to bed but his brain was still locked into overdrive. He fitted headphones into his ears and sat by the window looking out into the night, still consumed by a feeling of completeness. Outside a tree was swaying in the wind and occasional taxis splashed through the puddles. The music seemed to flow through his veins with his blood.

He had no recollection of getting into bed. When he woke his alarm clock said it was after one and a bright blue sky was framed in the window. After one? Surely not. He never slept in. He must have slept for hours and hours, and yet it didn't seem to have done any good. He felt shattered. Wrecked. It was like he hadn't slept for a month. Maybe it would be best just to roll over and sleep some more. But that was ridiculous. Not at one o'clock in the afternoon. What would his dad think?

That thought sent an ominous feeling through him. What would his dad think? Nothing good, that was for sure. And it would only get worse the longer he stayed in his bed. He needed to get up and get some cold water in his face and come up with a story to tell. Getting out of bed was anything but easy. It was like someone had poured lead into all his bones making his arms and legs feel almost too heavy to move. He trudged into the bathroom and fired ice cold water into his face to try and summon up some energy, but all it did was to make his face feel cold.

As he stood in front of the mirror he realised that it wasn't just his body that felt wrecked. It was his head as well. There was a feeling of total depression that ran all through him. He felt like bursting into tears. Stupid. Idiotic. He gave his cheek a slap and returned to his room to dress. Stupid. There wasn't anything to feel depressed about. Well was there? He forced his mind to replay the events of the last twenty-four hours. Football – brilliant! Sally – brilliant! Driving the night roads – brilliant! Coming up with a cover story for his dad? OK. Not so brilliant, but not bad enough for him to feel like this. He had never felt like this. Not ever. Not even when his mum had walked out all those years before. And he still felt like he wanted to cry.

Down the hall he could hear the radio. He couldn't hide away all day. Every minute he stayed in the room would only make it worse with his dad. Stupid. He braced himself and made his way into the kitchen where Bill McCann was reading the Sunday papers with a coffee.

"Bloody hell, it's Sleeping Beauty. Seen the time have you?"

Danny tried on a smile which felt like a new pair of shoes two sizes too small.

"I know. I must have been more knackered that I realised."

His father held him in a steady gaze whilst he took out a box of Cornflakes and busied himself with milk and sugar.

"Good night then was it?"

"Aye it was alright."

"Sally enjoy herself?"

"Aye. I think so."

Damn it, there were actually tears in his eyes now. For God's sake, what was going on? If his dad saw he was crying it would be a nightmare. He put the bowl down quickly and darted into the bathroom and wiped furiously at his eyes. What was the matter with him? He had never felt so bad. He took a few minutes and then flushed the toilet and went back.

"I feel a bit rough dad. Must have been the pie I had. I think I best go lie down for a while."

"The pie?"

Danny stared down at the lino floor. "Aye. The pie."

Escape. Escape. He rushed back to his room and closed the door with a feeling of panic. In the kitchen his dad stared straight ahead with a sinking feeling in his stomach.

By the next morning the black depression had more or less eased away and he told his dad that the effects of the bad pie seemed to have passed. By the time the morning break arrived, the world seemed to be back to normal. All the talk was about the semi final win and the big final that was now in the diary. And just as he was making his way to Home Economics he felt a light touch on his shoulder. It was Sally with glinting eyes.

"Are you avoiding me then?"

"No. Course not. I was just . . ."

She nodded. "Of course. You were just . . ."

"Aye, well."

"Aye, well."

She was mocking him and he couldn't seem to do anything much about it.

"Enjoy yourself then did you Danny? On Saturday night?"

"Yeah. Brilliant."

"So you'll be taking me out next weekend then?"

"Aye if you like."

"I like."

And she was gone, off to her Maths lesson.

Two mornings later the Postman brought the greatest letter that had ever landed on the mat. It was from the SFA and it was pleased to inform the reader that Daniel McCann had been selected for the Scotland Under 16's squad to play Wales at Rugby Park, Kilmarnock in a month-and-a-half's time. He had to read it three times before it sank in that he had actually made it. A dream that had grown for five years had started to turn into reality. At last the bleak misery that had so suffocated him on Sunday finally disappeared. Once again life was blindingly fantastic. Sunnybank were in the Rotary Cup Final, he was in the Scotland team and on Saturday night he was out with Sally again and his mind was already anticipating another journey into the dreamland he had found the weekend before.

PART TWO

There was sound. A distant sound. A sound that was trying to reach him from somewhere down near the core of the planet. Nagging. Hateful. Getting closer. Closing in. As threatening as a big guy with a twisted face and a baseball bat.

Slowly he peeled his eyes open. It was like opening the door to a garage that hadn't been used in about thirty years. And there, through bleary eyes, Danny stared at his alarm clock which was responsible for the sound that had dragged him back from the dead. His brain instructed his right arm to reach out and kill the sound with a tap to the button on the top of the clock. But someone had sneaked into his room in the night and replaced the blood in his veins with lead. His arm was too heavy. Impossibly heavy, and for a moment he wasn't sure if he could move it at all. At last it seemed to rouse itself and slowly but surely he guided his hand to the button that gave him silence.

Peace.

And the old garage door started to slide back closed again. But deep within the wet newspaper of his brain a determined voice was warning that going back to sleep wasn't an option. Not today. With a huge effort he stopped his eyes from closing out the world. With even greater effort he demanded that his clay body sit up. Wake up. Come alive. Become human.

One by one, he concentrated on small things. What time did it say on the clock that had dragged him up from the depths?

Nine o'clock.

What time had he finally managed to dampen down the blazing roar of last night's Ecstasy and Speed?

Must have been six. Maybe even later. He could remember sitting by his bedroom window watching the dark of the sky ease into light. Sitting and knowing that he had to find some sleep. Praying for it. Panicking about it. Begging for it. Sitting with tears of shame and frustration wandering down his cheeks as outside the birds woke up and sang out for a new day.

By the time the dawn had come he had been clear-headed enough to know that it was important that he set his alarm. He couldn't allow his father to be the one to pull him up out of the bottomless swamp of his sleep when it at last came. He couldn't allow his father to see what a complete car crash he was. Not again. Because that would only start the day with yet another row.

Danny's life seemed to have become a series of rows.

They had become events that happened every day and there seemed nothing he could do to stop them as he tried to keep everyone happy. For some time now the rows had been mainly with his father. They had focused on what the hell was the matter with him? Why couldn't he get out of his bed? What the hell was he up to every weekend? Couldn't he see that every morning after the night before he was like a walking zombie? And his dad had asked if Danny thought he was some sort of a mug? Well, did he? He wasn't born yesterday. He knew the score. Just like everyone on Sunnybank knew the score. There was no way Danny could be in such a state every Sunday after a few Pepsis at the St. Mary's disco.

He was on it, wasn't he? Bill didn't identify the 'it' part. The 'it' part was drugs. The Sunnybank plague. And Danny had reared-up and blown his top. Was he hell. No way. He was just tired. He must have caught a bug or something. There was loads of stuff going round. How come there were so many off school then? Why did his dad just assume he was using drugs because he was a bit tired . . .

A bit tired! Are you having a laugh. A bit tired doesn't meaning getting out of your pit at four in the afternoon and wandering about like the living dead . . .

Accusation and denial. Raised voices. His dad's anger driven by a terror that his son was on the slide. The Sunnybank slide. His own anger fuelled by shame at telling so many lies. Anger because deep down he knew how wrong he was to tell the lies.

And then the weekend before the rows hadn't been only about his dad and his fear. This time it was Sally. Sally like he had never seen her before. They had been to the St. Mary's disco on Friday night. Like they did every week. They had followed the usual routine. The ride out of town into the hills. Joints and alcopops and two eckies each. And then at half past eleven Sally had told him that her dad had given the OK for her to go and watch a film up in Glasgow the next night. Not that a film was what she really had in mind. They could try and get into some of the pubs. They could live it large on Sauchihall Street. She said it would be buzzing. Massive. And her Baz was going to take them in the Peugeot and her dad had said that since it was Glasgow and the film didn't finish till eleven they didn't have to be back until one because she had said that they would want to call in at McDonalds on the way home.

Her eyes had been so revved up with the whole thing that they looked like they were going to pop clean out of her head. He had told her that he couldn't. Because it was the Scotland Under 16's game on the Tuesday night and he needed a few days to get himself together for it. And the excitement in her eyes morphed into blazing rage. In about a second. It had been like flicking a light switch. One minute she was buzzing with it all, and all smiles. Then click. Raging. Red twisted face. Curled lips. Spitting anger. What was his problem? Pathetic. His stupid game wasn't till Tuesday. Tuesday! And she was talking Saturday. And not just any Saturday. A massive Saturday. A Glasgow Saturday. And she didn't know why she even bothered with him because he was just some pathetic kid. Well, wasn't he. Just because Mummy left. Just because Daddy will be cross. Pathetic. Well he could just get lost. She was sick of him. And all of a sudden she was storming across the dance floor and headed for the door and the Peugeot that was waiting outside. And Danny had panicked. Like completely panicked. Totally panicked. Because there was no way he was about to lose Sally Stamper for the sake of an early night. And he had legged it after her and said Ok, fine. Of course he'd go. Because he wasn't pathetic. No way. He was up for it. All of it. And his dad could shove it.

Switch. No more anger. Instead the gleaming shine of the 'E's. And she had wrapped herself around him and it had all been OK again.

Until Saturday morning. Well not the morning. It had been a while since Danny had seen a Saturday morning. It had been almost two when he had made it to the fridge in the kitchen to pour a tumbler of milk down his neck. And his dad had stared with that mixture of anger and worry. Hadn't he remembered? Danny had shaken his muzzy head. Remembered what? His dad had rolled his eyes and gripped the handle of his mug to hold onto his temper. The match. Gretna. They were going to watch them. For God's sake they had only been talking about it the day before. His dad had tried to wake him up at eleven but it had been like trying to wake a sack of potatoes.

And Danny had told him that he couldn't because he and Sally were off to Glasgow to see a film. Switch. All his dad's efforts to control himself were blown away. One minute he was tight-lipped. The next minute it was like a nuke went off in the kitchen. Was he mad? Had he forgotten what was happening on Tuesday night? This was his chance? It was the Scotland Under 16's for God's sake? Didn't that mean anything to him? And all he wanted to do was to go off to Glasgow with that Sally Stamper and take God knew what . . .

And suddenly the anger lit up Danny's brain to match that of his dad and now they were both yelling at each other. Red blazing faces. Neither listening to the other. Just shouting. Faces close. And Danny had stormed out and almost slammed the front door off its hinges.

By the time he met Sally he felt more washed-out than he had ever felt in his life. The gloom that had grown as he had killed the hours of the afternoon was almost as bad as it had been when his mum had left. Almost as bad as that day when the police and the social workers had come to take him to Stranraer. He had walked the streets of Sunnybank with the words of his dad rattling round his head like marbles in a jam jar. The worst of it was that he knew that his dad was right. Tuesday was the biggest day of his life. His chance. And maybe his only chance. Of course he was the big man down here in Dumfries. But Tuesday would be different. On Tuesday he would be out there with lads from Glasgow and Edinburgh and Dundee and Aberdeen. He knew he was good enough. He had been up for the training five times and he had held his own. But it wasn't easy. Not like playing for the school and Sunnybank. And he knew that to stand a chance he would have to be at the top of his game. Over the last couple of months he had come to know how the Eckie game worked.

CHAPTER TWO

The price for the weekend high was a two-day low. For a few hours he was Superman and the world was the best place in the universe and the Peugeot would fly through the night and the music would pour through his body. And there was Sally. Sally, Sally, Sally. Fantastic, blinding, unbelievable Sally. Cinderella Sally who would disappear at midnight to leave his brain racing like a Formula One car on an empty track. Round and round and round until it finally ran out of petrol.

Then would come the low. All through Saturday. And all through Sunday. And getting up for school on Monday would be harder than hard and the lessons would grind by without him taking on board a word of what the teachers were saying. And it wasn't just a physical low. A low that made his arms and legs feel like they were made out of clay and his brain feel like a soggy old sponge. It was a mental low as well. That was the worst of it. The wanting to cry all the time. The misery of seeing his dad eaten up with worry. And memories of his mum and days they would drive down to the coast for picnics. And no matter what he did he could never shake off the sadness that wrapped itself around him like cling film. And to try and make sure his dad didn't see it, he would hide away in his room until Monday night came along and the world around him started to seem less of a miserable place to be. He had learned the Ecstasy maths. Use on Friday. Washed out Saturday and Sunday. Half way human again by Monday night. More-or-less normal come Tuesday. But that was when he took the elevator to heaven on a Friday night. Taking the ride up to the top of the skyscraper on a Saturday night would change the maths. It would move the maths on an extra twenty-four hours. Which meant he would still be all washed out on Tuesday. Worse still was that this time the maths might be different because never before had he taken the elevator twice in two days. What would that mean? Would the double high lead to more than a double low?

As he had walked and walked, every instinct he had told him no. No, no and no. No and never. Not when on Tuesday night he was going to pull on the blue jersey of Scotland and take the first steps of a journey that could lead all the way to the dream he had lived for years. He knew what he had to do. He had to tell Sally that he was really sorry but there was no way. Not when he had such a big deal going down. And maybe when she was not buzzing quite so hard as she had been the night before she might understand a bit better. Surely she would. But the Ecstasy had drained him of that kind of optimism. By the middle of the afternoon it was raining and Sunnybank was grey all over and all his coats were still at home in his bedroom. Little by little the cold ate into his bones and a sense of utter gloom climbed in alongside. For a while he took some stolen warmth from the drying machines in the launderette until the owner came over to tell him to get lost and hang around somewhere else. He killed half an hour wandering aimlessly around the aisles of the supermarket until a security guard asked him if had any intention of buying anything and if he didn't maybe it would be a good idea if he left. More wet pavements. More quietly gurgling drains. Someone had dumped three bin liners off a bridge and onto the disused tracks of an old railway and a few crows were digging about in the mess. Someone had tossed a Kentucky Fried Chicken box into the gutter and now it had washed down to the drain. And now the light in the grey sky was beginning to smudge to black and the moment of truth was coming on fast. And of course she wouldn't understand. She would roll her eyes and slam the door in his face and Baz would spin the wheels and they would be gone. And he would be left standing on the pavement watching the tails lights swing around the corner and away into the night. And on Monday morning she would ignore him as if he wasn't there because he would have become nothing to her. And it was as certain as certain could be, because by the end of that leaky wet Saturday afternoon there was nothing in Danny's brain that wasn't bleak and bad.

So what would be the point of being sensible and going home to his father's anger and about a million acres of depression, because if Sally chucked him he would be good for nothing anyway. Sure, he would get a night's sleep and his body would be more ready for Tuesday but his body wouldn't matter because if she was gone then nothing would matter and he would play like a dog.

In the end he didn't want to be chucked. He couldn't face being chucked. He couldn't handle the idea of the empty hours in his room every Friday night as his mind wandered back to the hours of magic that he had learned to crave. He was too low. Too beaten. Too washed out. Too wet. Too everything.

So he went to Glasgow. And this time they took three each because Sally said they would need extra to get back up for another night. And Sunday was terrible. And Monday was worse. And on Tuesday morning he hauled himself out of bed and knew with a sinking certainty that he had blown it. That night he had only lasted thirty minutes before the coach had hauled him off with a slight shake of the head. His dad hadn't spoken a word all the way back to Dumfries and Danny McCann had cried himself to sleep because he had been handed the chance of a lifetime and blown it all away for the sake of three 'E's and a night out in Glasgow with Sally Stamper. Even though he had felt more tired than he had ever felt before in his life, he found the relief of sleep impossible to find. When he closed his eyes memories of his half-hour flashed before him. Memories of legs that were empty of all life. No pace. No stamina. No nothing. On the few occasions that he got the ball he had been tackled before his brain had the chance to decide what to try and do with it. He had been the worst player on the park. He had been useless. Worse than useless. And there was no way that they would be asking him back again.

School the next day was a torment. All of his mates wanted to know how it went. Did he score? How did he play? How good were the rest of the team? And Danny had spent the morning break and the lunch hour trying to keep tears in check as he fielded their questions with evasive actions and false confidence. He only told the truth to Sally when they shared a few snatched minutes between classes. He had hoped that there might be some sympathy in her sparkling green eyes. But like Danny, Sally was also still climbing out of the trough of their double night Ecstasy high at the weekend. She was strung out and tetchy and not in the mood for sympathy. She had merely given her shoulders an impatient shrug and uttered the dreaded thought that it was only a game, well, wasn't it, and then with a threatening pout she asked if he was still up for Friday night, and he was far, far too low to even think of saying that no he wasn't. He should have done of course because on Saturday morning part two of the biggest week in his football life was due to be played out. It was the Rotary Cup Final and Sunnybank Rovers were to play Springfield for the right to be crowned the under 16 champions of Dumfries. It was the time to draw a line in the sand. To take a firm stance and say sorry but no. He had already blown it once. No way was he about to do it again. But that would have meant risking her anger again. And he just couldn't bear to see the rage burn in her green eyes. He couldn't face her biting scorn. Not today. Not when he was on the floor.

And so he said yes. Course he was up for it. No problem. Usual time.

That night his father didn't speak to him at all. Not the next night either. An all-pervading silence settled all through the flat. Both of them knew that as soon as anything was said it would mean an eruption and neither could really face it. So Bill McCann kept his anger wrapped tight because he feared just how it would rage if he let his self control slip. When they had at last spoken it had been five o'clock on Friday night. Bill had cooked a pan of pasta because it was the right thing to eat on the eve of a big game. Danny had almost finished his plate when he steeled himself and told his dad that he was off out. Bill had felt a tension through his chest. The rage was there and ready for out. He took a breath and forced it back down.

"That a good idea with the final tomorrow?"

Danny shrugged. "I'll be alright."

"Like you were on Tuesday?"

"What do you mean by that?"

"You know exactly what I mean by that."

Danny tossed his fork down onto his plate. "Look I just played bad. That's all. It happens."

"Think I was born yesterday son?"

Danny didn't answer. Instead he sat back in his chair and folded his arms tight across his chest and stared down at the remains of pasta on his plate.

"Since I am almost sixteen I would be pretty stupid to think that wouldn't I?"

Bill held onto his anger but it was getting harder. It was like he had two Rottweilers on leads and they had just spotted a cat. He took a careful sip of his coffee and weighed his words.

"It's not too late you know."

"What isn't?"

"Look Danny, Tuesday night was bad. No point in pretending it wasn't. But that doesn't mean it's time to just give up. You will have tonnes of opportunities. But not if you carry on with all this."

"All what?"

"Oh for Christ's sake Danny, you know what. Out before games. Coming back all spaced-out then zombified for days after. Look I'm not saying there's anything wrong with going out with Sally. I never have. It's the drugs Danny. It's the drugs that are going to take it all away."

Still he stared down.

"What drugs?"

"You seem to forget I've known you all your life Danny. All the way back to day one. Minute one. And all that time I've known a lad who is out of bed at the crack of dawn. All energy. All go. And suddenly I see someone who can't make it out of his pit until halfway through the afternoon. And you really seriously think that I don't get to wondering why that might be. And then I look out of the window and wherever I look I see the walking-dead scurrying about the place, hunting out the next tenner bag. This is Sunnybank Danny. I'd have to be deaf, dumb and blind not to see it."

Danny started to get to his feet. "Look, I need to go. I'll be fine tomorrow. Wait and see."

To his surprise, Bill found that the anger was draining away. It was so easy to see what was coming because he was the wrong side of forty. It was something he had been seeing for years. Hell, he had been there himself. But would he have listened when he was fifteen? Had he listened when he was a grown man in his thirties with a son to look after and rent to pay? Instead he had dived into the bottom of a bottle and closed his ears to all around him who warned that his life was going to hell in a handcart. So was Danny about to listen? Not likely.

"Look Danny. It's your life. Not mine. She's a bonny lass and I guess that right now she seems to be everything. And I hope that in years to come the two of you get wed and have kids and go on to live happily ever after. The problem is that tends to be Disney Channel stuff. It costs £3.25 for two nights down at Blockbusters. All I see is that you have a one off chance to have one hell of a life getting paid a tonne of cash for playing the game you love. And you're about to blow it all away for Sally. But it's your choice. All your choice."

Nothing could have hurt Danny more than the reasonable calm in his dad's voice. He was ready for anger. And threats. And maybe even blows. He wasn't ready for understanding and advice. This meant it would be his choice. His fault. There would be no excuses after this. His dad was making sure that he did what he did with his eyes wide open. But these were things he had already thought through and he had decided to try to have his cake and eat it. He wasn't going to give up Sally and the weekend trips to a place far, far away from the Sunnybank and all that sailed in her. And he was going to keep playing football and some big club was going to spot him and it would all work out in the end.

"Look dad, I'll be fine tomorrow. I'm on top of it. Honest."

He pulled his jacket from the back of the chair and left without enduring the pain of his father's eyes.

And now he was sitting on the edge of the bed and it was 9.15 and they would be leaving the house for the final at ten and his body felt like it had been tied to the back of a tractor and dragged from Dumfries to Carlisle and back again. He had told his father that he was on top of it and now his solution was about to be put to the test. He was aware in advance that the Ecstasy maths were going to be all against him, just like he had known that Sally wouldn't accept him passing on the pills for no better reason than that it was the Rotary Cup final the next day. And so he had picked up the phone and called Baz for some advice. Man to man. And when Sally had done her weekly Cinderella act with a parting kiss, Baz had driven beyond the edge of town and passed two wraps of speed over the front seat.

"Know how to take it?"

Danny had nodded.

"Snort both bags about an hour before the kick off. You'll be like Ronaldino. Trust me bro. It'll be massive."

Danny pocketed the bags.

"What do I owe you?"

"Nothing bro. All in the cause of Sunnybank my man. My contribution. It's all good."

Now Danny eyed the two inconsequential bits of cling film suspiciously. If the powder they contained turned him into a human being again, it would be little short of a miracle. Well maybe it was the time for miracles. Five minutes later the speed was up his nose care of a new ten pound not that he had saved specially for the occasion and he was wiping away at his nostrils and blinking away the sharp biting taste of it. By the time he had changed, it was starting to kick in. As he came into the kitchen his dad looked up with a look of astonishment.

"I wasn't that confident you'd get up."

"Aye well, there you go. Never can tell can you, well you can't. I mean you think one thing but then another thing happens and you think I never would have thought it would be that way but there it is. We off then or what?"

CHAPTER TWO

The words spilled out like his mouth was a big hose pipe and there didn't seem much he could do to get things in the right order but it didn't matter much because he was revved up and rocking.

"What about breakfast?"

"Nah. I'm fine. Don't want to be weighed down. No way. Let's just go."

"You're pretty hyper."

"Course I am. Cup final isn't it. Who wouldn't be?"

Now he was facing a new and unpredicted problem. On the one hand he had about a zillion words that were pouring from all corners of his brain and dying to dive out of his mouth like a plague of gibbering locusts. On the other hand the way out wasn't that easy because for some reason his teeth were grinding together and blocking the way. Not that it mattered because all of a sudden his legs felt turbo charged and he couldn't wait to get out on the pitch. Ronaldino? Nae bother. He could do Ronaldino. Ronaldino R' Us. Ronaldino is basic.

The final was being played at a neutral venue where needles were not a problem and so they didn't need to go through the usual pre-match routine when they met Jimmy Doyle half an hour later. Danny took off onto the pitch with a ball and started beating imaginary defenders whilst his two coaches looked on.

"He's full of himself this morning." Jimmy said it in a way that wasn't much convinced.

"Too full." Bill spat the words out.

"How do you mean?"

For a moment Bill wanted to share the nightmare that had been growing every weekend since his son had first gone to the St. Mary's disco with Sally Stamper on the night of the semi-final. But it was neither the time or the place. They had both worked for this moment for many years and it wasn't right that he should put the knockers on things.

"Nothing. How we looking then?"

Jimmy gave a tentative smile. "So far so good. No calls as yet. Looks like we might just have a full squad."

"Well if we don't get a full squad for the final then I don't suppose we ever will."

As kick off time closed in there was indeed a full squad. Eleven players, three substitutes and even a modest group of supporters made up of a mixture of parents, brothers and sisters and mates. After the frantic tactical excitement that had preceded the semi-final, it all seemed a little dull. The first eleven were all present and correct and not one of them seemed to be about to die of Buckfast poisoning. It meant that defenders could be defenders and midfielders could be midfielders and strikers could play up front. Jimmy's team talk was all about remembering what they had talked about for two weeks. Shape. Discipline. Taking a second to think. Not just hoofing it. Keeping a straight line across the back. Covering the full back when they went forward. Staying onside. Not flying into any stupid tackles. Keeping the language down because people were watching. And in no time at all the lads were taking up their positions and the referee was setting his watch to zero. Bill gave him a nudge.

"We're honoured."

"What do you mean?"

"Look. Over there."

A man in his fifties with jeans, ponytail and anorak was making his way to the touchline whilst lighting up a cigarette at the same time having parked up a Transit van.

"I dunnae ken what you're on about."

"Him. Over there. That's Brooks Mileson."

"What, the guy who owns Gretna?"

"Aye."

Not only was it the guy who owned Gretna, but he was clearly making a beeline to where they were positioned by the halfway line."

"Morning lads."

"Morning."

"Is one of you Jimmy Doyle."

"Aye. I am." Jimmy was intrigued now. "Scouting are you?"

This induced a chuckle. Brooks tossed his cigarette and outed it with a scuff of his boot and immediately yanked another from the pack and lit up. "No. You must be joking. That's the gaffer's job. I'm just a fan. I was in town to collect the pies for the match this afternoon so I thought I'd catch the first half. Confident then are you?"

"Aye. Confident enough. Did I hear you right then?"

"What do you mean?"

"I thought I heard you say that you were in town to collect the pies for the game this afternoon."

"That's right enough. What's up with that then?"

"Nothing. I just couldn't see Roman Abramovich out and about in his Tranny van on match day, that's all."

"Well, he's not from Sunderland is he?"

"No. That he isn't."

For a moment Jimmy was somewhat waylaid by the thought that being a native of Sunderland made it perfectly normal for a multimillionaire football club chairman to be out and about in his van on Saturday morning on the pie run. Then all of his attention was taken by the referee blowing his whistle and setting the game into motion,

Brooks lit up his third cigarette in ten minutes. "Your lot in the white are they?"

"Aye. That's us. And Danny McCann is number seven, on the ball now."

"Danny who?"

"Danny McCann. He's who you've come to see isn't he?"

"No. Never heard of him. Like I said before, I leave all that stuff to the gaffer. No. It wasn't Danny McCann I came to see, though I'll have a look if you like."

Jimmy wasn't entirely convinced but he saw no reason why he shouldn't take what the man was saying at face value. "So who have you come to see then?"

"You."

"Me!"

"Aye. You."

"Why the hell do you want to see me?"

"To offer you a job actually."

Now this really knocked Jimmy back and pulled all his attention clear from a wild scramble by the far corner flag which was getting the referee into a high state of excitement.

"I've got a job." It was out of his mouth before he had chance to think what he was saying and he regretted it straight away. But Brooks wasn't remotely offended. He took a long pull on his cigarette and grinned.

"What do you do then?"

"I'm a postman."

"Well I'll match whatever you're earning plus a bit. How does that sound?"

This was crazy. Jimmy wasn't sure now if he was actually awake. Maybe in a second or two he would open his eyes to find it chucking down with rain and his whole team locked up for every kind of anti social behaviour.

"Doing what?"

"You've heard of our community programme. At Gretna?"

"Aye. Coaches in schools and stuff."

"Well. There you are then."

This was nuts. Completely nuts. "But you can't just offer me a job just like that. You don't even know me."

Another smoked cigarette hit the deck. Another fresh one was pulled from the pack. "I've asked about. People who know what's what. And I can see what I see out on the pitch."

Jimmy followed his gaze and all he saw was yet another whirling melee of young bodies hurling themselves at a football. Nobody would ever say it was like watching Brazil. "You've lost me Mr Mileson. What exactly do you see?"

"I grew up in a place like Sunnybank. In Sunderland. And what I see is eleven lads all keen as mustard. And three subs gagging to get a game. That doesn't just happen Jimmy. Not when they're fifteen. Not in places like Sunnybank. It takes someone special to make it happen. Especially to get them into the final. So that's what I see. Just think about it. Come down to Raydale next week if you like. I'm almost always about. Tell you what, that number seven of yours is a man on a mission."

To say that Danny McCann was a man on a mission was in fact something of an understatement. Everything about him was turbo charged. Normally he played with a steady, quiet focus but today he was loud. He howled for the ball and constantly roared on his team mates. He had always liked a tackle but today he was throwing himself at the ball with the manic zeal of a suicide bomber. Twice in the first five minutes the referee had to take him by the shoulder and warn him that if he didn't calm down a card would be coming out. Danny seemed as if he was covered from head to toe in ants and couldn't stand still for more than a second at a time. Then in the sixth minute he grabbed the ball as it broke out of a tackle on the halfway line and bore down on the goal. The central midfielder slid in on him but came nowhere close. Then the centre back made a better fist of his attempted tackle, but Danny nipped the ball by him and jumped over his sliding legs. Next came the keeper who bought a dummy hook, line and sinker to leave a vacant net for Danny to thrash the ball into. What followed next was the most demented goal celebration that any of the watching crowd had ever seen which took Danny all the way back to the edge of his own penalty area.

The next five minutes saw him complete his hat trick and each goal was better than the one that went before it. Brooks took it all in as cigarette number four came and went. When he spoke it was more or less to himself.

"Best bring the gaffer along next time."

Springfield by this stage were rattled to the core. Nothing had prepared them for such an onslaught. Their coach was yelling himself hoarse with instructions for the midfield and the back four, and none of it was making the slightest bit of difference. Seventeen minutes. Danny flattened the left midfielder with a murderously well-timed tackle and once again bore down on the goal. Once again he flew past the centre half but this time the lad decided that enough was enough. He was sick of being made to look like such a mug. More than that, he was sick of Danny's motor mouth. With a massive swipe of his leg he scythed Danny to the floor and them pushed his face into Danny's.

"Come on big mouth. You want some . . .?"

The centre half had enjoyed a big reputation in the playground for may years and he was accustomed to this kind of threat having a pretty drastic effect, especially when the lad on the receiving end was a good six inches and two stone smaller than him. Which all made it a major shock to the system when Danny flew to his feet as quick as a cat and floored him with a whipped right hook that Mohammed Ali would have been more than a little proud of. Once the centre half was down Danny was all over him, kicking and punching and screaming. For a brief moment both teams and the referee looked on in complete amazement. Then the spell was broken and all out war broke out. The referee was trying to get a near demented Danny into a half nelson but it was all but impossible. By now the centre half had curled up into the kind of position that he had last taken up in his mother's stomach in the last few days before he was born. Bill McCann arrived on the scene twenty yards ahead of Jimmy whose progress was severely hampered by his old leg injury. He dragged Danny clear of the prostrate figure on the ground and slapped him as hard as he could across the cheek. For a moment Danny's eyes blazed at his father and Bill readied himself for an assault. By now coaches and parents had managed to stabilise the situation and the kicks and punches had stopped. The referee was almost hyperventilating as he marched over to where Danny stared at his father with his heart beating at about ten million miles an hour.

"Right sunshine . . ." Danny saw him reaching into his breast pocket for a red card.

"Oh get stuffed."

And with that he was gone. Running. Away from the pitch. Away from the cup final. Away from six years of carefully nurtured dreams. Away from everything.

It took a few more minutes until a semblance of peace was restored. The game started back up and normality slowly took a hold. Bill McCann was white faced with fury and Jimmy decided it would be best to leave him be for a few minutes. He focused his attention on yelling out the tactical reshuffle that was now required to compensate for the absence of his star player. He withdrew one of his strikers and told him on threat of death to sit in front of the back four and not to go glory hunting. Springfield were suddenly filled with new hope now that their tormentor in chief had departed the scene. For the remainder of the half they pretty well laid siege to the Sunnybank box, but all their efforts only yielded a single goal. Half time gave Jimmy the chance to further organise his troops into an even tighter defensive formation which he hoped would shut out their victory.

Brooks had stood clear of the two coaches whilst the drama ran its course. Now he checked his watch and came back over as the Sunnybank players trotted out for the second half.

"I'll have to be off lads. You know. Pies. You'll have a think will you Jimmy?"

"I will. And I never said thanks. What with all the drama and all."

Brooks gave a rueful smile. "If we have half as much action this afternoon the fans will get their money's worth." He had been watching the agonised body language of Bill McCann and had guessed that it had been his son who had lost the plot in such spectacular fashion. "Was that your lad?"

CHAPTER TWO

Bill just nodded. Brooks quietly patted him on the shoulder. "Well if we can be of any help you know where to find us. It's not an easy time to be young."

Bill sensed the man's sincerity and muttered his thanks for the offer and Brooks departed to collect the pies as people from Sunderland do.

"Are you going to try and find him?" Jimmy really didn't quite know what to say. He had heard all about Danny's terrible debut for the Scottish under 16's earlier in the week and of course the Sunnybank grapevine had made him aware that his star man was spending his weekend nights with Sally Stamper. He had been wanting to say something for several weeks but had held his tongue. Now he wished he had opened his mouth.

Bill shook his head. "No point. I'll get him later."

Jimmy stared out at his new defensive set up that was showing every sign of holding back the tide of the Springfield comeback. He knew he was on thin ice. Bill was like an unexploded bomb and saying the wrong thing could easily set off the explosion.

"If I can help just ask OK. And I mean that."

For a moment his old friend looked at him very hard. Weighing the words. Wondering whether they were true. Then he nodded. "Thanks Jimmy. I might just take you up on that."

As it turned out the second half was a complete anti climax. After twenty minutes of fruitless pressure, Springfield started to run out of gas. In fact it was Sunnybank who scored the only goal of the half with a breakaway in the last ten minutes which induced a goalkeeping howler. The cup was presented and photos taken to commemorate the occasion. Win bonuses were paid out in McDonalds and the players drifted away one by one. Bill finished his coffee and took his leave leaving Jimmy to think about the extraordinary job offer that had come out of nowhere. He had told himself that he would give the whole thing long and careful consideration. Well obviously he would. It wasn't a thing to be taken lightly. He had been with the Post office for a lot of years. There was all the pension stuff to think about. And redundancy entitlement if things ever went wrong. This wasn't something to rush into. But as he carried his second coffee to the table outside and stirred in sugar he realised that these sensible thoughts were a complete and utter waste of time. If he said no to the offer he would regret it for the rest of his life. The choice was as simple as any choice could ever be. He could carry on pushing junk mail through letterboxes until retirement day. Or he could get back into full time football. With kids this time. And with no chance of a mistimed tackle taking the whole thing down in flames. So what was there to think about? Not a damn thing. He would drive down on Monday as soon as he had finished his shift. And he would sign there and then. And after a break of over twenty years he would at last be back in full time football. The sun burst out from between high white clouds and it carried the first warmth of spring. Jimmy Doyle had spent a lot of years looking over his shoulder and waiting to be hit by the next career ending tackle. It was time to put it all in the past. All of it. It was time for the future. And all of a sudden the future looked like a bright place to be. If anyone had noticed him sitting on his own outside McDonalds with a cup of black coffee, they might have noticed that he was smiling properly for the first time since 1985.

A couple of miles away Danny McCann was a million miles from smiling. For almost an hour after he stormed away from the cup final the speed had kept his body and brain locked into overdrive. He walked at a ferocious pace going nowhere in particular. One or two people stopped and watched him pass them by with looks of slight bemusement. Without realising it he was muttering to himself and gesticulating with thrashing hand signals. His mind was all over the place and he couldn't seem to hold a thought for more than a few seconds. But slowly the chemical began to loosen its grip and things started to slow down. The first sign of normality was the feeling of cold. He was still in his kit and his metal studs clattered along the pavement. He was back in Sunnybank by this time, having returned on some kind of auto pilot. Thankfully there was a spare key wedged into a crack in the wall in the back yard. Once inside he put on warm clothes and downed a pint of milk from the fridge. The next stage of normality was the tiredness that was now starting to seep through his bones with the inevitability of an incoming tide. He yearned to climb into bed and pull the covers over his head and escape the nightmare of life for the oblivion of sleep. But in his heart he knew that the sleep wouldn't come. It would be close, but not close enough. And then he would hear the front door open and he would have to face his dad and there was no way that he could face his dad because as well as the tiredness the despair was also starting to take a hold of him. It was a despair the like of which he had never even been close to before. Far, far worse than that morning when he had got back from school to find his dad sitting at the kitchen table with a note from his mum and tear streaks down his cheeks. Worse even than when the social workers had dragged him through the front door.

It was a complete despair. An unending wall to wall black despair that stretched all the way round the world and back again. So he couldn't face his father. Just like he couldn't face himself. But he could run from his father. If only he could run from himself. If only.

Outside again. Walking. Just walking, and with every step the darkness seemed to close in a little tighter. How had it all gone so wrong in just a few days? It was supposed to have been the best week of his life. He had hoped to finish the week well and truly on track to take up the life that he had dreamed about for years. He had hoped to have established himself in the national side and helped Sunnybank win the cup for the first time. And to make his dad proud. And Jimmy. And Sally. And to feel proud of himself. To feel like a somebody. To be one of those who soared clear of Sunnybank and its crumbling pebble dash walls.

Instead he had blown it. Absolutely blown it. Blown it into so many pieces that it could never be put back together again. Humpty Dumpty sat on a wall. A great fall. A completely massive fall. And all the king's horses and all the king's men would have as little luck trying to get his life back together as they had trying to put Humpty back together. And of course the tears were on their way again. It seemed like every week he went through hours of trying not to burst into tears. He needed to hide for a while. To escape all the eyes who would be watching him as he ground up and down the pavements. By the time the sun went down, the Sunnybank gossip machine would be working at full efficiency. The word would be out. Danny McCann lost the plot. I mean completely lost it. Flipped his lid, so he did. Attacked a lad. Like really attacked him. As in assaulted. If the cops had been there they would have lifted him. And they would have been right to. Going downhill, so he is. It's ever since he started knocking about with that Sally Stamper. That Danny McCann. Just like when his mother scarpered off to Australia. The cow. Got to feel for Bill though. Poor devil. Wouldn't be surprised if it all sent him back onto the drink. They're cursed that family. Cursed.

He was out now. Into country lanes with hedges and crows in the trees. Occasional cows gave him bored stares as he marched along. High above, a buzzard glided through the sky waiting for a mouse to get careless. One foot in front of the other. Walk. His legs were tired now. Really tired. But he knew if he sat down he wouldn't get up again. He knew if he stopped walking the depression would multiply by ten. So he kept moving, driving himself on. Not going anywhere. Just going. Running. At some stage he must have unconsciously started to loop his way back round to the town. The light was fading now and ahead an orange glow told him that he was headed back to town.

Then what? Home. Home was hell. And hell was home. Home was the nightmare at the end of the rainbow. Home was the searing misery in his dad's eyes. Home was the bedroom walls which would close in and squeeze his head until it would burst. Home was where everything would have to be faced up to.

Not yet.

Walk some more. Not anywhere in particular. Just anywhere. Everywhere. Everywhere but home. So he walked some. And then some more. And with every step a massive, overwhelming tiredness climbed into him until he knew that he couldn't walk any more. He would have to go home. After all, where else was there? Maybe it would be best to sit for a while first. Best to take a little time to gather up his thoughts into some kind of order. Somehow he would have to come up with something to say to his father although he couldn't begin to think what. There was a bench by a bus shelter which seemed as good a place as any. The back was split and the paint was peeling but it was usable. The unbreakable perspex on the bus shelter window had of course been broken into a crazy spider's web of splits. Someone had proudly spray painted 'Razzo'. Had it maybe been Razzo himself who had taken on the challenge of breaking the unbreakable perspex? Or maybe the perspex had been intact when Razzo had gone to work with an aerosol and then later somebody who really hated Razzo's guts had come along and been so enraged at the sight of the name that they had kicked it hard enough to break the unbreakable. Another Sunnybank mystery.

"Danny!!"

He had been away with the fairies thinking about Razzo. Not his dad's voice. Thank god. Baz. Baz leaning out of the driver's window of his Peugeot. And beyond Baz the faint outline of his sister on the passenger seat.

"Jesus Danny, you were all zoned out somewhere completely else there man. What you up to?"

"Nothing. Just sitting."

"Fancy a burn? Me and Sal are taking a ride. Few tunes. Couple of spliffs. Just chilling, yeah? Nothing heavy. You good?"

Nothing heavy sounded good enough to Danny. Because right at that moment just about everything in his whole, lousy, miserable life was heavy.

"I'm good."

"Then jump in Danny boy."

It was the usual routine. The tired orange lit streets of Sunnybank gave way to the empty blackness of the countryside that spread uninterrupted into the north for millions and millions of acres. Nobody was talking because the music was louder than a fighter jet at twenty feet. Danny was happy enough to take his turn on the joint and sink his head back into the seat so that he could look up and out into the sky which was filled with stars. The car was warm and the joint made the back seat seem like the most comfortable seat that anyone had ever sat on. He passed the joint on to Sally and allowed his eyes to close for a few moments. Why not? Take a time out. Later would come along later. It always did. And later was going to be an utter nightmare. So now could be now. And later could be later. The moronic simplicity of his befuddled thinking made him smile to himself. Now and later. Later and now. All that mattered was the in between.

Because he was drifting off into sleep Danny never saw the young red deer as it jumped out from the pine trees. Baz saw it and he dragged down hard on the steering wheel to avoid it. The small car managed to adjust its course sufficiently to avoid the terrified animal but it was all much too sudden. Had they been wandering along at a sedate forty, then it would have probably been OK. But Baz wasn't a sedate forty type of lad. He had his tunes as loud as they would go and his cap pulled back to front and his right foot jammed hard down to the floor. The speedo read 77 mph at the moment that he jumped the car away from the deer and it was all too much. The Peugeot flipped and rolled over three times before coming to rest against a four-year-old pine tree.

The tiredness was ripped away. In a second adrenaline was flying through Danny as he tried to make sense of what was happening. For a second or two, the world was a mad, rolling place full of the sound of screaming and metal scraping on tarmac. Then silence. The radio must have been smashed. No more banging sound. Had he really listened, he might had heard the soft sound of the deer as it hopped away through the pine trees. Why did he feel so weird? Everything seemed wrong. His head felt like a balloon being filled from a kitchen tap. Then at last his brain started to find its bearings. The reason for his weirdness was that he was upside down. The car had come to rest on its roof and his seatbelt was holding him. Once he had worked out that much, he started to think more logically. He found the seatbelt catch and pressed it. Once free of its hold he fell to the roof which of course was the floor. It was hard to organise his limbs in the confined space, but he managed it after a few seconds and then he felt about the door until he located the handle. Click. It worked. Thank God. Then a firm push opened the door and the crisp air of the night flowed in. Once he was out of the car he gingerly ran his hands up and down his body to confirm that nothing was broken or missing. It wasn't. Parts of him hurt like hell but everything seemed in one piece.

With a sense of dread he dragged at the driver's door which was stubborn at first but opened with a good yank. There was no moon and the starlight was all but worthless. He couldn't make anything out, but he could feel Baz. And Baz was sticky. And there was a metallic smell to the stickiness. Oh Christ no. He forced down a feeling of rising panic. Think Danny. Think. He did. Next he ran his hand along the floor until he found the light switch. Click. It worked. Straight away he wished it hadn't. Baz and Sally were both out cold. Neither had been wearing seat belts and their bodies were covered in blood. He wanted to run. To scream. To hide. To see if he could manage five hundred kick ups with his left foot. Instead he gritted his teeth and carefully frisked Baz until he found his mobile phone.

The ambulance driver must have driven even faster than Baz. They arrived in under twenty-five minutes. The police landed five minutes later. Danny sat by the roadside with his head in his hands whilst they pulled out his fellow night riders and gently transferred them to stretchers. There was a voice now. Close. Not loud. Quite gentle really.

CHAPTER TWO

" . . . listen son, I really need you to help me out here. You need to tell me their names. So I can tell their parents. You hear me son? I know it's hard but you need to try. Come on. Lift your head now….."

He didn't lift his head. Instead he talked to the floor.

"Stamper. Baz and Sally Stamper."

This brought on a sharp intake of breath.

"What? Les Stamper's kids?"

Danny nodded.

"Bloody hell. Right. Just sit tight son. I'll be back in a . . ."

In one way it almost turned out well. His dad was so relieved that he wasn't dead that he wasn't about to tear into him. Danny was still in a semi-trance as he walked into the flat. He stared down at the kitchen table whilst the two officers gave Bill the main facts about what had happened. The lad must have been going like the clappers. The car was a complete write off. Both the kids looked like they would be OK. The lad had a broken collar bone. The lass seemed pretty well untouched. Apart from cuts and bruises of course. They both had plenty of cuts and bruises. Probably concussion as well. But they had been lucky. No doubt about that. Really lucky . . .

Bill offered to make tea and both policemen accepted. Once they were sipping at their steaming mugs they seemed to exchange a glance. The older of the two assumed the face of a man who was about to have to say something difficult: something that nobody would really want to hear.

"I'm afraid there is some more sir. I'm sorry to have to go into it now, but . . ."

Bill gritted his teeth and gave a resigned wave of his hand. Danny just stared.

"I'm afraid we found drugs in the car sir. Not huge amounts. But there will be questions. Not tonight. Danny here has been through enough for one night. We would like you call us. Arrange a time. There's no need to come to the station. We'll come to you . . ."

On any other night Danny would have found sleep impossible with the worry of the police, but not on that night. His body and brain had taken all they could stand and he was out cold within seconds of his head hitting the pillow. His father shook him awake a little after eleven to tell him the policemen would be back in two hours time. It gave him time to take a shower and clear his head. He was once again back in the grip of black depression, but this time it was the worst he had ever known. Before there had been no particular reason for feeling so low. Before he had the prospect of a football career and Sally Stamper was his girlfriend. So things weren't bad. Not remotely. They just felt bad as he slowly climbed out of the chemical low that followed the chemical high as sure as night followed day. But this was different. His tears mixed with the hot water from the shower as the consequences of what had happened smacked into him one by one. He'd blown his chance with Scotland. He'd blown it with Sunnybank Rovers and there was no doubt that some kind of lengthy ban would be in the pipeline. And all his instincts told him that it would be over with Sally. It hadn't been his fault that Baz had pranged the car, but he didn't expect that Les Stamper would see it that way. As he towelled himself down the realisation hit him that he hadn't even bothered to find out the final score from game. What was he turning into?

When he did ask over a bowl of cereal, his dad hadn't wanted to go into any great detail. He had just muttered. "We won. 4 – 1."

The police arrived at one and accepted more tea. Danny stuck hard to a simple story. He hadn't seen any drugs. He didn't know about any drugs. He had just gone for a drive. That was it. No, he had never seen Basil Stamper taking drugs. No, he had never seen Sally Stamper taking drugs. No, he had never taken drugs himself. No, he didn't know anything about Les Stamper. No, he didn't think that Baz had been going too fast.

The policemen had expected nothing else. They scribbled a few notes down and finished their tea. It was the usual Sunnybank story. Sorry officer, but I didn't see anything. I was watching the TV. I was in the bath. I was on the phone. If a full battalion of the Iraqi army bombarded the place, nobody would have seen a thing. Not if Les Stamper had anything to do with it. In a way, his steadfast lies suited them well enough. There had been a meeting that morning and it had been decided that the matter should be forgotten and filed. They had gone through the wrecked car with a fine-toothed comb and had found next to nothing. All that they could charge anyone with would be possession. Les Stamper would field some £500 an hour lawyer down from Glasgow and it was a racing certainty that he would find some faults in the paperwork because the officers at the crash scene hadn't been interested in paperwork. Their priority had been helping the ambulance crew to save the kids' lives. So they decided to let the thing drop. They had all had to suffer Les Stamper's smug smile as he beat the rap in the past. They had no wish to do it again.

When the policemen left after half an hour, Danny braced himself for the inevitable onslaught from his dad. But the onslaught never came. Just a sentence which was about a hundred times worse.

"I'm not going to go on and on Danny. No point. You're sixteen now. Almost a man. I'll just say this. I'm disgusted. Completely disgusted. You've let everyone down. Me. Yourself. Jimmy. Your team mates. Everyone. You're a disgrace. A bloody disgrace. You make me sick. I just hope you make yourself sick."

And that was it. And the quietly spoken words hit home harder than any shouting could ever have done. The silence that settled into the flat lasted for days. Danny went to school and returned to his room. In the playground his mates were slightly wary of him. All the talk was of the victory in the final. But it was like his hat trick had been forgotten. What was remembered was the ten-man rearguard that kept Springfield at bay.

And Sally was nowhere to be seen. After a few days he took a walk across town to the hospital, but they told him that she had been checked out two days earlier. He thought about going round to her house and knocking on the door but every instinct told him it would be the mother of bad ideas. So instead he waited for her to return to school and wondered if they would ever go out with each other again.

It was ten days after the accident that a line was drawn under things. He was halfway home from school when he turned a corner to find Les Stamper's blue Range Rover waiting by the pavement with the engine on. As he approached, Les reached over and popped open the passenger door.

"Get in Danny."

Danny got in. Les seemed to look him over for a moment and then sighed and lit a cigarette.

"OK. Listen and listen well. Sally's OK. She came home two days ago. She's not coming back to Sunnybank School. She's off to England. A private place. Boarding school. But she will be coming home in the holidays. And you won't be seeing her. I'll repeat that just so we're nice and clear. You won't be seeing her. Now. You weren't driving the car. Fair enough. You did well in fact. You did all the right things. And you played a blinder with the cops from what I hear. So you and me are square. You stay away from Sally and we'll stay square. Simple as that. You go against me and I'll pull your fingernails out. As for Baz. See him if you like. It's nothing to me. Me and Baz are finished. Done. He's nothing to me. Not any more. OK. That's it. You can get out."

Danny got out. He stood and watched as the big car drew away from the kerb and eased away. He would do as he was told. There would be no more Friday nights with Sally at the St. Mary's disco. There would be no more nights hurtling down dark country roads with the music bouncing around his skull. There would be no more chances with Scotland. The school team season was over. The Sunnybank Rovers season was over and he was banned for six months when the next season started. His father hated him. His mates were nervous of him.

And he hated himself.

Loathed himself more than he dreamed he could ever loathe anyone.

Summer had arrived in Sunnybank during the first week of July and had liked it so much that it had stayed for over a month. A hot dry wind was rolling an empty crisp packet along the pavement. This attracted the attention of a panting dog halfway through an afternoon walk. For a moment it seemed like it might give its lead an extra tug to see if it could catch the bag as if wafted along. But then the breeze stepped up a notch and the crisp bag was lifted clear of a broken wooden fence and dropped onto a pile of similarly wind blown rubbish which had gathered between a wheelie bin and a long ago junked bike. The dog owner gave Danny and his two mates a nervous glance from the corner of her eye. She tightened her grip on the lead and quickened her step, moving to the edge of the pavement, putting the maximum distance she could between them. The dog on the other hand had no such worries about the three teenagers who sat on a low wall in their baseball caps. It took a lunge toward them, hopeful of a morsel of food at best or, if not that, at least a bit of fuss. The owner was having none of it. She pulled the dog clear with a ferocious yank on the lead before it got the chance to stick its head under Danny's outstretched hand.

CHAPTER TWO

The three lads watched her clatter away down the pavement with bored eyes. Every inch of them spoke of boredom. Of empty hours that crawled through day after day of nothing happening. Danny was idly flicking pieces of gravel at a post which held up a tired looking sign that informed anyone who cared to read it that ball games were not allowed. It wasn't just ball games. It seemed at times as if there was nothing that was allowed on Sunnybank. Not if you happened to be between 13 and 19. No ball games. No hanging out in groups of more than two. No shouting. No messing about. No being disrespectful. No nothing.

Their attention was taken up by the sight of a figure who turned the corner fifty yards away and made his way toward them with a jaded sort of trudge. It was Deano. He had spent the morning helping his dad move an old settee to the dump on the edge of town. Now he was back. And so now they were the usual four. They had kind of fallen together in the weeks after they walked out of the gates of Sunnybank High School for the final time. There had been some who were on line to return for the autumn term to study Highers. Others were lined up for college. Others were to get a start with a relative in the building game. Or joinery. Or plumbing. A couple were set to start work on farms. And then there were those who weren't due to return to school or head on to college. Those who didn't have a handy uncle to give them a start. Those who simply dropped off the map and onto the baked streets of Sunnybank.

The four of them had all been school team players. Billy Dean AKA Deano had been a right back of limited talent who compensated for lack of natural ability with enthusiasm that occasionally crossed the line into downright violence. To the right of Danny on the wall was Terry Bancroft AKA Chewit. When he had been in primary school his dad had bought up a job lot of Chewits at the Barrowlands market up in Glasgow. For several weeks his son had Chewits to spare with his packed lunch every day of the week. His mother had given his dad a hard time about it and said that the lad would end up looking like a Chewit. He didn't. But he ended up being called Chewit and it had been many years since anyone under the age of twenty had called him Terry. His role with team had generally been to mope about on the touchline as a substitute. On the few occasions that he made it onto the pitch he never made any kind of impact.

Then to Danny's left was Steve McAndrew AKA Nokey who had been the team's goalie all the way from S1. Like Chewit, Nokey's nickname was a souvenir of his primary school days. It had no doubt been obvious from the moment he was born that Steve McAndrew was going to have a larger than average nose. This of course made it a racing certainty that at some stage he would be called Pinocchio and this duly happened just a few weeks into his time in Primary One. He had no recollection of how Pinocchio came to be shortened to Nokey. It just did and it had been that way for over a decade.

None of the four had been particularly close at school. They had been in the team together. They had kicked a ball about in the lunch break together. Some evenings they had walked home together. And now they had fallen into each other's company because they had fallen off the map together. None of them were due to go off on a family holiday. They had tried to get jobs. And they had failed to get jobs. And so now they spent their days hanging around killing time. Sometimes they would kick a ball about. Other times they would walk into town and back. Most of the time they would find a wall to sit on and watch the world go by. Not that there was much of a world to watch. A few cars. Mothers with prams. Dog walkers. Other groups of bored teenagers. Stray cats. A few pigeons. Mumbling drunks. Scared pensioners. Squad cars. Council vans.

Mainly they watched out for the community wardens. None of them had managed to pass Standard Grade Maths, but they could all do the sums that counted. They were four, and four was two too many. Groups of two was all that was allowed, so if a pair of wardens came along they would be moved along and told to watch it. And if they answered back, the wardens would call up a squad car and names would be written down. It was a no winner. So they kept an eye out for the familiar uniforms and would duck away before anything could kick off.

It had taken Danny a while to get his head round the idea that the long empty days were what his life had come to. Everything was different this time. Always before, the summer holidays had a start date and a finish date. At the end of August the uniform would come out of the cupboard and another academic year would begin. It ensured that life always had a structure. Not this time. This time the uniform would stay in the cupboard until one day being taken to one of the town's charity shops. There was nothing at the end of August. Or the end of September. Or the end of any month for the rest of his life. There was only a blank sheet of paper and no matter how he tried he couldn't think of anything to write on it. To start with he had been reasonably confident that he would be able to get some sort of job. A job would mean a pay packet at the end of the week and that would mean his life would have a kind of direction. He could go out, buy a few clothes, some music. Whatever. He would have some options.

But there had been over twenty applicants for every one of the jobs he had tried for and the answer had always been no. After a month he had decided that it was hopeless. What was the point? Nobody was going to give him a job. Of course not. They all saw him as typical Sunnybank trouble. Not worth the risk. Not worth anything.

Money was a nightmare. None of them were eligible for any benefits so they had to rely on whatever their parents gave them. Bill McCann wasn't much in the mood to give a penny. The flat had become a place of quiet hostility ever since Danny's brief but dramatic appearance in the Rotary Cup Final. Father and son had got themselves into a vicious circle. Danny couldn't bear the look of disgusted disappointment in his dad's eyes and so he avoided it. He never got out of bed before his dad went off to work and after a while he could see little point in getting out of bed at all. What for? All it did was add a few more empty hours to kill on the dusty streets. Soon he was sleeping in until one and two in the afternoon. Sometimes Bill would call home to make himself a sandwich and a cup of tea. When he discovered his son still asleep, he would flip and yell at him for a few minutes before crashing the front door and heading back to the bins. The evenings told a similar story. By six o'clock, Danny would be bored to tears with hanging around doing nothing. But it was hard to face the idea of going home and being lectured all night. So he would stay out. Until ten. Until eleven. Often until after midnight by which time his dad would be asleep because he had to be up and about early.

It didn't take long for all of them to get fed up with kicking a football about in endless games of two a side. It was too hot. And what was the point anyway. There was no school team season to look forward to. They talked vaguely of joining a club in the Autumn but none of them really believed that they would. Gradually as each hot summer week melted into the next they found there was only one way to escape the mind-numbing boredom of their lives. And that was the pills, powders and bottles which were always available to be purchased from Baz Stamper.

Whatever cash they could scrape up inevitably went to Baz. Although Les Stamper had indeed disowned his son, he hadn't left him completely on his uppers. Before kicking his son out he had set him up with a flat and a few hundred quid to send him on his way. There had been no question of the treasured Peugeot 206 being replaced. Baz had sulked for a week or two and then he had decided to get down to business. His choice of trade was never likely to be anything like window cleaning or joinery or dry stone walling. He had set himself up as a purveyor of Class A, B and C narcotics in the long tradition of his family. He knew that it would be complete madness to step on his father's toes and so he avoided the Heroin market and focused entirely on the youth market. The customers that Baz sought out were more likely to spend £3 per week rather than his father's favoured clients who averaged £40 a day. It meant lots and lots of work but it beat the pants off turning up at the Job Centre and being sent out on some New Deal project.

What was in his favour was that he was based in one of the best possible market places for his new venture. All over Sunnybank were potential customers who spent day after day of mind-numbing boredom with nothing to do and nowhere to go. A couple of pounds in the pocket was never enough to get into the cinema, or get a ride on a bus down to the beach or to spend a few hours in the ice ring. But Baz prided himself on being able to supply little trips away from the grinding emptiness of the Sunnybank summer days for bargain prices. He liked to tell his customers that he was their Lunn Poly. He arranged excursions at rock bottom prices. He could set up a few hours of entertainment at a price that nobody in town could match. Package tours. All inclusive. Different every time. And like anyone else involved in the charter business, he based his operation on group buying. He would encourage groups of four or five to pool their money and buy together to get maximum value for their money.

And it was a ready market. Ready, eager and hungry for what he had to offer. He spent time planning each days' new campaign. He liked to mix and match. Where his father's business revolved around the sale of tenner bags of Heroin, Baz came up with different daily specials that would take a group of four Sunnybank lads on a journey for ten pounds all inclusive.

It hadn't taken very long for Danny, Deano, Chewit and Nokey to become bored with endlessly kicking a football around. They were more than happy to listen to Baz give his sales pitch. And as the slow weeks of the summer trundled by, their lives came to revolve around dredging up enough cash to pay for Baz's deal of the day.

Now as they watched him walk up the road to where they were sitting, they wished that their combined cash reserves were rather more than 67p. £9.33 more to be precise.

"Afternoon boys. All good?"

Danny gave a rueful grin. "Yeah right. Brilliant. What else?"

"Can I run you through the details of today's special, which, even if I say it myself, offers even better value than normal."

Chewit kicked a stone across the pavement and into the gutter. "Only got 67p haven't we Baz."

Baz's face took on a frown at this unwelcome news. "Not good boys. Not good at all. You know how much I pride myself on being able to cater for clients who are financially stretched, but 67p . . ."

His voice trailed off.

"What is it anyway?" Deano wanted to window shop.

Baz gave a what can you do kind of shrug. "One two litre bottle of white Lightning – a fine, crisp cider fresh out of my fridge and perfect for such a warm day. Also an ideal way to wash down two vallies each and a Baz eight skin spliff to top it all off. I'm sure you will all agree that such a package offers an absolute bargain for £10. I'm only sorry that you boys aren't in the game today. But, like they say, life's a bitch . . ."

They all stared down at the pavement, each with thoughts of ice-cold cider and the comfort blanket of two vallies each. Like the man said. Life was a bitch.

"Can I get a word Danny?"

Danny shrugged and eased himself to his feet and walked a few yards out of the earshot of the others.

Baz pulled out a packet of cigarettes and passed one over before lighting both. "Maybe I can help out here Danny boy."

"Go on."

"A bit of intelligence my man. The germ of an idea. A plan of attack . . ."

"Yeah, yeah. Just spit it out will you."

Baz looked a little miffed for a moment. He had been on a roll.

"Know that frozen food place on the way into town?"

"Sure. I know it. So what?"

"They have whole legs of lamb in there. Frozen like. Well. I know a man who pays a fiver a go for them. As many as he can get. So maybe you lads should give it some thought. One trip for two legs. The security's a joke. It's an in and outer. Easy, easy. Call me if you get a result. Know what I mean?"

Danny nodded. He knew. "I'll think about it."

"Course you will Danny Boy. Course you will."

Once Baz had made his exit on the hunt for his next trade, Danny put the plan to the others. They decided that the best thing would be take a walk down to the frozen food store and take a look and then make up their minds. There wasn't really a great deal of point in this. They had been walking past the place for years and all of them had been in on numerous occasions whilst pushing trolleys around for parents. But a walk to the shop would kill a bit of time. And it put off the moment of decision. So they walked. And when they got there, they walked past it three times, casing the big front window that advertised 25 burgers for 99p and the chance to buy one litre tub of ice cream and thereby get one free. After the third pass they retired to a small play area and started the process of coming up with a plan. Danny was the man on the planning front. He laid out the stages of the operation carefully so that there would be no misunderstanding. Stage one. Deano would leg it up the street like a boy who was scared for his life. Stage two Chewit and Nokey would chase him, just a few yards behind. Stage three, Deano would dive in through the doors of the frozen food place to find sanctuary. Stage four. Nokey and Chewit would follow him in, chase him up one of the aisles and catch him. They would grab him by the shirt and pin him against one of the freezers and pretend to pummel his stomach whilst they yelled at him and he screamed for mercy. Stage five, whilst the staff were distracted by all the commotion, Danny would walk in, find the right freezer, get two legs of lamb under his top and walk out. As soon as he was out of the door, Deano would be allowed to wriggle free and the others would chase him from the shop.

CHAPTER TWO

Once they had been over all five stages several times, it was time to put the thing into action. They gave each other high fives like they had seen in the movies and got to it. A few minutes later Danny waited in the doorway of the next door shop as a terrified Deano flew up the street and crashed through the door to the frozen food store closely pursued by his attackers. He took a deep breath and followed them in a few seconds later. He forced himself to ignore the racket that was coming from the far end of the shop. It took him less than thirty seconds to get two legs of lamb under his top and make for the door. The ice-cold packaging on his bare skin took his breath away but thankfully there was no sign of any shop employees. No doubt they had all been drawn to what was going on down at the end of the aisle. Ten more steps. Five more steps. Door. Door open. A blast of hot air from outside. Into the hot air. A surge of relief. A feeling like he had known once upon a time when the ball smacked the back of the net...

And then he was stopped. Someone had hold of the hood at the back of his jacket. And someone was in front of him. A woman. Reaching out and feeling the shape of the legs of lamb. Smiling now.

Crash. The door behind him flew open and the others burst out and ran away up the street.

A voice behind him. "Just leave them. They're only the decoy."

The woman nodded. "Now then, I think we better take a look at what you have under that jacket sunshine."

Danny tried to break free but the grip from behind was iron clad. "Don't bother lad. You're not going anywhere."

The woman tugged up his top and the two legs of lamb dropped to the pavement. She rolled her eyes. "I would never have thought that so many youngsters would have got such a taste for New Zealand lamb. Amazing. I would have thought McDonalds would have been more to your taste. Or a chippy roll. But no. All of a sudden it seems like half the lads in Dumfries want a leg of lamb for their tea. Extraordinary. But then again, it's a funny old world isn't it . . . I didn't get your name . . ."

"Danny."

"Right. Danny. A funny old world. I'm DC Jean Billows by the way. Now. We have two choices here. Nice and easy. You choose A or you choose B. Just like that. Choice A. You tell me who wants to buy those legs of lamb and we send you on your way. I'll be clear here.

You'll tell us at the station where we'll write it down and you will sign the piece of paper. And that will be that. Choice B. You tell us that the lamb is just for yourself and nobody else, in which case we read you your rights and arrest you. So Danny. There you are. Nice and easy. Two, simple choices. Of course, you should know that you have been set up good and proper. Whoever told you that it would be a good idea to pop a couple of legs of New Zealand under your jacket also seems to have told about half of Sunnybank Estate. Maybe the ones who came earlier might have got lucky. But not you Danny. Not you at all. You're the one who has been played for a mug. So maybe the best choice is Choice A, because who ever sent you down here has dropped you right in it as far as I can tell."

Danny clenched his eyes shut. What planet was the stupid copper living on? Somewhere about a zillion miles past Mars as far as he could tell. As if grassing up Les Stamper's son was an option. Choice A. What a complete joke.

"It was for my tea. Just me."

He heard a snort of contempt from behind him. "Come on Jean. Let's book the little pratt."

His rights were read and then it was a short ride through the town centre to the main police station. There were forms and more questions and after a couple of hours his dad arrived with a face that was sheet white with fury. The paperwork was all wrapped up and they were allowed to go. They would be hearing from the Children's Reporter in due course. Jean Billows had a private chat with Bill whilst Danny waited by the front door and stared at a poster that warned of all the bad things that would happen to those who risked having a drink and driving. Then they were out in the cool of the evening and taking the long walk back to Sunnybank in silence.

Danny was expecting the greatest row of his life once his father closed the front door on the world outside. Instead Bill quietly nodded to the stool by the kitchen table. When he spoke he sounded more tired than angry. The anger which had been furnace hot when he had received a call to inform him that his son was at the police station had slowly but surely evaporated. Now he was just sick to the stomach with all of it.

"I'm not going to go on and on. What's the point? You're not about to listen, I've learned that much. What I have to say is dead simple. If

I EVER get a call from a police station again that will be you and me finished. End of story Danny. Once more and you can find somewhere else to live. Now I don't want to talk about it. I don't want to pick it apart piece by piece. Just get out of my sight. You make me want to throw up."

For a few moments Danny wasn't sure if it was finished. He watched the stiff set of his dad's shoulders as he waited for the kettle to boil. Then he got to his feet and slipped out of the kitchen and went to his room. It would have made things easier if he could have found a way of being angry about what his dad had said. But he couldn't because it merely mirrored how he felt himself. There was no escaping the truth. He had been caught trying to nick a couple of legs of frozen New Zealand lamb. And for what? So that he could hawk them for a tenner which would have meant the four of them could have got clean out of their faces on vallies and cider and dope. And that was it. Completely pathetic. A few months earlier he had turned out for the Scotland under 16's. Now the summit of his ambition was to steal his way into enough drugs and booze to blank everything out. He buried his face in the pillow and yearned for the release of sleep.

A few days later he was wandering around aimlessly when a shout caught his attention.

It was Baz, looking rather sheepish.

"Yo. Danny boy. How's it hanging man?"

Sometimes Baz's pseudo-American nonsense made him want to scream.

"How do you think Baz. I'm waiting on my summons and my dad's about to sling me out. I've got nae job, nae money, nae prospects, nae nothing. Other than that Baz, I'm in the pink."

Baz kicked at a stone and pushed his hands deep into his pockets. "Look Danny man. I heard about the lamb thing. My fault, OK. I never figured they would get their acts together for a few lousy legs of lamb. Plain clothes were they?"

"Aye."

"That's heavy. Way too heavy man."

Danny rolled his eyes and started to walk.

"Hey Danny. Hang a second man. Be cool. I need to make it right, OK. Fair enough. I gave you a bum call. I hold my hands up. But you took it fair and square and kept buttoned up and I appreciate that. Ken what I mean?"

Danny nodded. Baz relaxed a little now it was looking like Danny wasn't about to take a hike.

"So look. I want to square up man. Make a contribution."

"Just get on with it Baz."

Baz reached into his jacket pocket and crashed the fags. Once they were lit, he carried on.

"Look Danny, I'm doing OK. You know me, yeah. A wheel here, a deal there. It's all good man. Top. So I got to thinking maybe I should cut you on some of it. You ken what I mean. A piece. A chance to put a bit of cash together."

Danny was very much in once-bitten-twice-shy mode after the doomed legs of New Zealand lamb. "Go on then.

"Wholesale man. A concession. I'll give you vallies at 40p each. You knock them out at a oner and that gives you 60p a pop. Knock out fifty a day and you're into thirty quid. Knock out a hundred and you doing sixty. It's simple as, Danny boy. Simple as. I mean look at me yeah. Nice togs. Nice shoes. Bit of bling. Tasty phone. Like I said. It's all good man. All good. And you have just proved to me that you're a dude who knows how to zip it when the pigs come calling. And that's good Danny boy. It counts big time."

Danny took a pull at his cigarette and blew smoke out through his nose angrily.

"All very nice Baz, but it doesn't matter if your pills ore 40p a pop or 4p. I'm skint. Flat broke."

"Course your broke Danny boy, because life is too slow man. I know that. I appreciate that. So I'll boost you OK. I'll lay you on £40 credit. A hundred Scrappy Do's. Right here, right now man. You get out there and turn that into a £100 then we'll talk again. They're in my pocket man. Weighing me down. So come on Danny boy. We going to roll?"

Again the little voice was there. It was over the far side of a hill now and the wind was blowing its words away. By now the voice was so small that he could hardly hear it at all. But he could hear it. And the words were the same as ever. "No, no, no...."

But what was the point in no? Where would 'no' get him? A start on the New Deal? Some poxy losers course at the college? Another six months of sitting on walls and kicking stones about? Yeah, right. Some choice. Either way was loser's alley. At least this way he might just have a quid or two in his pocket for once in his life. So stuff the voice. Stuff it all. He reached out an open palm and slowly allowed his mouth to open into a grin.

"OK Baz. We're on."

"Yo. Danny'O. I knew you were sound man. Knew it. Nice one man. Really nice."

The change in Danny's life had been more or less instant. One day he had been wondering if time was about to stop altogether as the hours crawled by as slow as centuries. And then suddenly his life was full. Busy. It was nought to sixty in under five seconds. The first couple of days had been tough as he had to swallow down his nerves when approaching small groups of lads who he vaguely knew from school. But he soon learned that the words 'I've got a few vallies about me if any of you are interested' had an almost magical effect on just about everyone he talked to. Sunnybank had gone Valium mad. At a pound a pill it had become the drug of choice for those with next to nothing in their pockets. As he wandered around the baked streets, it seemed to Danny that there was hardly a youngster on the estate who wasn't rolling their pocket money into the nondescript little pills. Not that he was complaining. It only took him three days to turn his £40 start up stock into £100 cash. He repaid his stake money, bought another hundred pills and kept a crisp £20 note in his pocket. In a further two days he took on another consignment of a hundred pills and bought a knocked off mobile phone for £30 which Baz told him would cost £200 plus on the High Street.

Once he had the phone, everything became ten times easier. And busier. Texts and calls. Ten here. Twenty there. See you at the back of the post office. See you at that old pavilion. By the bus stop up the road from the Spar. I'll have six. No make it eight. At the end of our road good for you?

Within a fortnight he had bought a mountain bike from Baz for fifty quid which he was reliably informed would have set him back more than four hundred in Halfords. And soon he was buying in two hundreds rather than hundreds. Then five hundreds. All day the phone trilled and beeped. All day every day. More gear followed, mostly from Baz. Nike trainers. A new jacket. An iPod. And for a month he felt like a king. Soon he had a carrier bag hidden under a floorboard in his room that was full of cash. By the time the school holidays were over the bag had over £500 inside. As he rode the closes, he started making plans for a holiday. Or a motor bike. Or a widescreen TV. And what would his dad say if he volunteered to cough up the money for a Sky dish? And a subscription. No way. It would be so where has all the money come from Danny? Just the same as it was every time he spoke with his dad. But that wasn't very often because Danny made sure he avoided him most of the time.

But it was the time when there was no way he could avoid a conversation in the kitchen that the paranoia started to get its hooks into him. His dad had sat with a cup of tea and a look of total disgust in his eyes. Do you really think that nobody notices Danny? Well, do you? Do you think they can't see the new bike and the fancy clothes and the iPod? Well, I have some news for you son. They see. And they talk. How come that little toe-rag is suddenly so loaded? Not hard to guess though, is it Danny? Not on Sunnybank. I mean they don't think that you've become a lawyer do they? Or a market research consultant? Well do they? Not a chance. There is only one way that lads like you suddenly start strutting their stuff in all the designer gear. So think about it. Think about it long and hard.

Once his father had sown the thought in his head, Danny's mind was filled with nothing else. And the more he thought about it, the more impossible the situation seemed to become. Suddenly he hated riding around Sunnybank making his deliveries. He could sense eyes on him all the time. Watching. And watching. People at bus stops. Men out washing their cars. Grandmothers taking their grand kids to the swings. Mothers pushing prams. Postmen delivering the mail. Bin men emptying bins. He felt eyes on him from the drivers of cars. He sensed curtains twitching down every street. Occasionally when the air thumped with the sound of a helicopter overhead, he would be convinced that it was up in the sky to watch him. Soon he didn't want to go out at all, but if he didn't go out he wouldn't sell, and by now his phone never stopped ringing. So he started to go around on foot thinking that it would make him less conspicuous. But it didn't feel that way. Not even nearly. It just seemed to take longer to get clear of watching eyes. And it took too long. And without the bike he couldn't keep up with the deliveries. Baz had told him the golden rule. The absolute golden rule of every golden rule there ever was. Never, ever go about it more than five pills at once. If you were lifted with five, you could pass it off as for your own personal use. Well, your lawyer would. And no matter what the coppers thought they knew, there wasn't a thing they could do about it. More than five, and they would bust a gut to have you for dealing and if the Sheriff got out of bed the wrong side you would be in for a serious lump of time, first offence or no first offence.

Baz told him how it was done. You take the order. You fetch it from your stash, never more than five at a time. You do the deal. Then you do the next order. Don't go about with a fat wad of notes in your pocket because it can be hard to explain to the law how as an unemployed sixteen-year-old you have a couple of hundred pictures of the queen in your pocket. The key was to be smart. Understand the rules. Stick to the rules. Never make an exception. It was why he had taken Baz's advice and bought the bike. It speeded him up. Helped him to do more deals in a day. Helped him to maximise his income.

For a while it had seemed almost perfect. He was working hard and earning good money. But once his dad had said his piece, all the joy went out of his new career. Every morning he found it harder to get up and out to face the eyes which were on him all the time. Sometimes he felt so nervous that his heart rattled his ribcage. Every time he turned a corner he expected to finds a parked squad car waiting for him. And if not a squad car, then a gang of older lads with knives and baseball bats ready to stove his head in to get his cash. And if not a gang of muggers, maybe a gang of fathers all fired up with rage that he was dealing drugs to their kids.

More and more he could only find one way to overcome the constant state of panic. The answer was in his pocket every day. The answer was to be found in the little pills that he bought for 40p and sold for a pound. Soon he got to taking three before he got out of his bed in the morning. Then there would be at least one every couple of hours as he made his rounds. By the time the first wet winds of the autumn swept in from the Irish Sea, he was up to ten a day. By the time the first frosty night of October came along, he was doing fifteen and at least four big joints at night. To help him to sleep. Or at least that was the theory. But it never seemed to work. No matter how tired he felt it always seemed impossible to find sleep. Whenever his eyes were about to close out the day, new images would jump into his mind. A squad car screaming to a halt in the street outside. Flashing blue lights through the curtains. The sound of the front door flying off its hinges. The sound of heavy boots in the landing outside. His own door flying in at him. Big men with hard hands. Cuffs on his wrists. And the bed pulled clear of the wall. And the floorboard dragged up. And the carrier bag pulled out. How much now? Over two grand. All that work. All the fear and all the staring eyes. And a stash of three hundred pills. And they would send him down harder than hard. And by now he would be wide awake and sweating with fear and so he would pop another couple of pills and make up a joint with trembling fingers, but it would only make things worse. And worse. And the lack of sleep made him even more edgy and up tight. He felt like he was stretched to breaking point.

Baz saw it of course. He knew the signs well enough. He tried to tell Danny that sampling too many of the goods was the mother of bad ideas. And Danny had said that he wasn't doing very many. Just a couple a day. Just enough to mellow him out a bit. He tried to explain that without a couple of pills he was getting really nervous about things. Jumpy. And Baz had tried to be patient and point out that the very reason that Danny was getting paranoid was because he was dropping way too many vallies. Didn't he know that? It was why they were called Scrappys, yeah. Scrappy as in Scrappy Do? As in getting into loads of scraps because you're so paranoid that everyone is after you. Watching you. Having a laugh at you. Judging you. Plotting how to take you down. He told Danny that he'd seen it a thousand times before. Lads who were normally steady away suddenly flipping their lids and carving the faces of complete strangers just because they had looked at them the wrong way.

Danny had said cheers mate, thanks for that, nae bother, he'd knock them on the head. And the dope as well. Because Baz had warned that the weed was as bad as the vallies for making you all paranoid and miserable. Sure it was OK when you were out with the lads or flying through an avenue of pine trees with a girl called Sally. Not so great when you're on your own in your bedroom waiting for the drugs squad to crash the door in. So he had been adamant. He would knock it on the head. Lay off. Clean up his act. And Baz had gone further. He

CHAPTER TWO

had said that Danny must have a bunch of cash put to one side by now. Why not take a holiday for a few days? Get out of Sunnybank. Let his hair down. Pull a few birds. Have a laugh.

Danny had genuinely taken the advice on board. He had booked a B&B in Blackpool for the weekend and told Deano, Chewit and Nokey that the lads were on for a bit of a trip. His treat. And he had really tried to ease back on the vallies, but that had been a much harder task than booking the B&B. As soon as he eased off, he felt as if all his clothes had been taken away. Anxiety gave way to pure terror. What made it worse was that he felt really ill as well. For three days he cut back, but then he was soon back to using more than before he had eased off. By the time they arrived at the station for the train to Carlisle which was the first step on their Blackpool adventure, he was using over twenty a day. But wouldn't be for long. All he needed was a break from Sunnybank for a while. Blackpool would see to that. A couple of nights in the clubs. The Pleasure Beach. A few games of pool. Maybe even a kickaround on the beach. A ride along the front on the tram to look at the illuminations like they had once done before his mum ran away. He would clear his head of lots of junk. And when he got back he would be stronger. The demons would be away and he could get on again.

They had arrived with plenty of time to spare. The holiday mood was on them as they sat down on a bench and Danny rooted out a lager each from one of the two carrier bags of cans that he had bought from Baz earlier. They popped the ring pulls and toasted each other before drinking deep. Before leaving Sunnybank they had already had three cans each and Danny had passed around the Valium. By the time they made it to the platform they were on a complete roll, no-one more so than Danny who had already popped ten pills. His brain felt like it was about to split like a log. Part of him was infected by the buzzing spirits of his mates who were loudly telling the world that they were about to live it large. Yet the other half of his head was almost paralysed by paranoid nerves. He had well over a hundred pills in his back pack as well as two carrier bags of cans at his feet and half an ounce of blow in his jeans pocket. What if they came now? What if they came from either end of the platform? Or maybe on the train, when it was clattering along the tracks at eighty and there was no way of getting off? Or maybe they would be waiting at Carlisle? Or even Blackpool?

As all of these thoughts scratched around his head like an army of ants, his eyes flicked about the station looking for danger.

Then his gaze landed on the figure of the stationmaster. And the stationmaster was staring right back at him. His face was angry. Set like stone. His eyes were taking in the carrier bags. His ears were logging their loud voices. And now his hand was moving to his pocket. Slowly. Deliberately. What was in there? The man's eyes were locked on to him. Maybe he was about to have a smoke. Or maybe a stick of chewing gum. A Mars bar. A tissue for a runny nose. What was it? What was it? Danny's heart was starting to bang harder and harder. What was the swine up to? Pig. Swine. All they wanted to do was to go away for a few days. To get away from Sunnybank for a while. To play pool and act stupid on the rollercoasters and try to win useless teddy bears on shooting games. What business was it of his? Why couldn't he just leave them be? Why couldn't anyone just leave them be? Why did they always have to watch? All the time. Everywhere he went. On foot. On his bike. Everywhere.

A phone. A mobile phone. Not chewing gum. Not a smoke. Not a tissue. And still the man's eyes were locked on. His index finger was on the key pad now. Pressing buttons. He just wouldn't leave it alone would he? Had to stick his nose in. Had to mess it all up. And now a boiling rage was rising up from somewhere in Danny's stomach and there was nothing that was going to stop it. Because all of a sudden Danny McCann was sick of it all. How many nights had it been since they had allowed him a decent sleep? Weeks. Months. Centuries. Never a chance to close his eyes. Because they were there all the time. Waiting and watching. Biding their time. Sticking their noses in. A voice from the middle of the army of ants howled very loud. No more. No more. NO MORE!!!

Suddenly he was on his feet. Running. Bearing down. And the man's face was different now. The cold anger was all gone. Instead his face was an open book of fear. Danny suddenly realised that the voice in his head had got out. Now it was his own voice that was screaming.

"NO MORE!!! NO MORE!!! NO MORE!!! . . ."

The man was trying to turn and run. No chance. He was old. He was too fat. He was nothing. He was interfering scum. He should have thought about it before staring. He should have thought about it before taking the phone from his pocket. He only made it five yards before he tripped and fell. And Danny was on him. All over him. Beating. Pummelling. Howling.

"NO MORE!!! NO MORE!!! NO MORE!!! . ."

And the man was screaming. Begging. Crying. Pathetic. Crying like a baby. As if that was going to get him off the hook. Forget it pal. Too late for tears pal. Should have thought about that before . . .

But he couldn't hit any more because his arm wouldn't move. Why wouldn't his arm move? It was stuck somehow. What...

He half-turned and found that Deano had a hold of his arm. And Deano was trying to say something to him but he couldn't hear because his own voice was far to loud in his head. His voice and about twenty zillion angry little ants. And what was Deano doing? He was with them. Even Deano. The others were there as well. Trying to drag him off the crying man. Yanking at him. Heaving at him. He fought them with everything he had and for a second their grip loosened and he was able to kick the man in the head. Hard. Really hard. Hard enough to feel the crunch of the man's nose through his shoe. And now there was more sound. A howling, wailing end of the world sound. Sirens. And a car skidding to a halt of the other side of the station building. And the heavy sound of footsteps thundering along the platform. Just like the footsteps that thundered through his mind every night when sleep wouldn't come.

Policemen. Three of them. Their faces were red with exertion. On him now. Slamming him down to the platform. Rolling him over. Pushing his cheek down hard into the concrete. Yanking his arms together behind his back. Snap. Handcuffs on. Heave. Lifted to his feet. His brain had more or less completely flipped. He vaguely registered one of the policemen crouched down over the stricken figure of the stationmaster. Other policemen were cuffing the other lads. A small crowd had gathered. Staring. Gloating. Loving every minute of the spectacle. Better than tele so it was. Something to tell them all about later in the pub. His ears were full of voices but all of the words were tangled up. He knew he was expected to walk because there was a policeman behind him pushing him. Another siren. More lights. Ambulance men running fast, passing him on the platform. A radio was crackling somewhere. One of the other lads was crying. And slowly the adrenaline was fading out and his brain started to put together what a complete and utter mess he was in.

What had he done?

What had he done?

Oh Christ.

What had he done.

The streets outside the back window of the squad car were absurdly normal. People were just getting on with their lives as if nothing had happened. A seagull sat on a telegraph pole. A kid screamed at his mum for a bag of sweets. A man in a suit was firing words into a mobile phone.

What had he done?

Out of the car. Into the station. Into a cell. Out of the cell. Name. Address. Next of kin. Date of birth. And we'll take your shoes please. And the belt please. And could you empty your pockets please? Oh dear, oh dear. What have we got here. A small brown lump. Sniff, sniff. Oh dear, oh dear. Cell. Slamming heart. Overwhelming depression. Remorse and guilt. Guilt and remorse. And zillion upon zillion ferocious little ants scurrying about his head, nipping and biting.

What had he done?

He had a headache now. Too much lager. Too many vallies. And the harsh light in the ceiling of the cell seemed to burn into his eyes. Later he found it hard to piece together the hours that followed his arrest. He was interviewed. They told him that they had spoken with his dad and that his dad had said that he wouldn't be coming. There was another man. A duty lawyer apparently. They listened to what he had to say. It can't have made any sense. He couldn't remember much of it. Was he using drugs? No, he wasn't using drugs. What about the cannabis in his pocket? It wasn't his. Whose cannabis was it then? He didn't know. Where did he buy the lager? A guy. Who was the guy? He didn't know. Why did he hit the stationmaster? He didn't know. And then he had signed where they had written it all down. Next came a doctor. Was he using drugs? No. Was he sure that he wasn't using drugs? Yes. He was sure.

They explained that it was Friday. But he knew that already. He wasn't that far gone. They explained that he would be with them all weekend. And Monday as well because Monday was a Bank Holiday. And the Sheriff didn't sit in court on a Bank Holiday Monday. So it would be Tuesday. Did he understand that? Yes. He understood that.

CHAPTER TWO

The cell again. Some food which he couldn't face. A tepid cup of tea. And suddenly his eyes were heavy. He dragged the blanket over his head to block out the light. And for the first time in weeks, sleep came. Real sleep. Because what was the point getting into a terrified sweat that the police were coming for him because the police were already here. He was in a cell. They would have found the Valium by now. And they had found the cannabis. And the lager. And next they would get a warrant to search the flat and they would find the carrier bag under the floor board. And more Valium. And the phone he had bought from Baz. And the bike. And then there was the stationmaster. As the world slowly faded to black, he saw an image of the older man's face; terrified. And crying. Crying out of fear. And he remembered the feel of the man's nose breaking under his foot . . .

What had he done?

What had he done?

Sliding. Fading.

What had he done?

What had he done?

All black now.

All quiet.

Nothing.

They woke him to feed him, but he had no appetite. He hadn't really any idea if it was night or day. He gulped down some tea and tried to find his bearings. That was easy enough. He was in a police cell. He had given some kind of a statement but he couldn't remember what he had said. Whatever it had been, he had signed it. They had taken his shoelaces and his belt. And he had slept. He had no idea how long he had slept. There had been no dreams. Just a long blackness. But he knew that sleep could be deceptive. Sometimes you slept for an hour, and it seemed like a whole week. Other times ten hours felt like nothing more than a short nap. So maybe it was still Friday night. Or maybe it was Saturday morning. Possibly even Saturday afternoon.

What he did know was he was feeling lousy and he had a pretty good idea that his body was starting to scream out for some Valium. It was the same feeling that had come when he had tried to cut down after Baz had given him his little pep talk. Then he had not been able to see it through. No choice this time. No doubt the hundred pills in his backpack for the Blackpool trip would already be bagged and tagged in a police evidence cabinet. It was still only Saturday. Then it would be Sunday. And then Monday . . .

He pulled the blanket back over his head and tried to sleep again. What had he done?

Sunday lasted forever. With every minute that passed, he was feeling worse. They brought him food but he didn't want it. The walls of the cell seemed to be closing in on him and slowly a feeling of complete panic started to grow. What if he was going to be really ill? Would anyone notice? What if it was the middle of the night and there was nobody out there? And as the panic grew, he tried to pace the small cell to loosen himself. He remembered watching a tiger in a zoo marching endlessly from one side of its cage to another. Trapped. Enclosed. And he was sweating even though inside his bones felt as cold as ice.

One, two, three, turn. One two, three, turn. . One, two, three, turn. One, two, three, turn.

If he kept walking all the way through to Tuesday morning how far would that be? Three paces across the cell. Six paces there and back. Go there and back a thousand times and that was 6000 metres. Six kilometres. How many miles in a kilometre? He dredged his memory for maths lessons at Sunnybank High. What was it? About one-and-a-half kilometres to a mile. So six kilometres was four miles. And how long to cross the cell? He was walking fast. Maybe a couple of seconds. So four seconds for six metres. Ninety metres in a minute. Five thousand and something metres in an hour. Fifty kilometres in ten hours. Over a hundred in a day. And no matter how he walked, the panic seemed to get worse. And the sweat was splashing onto the floor. And he could sense a massive great blackness starting to swallow him up . . .

Had he slept at all? Maybe. It didn't seem like he had. He had walked and walked until his legs would no longer carry him. It had fallen very quiet outside. Night. Sunday night. Then it would be Monday and only one more night to go. His body was tired from head to toe, but sleep was still a near impossibility. The panic was changing now. He felt edgy. Twitchy. The light seemed to have become ten times brighter. There might have been a power surge. Now it was so bright that he was convinced that it was burning his skin. He closed his eyes because it felt like it might burn all the way through to his brain. A door clanked shut outside and the noise sounded like a gun going off and made him jump upright on his bed. He snapped his head from side to side, checking for danger. Nothing. Four walls. One floor. One ceiling. One light that felt like a laser. Nothing. And yet he was sure there was danger all around him. Two voices outside. They sounded incredibly loud. Were they shouting? Were they coming for him? Were they going to beat him? He suddenly thought of the pictures he had seen on the news of the Iraqi prisoners in the American prison. Was that what was about to happen to him? They had left him alone to soften him up. That was it. And that was why they had turned up the power in the light so that it scorched him. And that was why the officers outside were speaking through megaphones. Because they were coming. Coming. And the light was so hot now that it felt like it would melt the skin from his flesh. And the voices screaming. And the panic was crashing up through his body like some great train roaring through the night. And suddenly he felt himself fading.

Fading.

Slipping.

Fading

A voice brought him back. At first it seemed as if it was a very long way, almost too far away to be heard. But it was getting closer. He could just about make out what it was saying now. It was getting clearer. Little by little. Taking shape. Letters turning into words.

"Daniel . . . Can you hear me Daniel . . . Daniel . . ."

He realised that the voice was really very close. It was only inches away from his face. He opened his eyes to find the face of a man looking into his. No uniform. An old tweed jacked and a wool tie. The man looked like a teacher. Behind the man's head was the ceiling of the cell and the eye ball burning light. Why was the ceiling behind the man's face? Danny realised that it was because he was lying on his back. On the floor. Why was he lying on the floor of the cell? Why wasn't he on his bed? And why did he feel so completely weird from head to toe . . .

"It's all right Daniel . . . Just try to relax . . . try to take deep breaths . . . When I say 'in', you breathe in, OK . . .? Just nod . . . excellent . . . Right . . . In, one two, three, four . . . Out, one two, three, four . . .

Danny focused on doing like the man said and pulling in the stale air of the cell and then pushing it back out again.

"That's excellent Daniel . . . Really good. do you think you can speak Daniel?"

Danny nodded. He was pretty sure that he could speak.

"Have you been taking Valium Daniel?"

He tried to say 'yes' but it came out as a croak. The man half-turned and spoke to a policeman who was standing behind him. "Bring some water please."

The water came and the man helped Danny to take a few gulps.

"Better?"

"Yeah." A word this time. Not a croak.

"Good. Now Daniel. I am a doctor. Doctor Brooks. I really need you to answer my questions as honestly as you can. Can you do that for me Daniel?"

A doctor. Why was there a doctor? What was wrong with him?

"What happened? Am I sick . . ."

"Try and stay calm Daniel. You had a fit. Rather a severe one. Do you know what a fit is Daniel?"

Danny nodded. The doctor continued.

"The officers tell me that they found quite a lot of Valium in your bag. Have you been taking many Daniel?"

Danny could see no point in lying. They already had the bag. And it wasn't like he was grassing anyone up. Only himself. "Fifteen most days. Sometimes twenty."

Dr Brooks nodded to himself. "I thought as much. Didn't anyone tell you what might happen if you stopped taking the pills Daniel?"

Danny shook his head. The Doctor suddenly looked tired.

"No I don't suppose they did. Well you have just discovered what can happen when you suddenly withdraw from huge doses of Benzodiazepam. I am going to insist that you are transferred to the hospital now. There is no need to worry too much. It doesn't mean you will have another fit. It just means that there will be trained medical staff to keep a proper eye on you. Are you going to learn from this

Daniel? You were lucky this time. It probably doesn't feel that way, but a police cell is one of the better places to take a fit. If you had been outside somewhere, well, who knows? Think about it Daniel. You'll do that?"

"I will."

"Good. Now let's get you up and onto the bed."

It was all that he could do to stay awake as they helped him out of the police station and into the back of the ambulance that was waiting outside. He was asleep again by the time it was half way to the hospital. He slept as they wheeled him to the ward. He slept as they lifted him onto the bed. When he woke, he was once again disorientated. Where? No wall close to him. Instead there were other beds. People sleeping. Machinery. A dim soft light. A hospital. Why was he in hospital? A memory of a man in a tweed jacket and a wool tie . . .

In the end it was Wednesday before the hospital were happy for him to be taken to meet the Sheriff. The police collected him and delivered him to the court on Buccleuch Street. The lawyer who had been there on Friday night met him and asked if he was OK to talk things through. Danny said he was. His head was more or less clear now. The lawyer said that there really was no point in not pleading guilty. He explained that Danny had more or less admitted everything in his statement. He pointed out that there were several witnesses as well as CCTV footage of his assault on the stationmaster. He confirmed that the police had found 100 ten mill Benzodiazepam in his back pack. They hadn't needed a warrant to search the flat. Bill McCann had let them in. And they had found the carrier bag of cash under the floor board. And another substantial quantity of Benzodiazepam. So there was no point in pleading not guilty. Things would be better if he owned up to it.

The Sheriff seemed to take a long time with the papers in front of him. Danny scanned the small court room for the fifth time since the police officer had led him to the dock and told him where to stand. But even if he had scanned the room a hundred times he knew that his father would not be there. Nobody was there. He was completely alone. At last the Sheriff looked up and seemed to examine him.

"I gather that it is your intention to plead guilty Daniel?"

"Yes sir."

A grim sort of nod. "Well, that at least is something. Now I am also led to believe that your father is not here this morning?"

"No sir."

"Do you realise why that is Daniel?"

"I think he's washed his hands of me sir."

The Sheriff looked back down at his papers and spoke more or less to himself. "Washed his hands of you...."

He looked up again. "And your mother?"

"She's in Australia. She left us. When I was nine."

"Australia. I see."

"Sir."

"Daniel, I hope that you realise that the charges you have admitted to are serious. Extremely serious."

"Sir."

"What happens now is this. Before passing sentence I need to see what we call social enquiry reports. These will tell me what sort of a lad you are. If you have done this sort of thing before. Do you understand that?"

"Yes sir."

"Now while these reports are being prepared, I have to decide what we are going to do with you. I don't like sending a boy of your age to spend remand time in prison but I am afraid that I have no choice. Not with your father refusing to allow you to come back home. I'm afraid that you are going to have to accept that there will be very serious consequences for what you have done Daniel. Very serious. May I ask the officers of the court to do all they can to ensure that all the paperwork in this case is brought to me as quickly as possible. Dismissed."

Danny wasn't sure for a moment if it was finished or not. Then the policeman who stood next to him tugged at his wrist with the handcuffs that joined them.

"Come on sunshine. You're done here."

They departed the court down a flight of stairs that descended through the floor. The next day Danny watched the familiar streets of Dumfries through the barred window of a prison van. And very soon the streets turned into fields as the van headed north to the Young Offenders Institute where he would serve his remand time until the Sheriff had the paperwork he needed.

PART THREE

The warder led him along the corridor to a cell about halfway along. Then he chose a key, unlocked and opened up.

"OK McCann. Home sweet home. In you go."

Danny did as he was told and stepped into the cell. It was the same as the one he had been in during the weeks of his remand. A double bunk bed. A desk. A toilet in the corner. A small window. A TV showing a game show with the sound muted. Somebody else's clutter. The somebody else was on the top bunk and looking down at him with a look of mild interest. The boy was older then Danny. Nineteen. Maybe even twenty. He was lightly built and there didn't seem to be any great aggression about him.

Danny hoped not. For six weeks before reappearing in front of the Sheriff to receive an eighteen month sentence, he had been sharing a cell with a lad from Pollock called Eric. Eric was seventeen and his life ran on hate. He hated Celtic fans, Catholics, asylum seekers, the police force, social workers, prison workers, Pakis, anyone who wasn't from Pollock, nonces, Big Brother contestants, the English, in fact it seemed to Danny that Eric more or less hated everyone on the whole planet apart from himself. Once Eric had established that Danny was from Dumfries, he had made it more than clear that he had no time for anyone from poxy little towns in the countryside. Luckily, the Dumfries postcode was one of the more minor crimes. He wasn't a catholic, Paki, Celtic fan, policeman, social worker, Englishman or prison officer and so Eric grudgingly allowed him to live. After three weeks they even managed an occasional conversation, though they never hit it off well enough for Danny to have a go with the remote control that changed TV channels. After a month and a half Danny was positively looking forward to getting back in front of the Sheriff so that he would be moved into another cell. As the van had taken him away from the court he had crossed fingers, toes and any other part of the body he could think of and hoped that his next cell mate might be a little better.

He was realistic enough to know that it was probably a hope which would be dashed. Seventy percent of the inmates of the young offenders prison seemed to be from Glasgow and they all had a very low opinion of the few who came from small towns all across Scotland. There had been a few others in the same boat when he had first arrived. They were the ones who seemed completely lost in the exercise yard, constantly close to tears, living in constant fear of the boys from the big cities. Danny had looked on as others had let the whole thing get on top of them until finally the damn burst and the tears came which of course only made everything a million times worse. He was better off than most. He knew all about what it was like to be excluded. It was something that he had learned to live with at ten years old when every door in Sunnybank was closed in his face. Now he had been able to draw on the inner strength that he had built up in his days as 'that' Danny McCann. It wasn't great. But he could handle it. And he did handle it.

Then one day a football burst out of a frantic game and he flipped it up and juggled it to the grudging appreciation of the watching players before kicking it back and saying,

"Any chance of a game then?"

A huge boy called Taz from Easterhouse stepped forward and looked him up and down as if he was a slug.

"Where you from then, pal?"

"Dumfries."

Taz spat. "Well this is Glasgow against Edinburgh. Where does poxy Dumfries come into that?"

Danny shrugged. "No idea. I'll play for whoever's losing."

This made the bigger boy smirk. "Edinburgh then. Just like always. Go on then country boy. You play for Edinburgh."

A minute or two later Danny collected the ball and drifted past two attempted tackles before coming up against Taz, who was the last line of defence. A dummy sent the Easterhouse stopper the wrong way and he lost his balance and slipped. Danny put a foot on the ball and waited for him to get to his feet. This time he lunged into a tackle that was more about maiming than getting the ball. Danny flicked the ball aside and jumped clear of the scything leg. He gave a tut-tutting sound and then turned to crash the ball into the corner.

"Nice try big man."

For the next twenty minutes Taz tried and failed to kill Danny in every manner he could think of, but he never got close. In fact when the Glasgow keeper rolled a ball out to his centre half, it was the big man who was completely floored as Danny bit into a two-footed tackle. By the time Edinburgh completed their first victory in living memory, Taz walked up to Danny and gave him a matey bash on the back

"Been thinking. Dumfries is nearer to Glasgow than Edinburgh. You play for us next time."

From then on the exercise yard was an OK place to be. The lads got to asking if Danny had ever had a chance of making it as a pro. He told them that he had blown it. That was fair enough. Everyone in the yard was familiar with blowing it. It was why they were there.

After that, the place had felt easier. On the one hand he found the whole regime as oppressive as each and every one of the prisoners. But on the other hand he found the prison environment made him feel oddly safe. It was a relief not to have to spend his days being chewed up with the worry of a squad car waiting around every corner. Or robbers with baseball bats. Or vigilante groups of fathers. Or his own father, tight-lipped and white-faced with anger. Prison kept all these fears safely locked outside. All he needed to do was go with the flow. It was a strictly regimented flow which ran the same through every day. Wash. Breakfast. Work. Exercise. Work. Tea. Association. Lock down. Soon he found the routine to be comforting. The worst part of the whole experience was having to spend so many hours of every day in the company of Eric and all his hate.

Now there was a chance for all of that to change. The new cell mate on the top bunk certainly didn't look much like Eric. He gave off a laid back vibe rather than looking like he wanted to put a brick through every window he could find. Danny gave him a nod as the cell door closed behind him and the key clanked in the lock.

"Bottom bunk is it?"

"It is. Hang on. I'll get rid of my stuff. I wasn't expecting you."

The boy swung himself down and gathered up an armful of clothes, magazines and a CD player.

"There you go. I'm Rico." A hand was held out. Danny shook.

"Danny. Danny McCann."

"The footballer."

Danny raised a surprised eyebrow.

"Seen you in the exercise yard. Impressive."

"Cheers."

Danny put away his bits and pieces. There wasn't much. Some washing gear. A couple of magazines. Spare socks.

"You Italian or something then?"

Rico shook his head. "No man. I'm Richard. Richard Hughes. From Kilmarnock. I just hate being called Richard, that's all. Poxy name. Rico's loads better."

"Right."

"You want a roly?"

"Yeah. Go on. Cheers."

Danny caught a tobacco pouch and Rizzlas and sat on his bunk and started rolling a thin smoke.

"So Danny. What are you here for? I gather you're here for good now, yeah? No more remand?"

Danny nodded as he licked the papers. "Eighteen months."

"You must have been a bad boy then."

"I was."

He took the offered lighter and got the smoke going.

"Well, go on then."

"Go on what?"

Rico rolled his eyes. "You know. What did you go down for?"

"This twenty questions or something mate?"

"Ah don't get touchy. Look. I'm in for two years on possession of Class A substances with intent to supply. I've done three months which means that if I keep my nose clean I'll be back out in the fresh air in nine months. If you are a good lad and don't forget to tuck your shirt in, you'll be away in seven-and-a-half-months. Which all means that you and I will be spending a lot of time in each other's company.

So we might as well find out who the hell we are and if we're going to batter each other to bits, why not do it sooner rather than later. Anything wrong with that?"

"No. Sounds OK to me."

"Want a coke?"

"Aye. I'll have a coke."

Rico poured from a plastic bottle into a plastic cup. Danny took an appreciative sip.

"Fair enough. I'm here for battering someone, possession with intent to supply, being in possession of stolen property and nicking two legs of frozen lamb. Happy now."

Rico grinned. "A very, very, very bad boy."

"Not as bad as you. Eighteen months is six months less than two years."

They lapsed into silence for a while. Eventually Rico said.

"What were you possessing with intent to supply?"

"Vallies. Three hundred. You?"

"Smack. Ten grand's worth."

Danny almost spat out a mouthful of coke.

"Ten grand! Bloody hell."

"Wasn't mine. It was my brother's. The cops had his place under surveillance. He got a tip off that they were about to put the front door in so he asked me to hold onto it for a couple of days. And they only went and put my door in instead. Typical."

"We're you not selling any then?"

"No. Not really. The odd bag here and there. I used plenty though."

"What? Smack?"

Rico nodded and started rolling a smoke of his own.

"Yeah. Started when I was fifteen."

Danny studied his cell mate through new eyes.

"You look better than most. How long is that then? Four years?"

"Five. I'm twenty. Smoke it, don't I? Never jack it up. You don't look like death warmed up if you smoke it."

Danny shrugged. "You must have been OK for cash. Lads tell me that it's more expensive. Smoking it."

Rico gave him a faint smile. "Not really. Smack's our family business you see. My dad and my two older brothers. They always see me right."

Danny thought of the Stamper family. Sally was nothing more than a distant memory now. Sunnybank rumour had it that she was at some fancy school down in England. He had spotted her a couple of times but they hadn't spoken since the night Baz had written the car off. Baz never spoke of her.

"But you don't get into the dealing then?"

Rico shook his head. "Nah. Not my scene man."

Danny allowed a long drag of smoke to wander out of his nose and felt his body relax. Rico gave him all the right first impressions. Life looked like it might be much more tolerable that it had been cooped up with Mr Hatred from Pollock. The doors of the cell were closed for the night and they idled away the time getting to know each other. The muted TV moved from programme to programme without either of them paying too much attention. Rico explained that he had done better at school than either of his brothers. A lot better. He had stayed on to do Highers and had got decent grades. His dad wanted him to go on to college and he had done as instructed. He explained with a wry grin that his dad wasn't the sort of bloke you argued with. Besides he was the man with the smack and so he had to stay the right side of him.

"Isn't he bothered then? About you having a habit?"

"He hates it. He went clean ballistic when he first found out. Battered me good and proper. Neither of my brothers use. He's tried everything. Locked me in the house. Sent me off to rehab. The lot."

"It's never worked then?"

"No. I've sometimes stayed clean for a few months, but I always go back."

Danny found it something hard to get his head round. Fair enough, he had got to needing the vallies every hour on the hour, but now he was off them there was no way he was going back down that road.

"Why does he let you have it then?"

"Because if he doesn't give it me he knows I will get it somewhere else. And if I go somewhere else I'll have to pay for it. About forty quid a day. And I don't have forty quid a day, so I'll have to go out shoplifting and I'll get caught and end up in jail. So to avoid that he gives me the gear. That way he thinks he can keep me out of bother and I can finish my college and go on to have a proper life. Crazy isn't it. All that effort and I wind up in here anyway for looking after some kit for my brother."

"Your dad must have been raging."

Rico chuckled. "Let's just say it wasn't the happiest week of my brother's life."

"The cops never got your brother then?"

"Nah. They messed up the arrest. Got the paperwork wrong. My dad has a big-hitting brief up in Glasgow and he got my brother off. Not me though. With me they dotted every 'i' and crossed every 't'. So here I am. Looks like your lawyer didn't have any luck either"

This made Danny laugh. "I just had some duty lawyer. My dad works on the bins. No big-hitting brief for me. Mind you, even if he won the lottery he wouldn't pay for one. He's washed his hands of me. Not that it would have made any difference. I pleaded guilty to all of it."

"So your dad doesn't come to visit?"

Danny shook his head. "Doesn't visit. Doesn't phone. Doesn't write. Actually, that's a lie. He wrote once. Half a page saying not to come back home once they let me out."

"What about your mum?"

Another shake of the head. "She's gone. Left when I was nine. Legged it to Australia with some bloke."

Rico gave a low whistle. "That must have been hard."

"It was."

They didn't talk for a while. Outside the prison was falling into the edgy silence of the night. In the distance a door banged closed. There were occasional shouts. Then nothing. Somewhere far into the night it was possible to hear wagons rolling down the motorway. Danny could sense that Rico had something to say. Something he was biding his time with. Waiting for the right moment. Then at last it came.

"Look Danny. I'm going to need some co-operation. If we're cell mates and that."

"Go on."

"I'm still using, OK."

"What? The smack?"

"Yeah."

"How the hell do you manage that?"

"Ways and means. There's loads of drugs in prison. You know that."

"S'pose so. I've never bothered looking. No money have I."

"My dad gets it sent in."

Danny sat up, intrigued. "How the hell does he manage that?"

"There's a lot of boys in here from round Kilmarnock. He gets their mates to smuggle in gear. Then he pays them on the out."

"What? The mates?"

"Yeah. The mates. Most of them use kit. He gives them a few free bags if they smuggle stuff in."

Once again Danny thought of Les Stamper. Men like Les and Rico's dad lived in a different world where organising for Heroin to be taken into a prison was as easy as buying the weekly groceries at Tesco.

"So what's it got to do with me then?"

Rico leaned over the edge of the bunk and looked down. "The only place I can smoke is in the cell. And if I'm in the cell, you're in the cell. So I need you to watch my back. Turn a blind eye. You know."

Danny shrugged. "You don't have to worry about me. I'm not a grass. You can do what you want."

Rico nodded. "I've got plenty. If you want a taste just say. It's up to you."

This made Danny laugh. "The only reason I'm here is the vallies. I'm off them now. I don't want to replace them with smack do I?"

"Like I said. It's up to you. But smack's different to vallies."

"So they say."

"I'm serious. Vallies just get you paranoid all the time and make you want to pick a fight with everyone."

"I'm not arguing with that."

"Smack makes everything right. Not wrong. When I have a smoke I couldn't care less if I'm in here or on the out. Makes no difference. You want to make the time go easy, then that's the way. But like I said. It's up to you. Just let me know."

"I will."

The next few weeks drifted by easily enough. The time was slow, but not particularly bad. Danny dropped into the steady routine of prison life and felt like his life was on hold. After a while, he gave up wondering if there would be another letter from his father. In his heart he knew there wouldn't be. He knew what his dad was like when he made his mind up. It would be a long, long time before there would be a chance to build any bridges. Danny knew well enough what he would have to do. He would have to serve out his time, get back home, get some accommodation, then a job, and then prove that he had put all the bad stuff behind him and turned things around. And it wouldn't just be for a few weeks. His dad would never be convinced by a few weeks. It would have to be months. Maybe years.

Strangely enough as he passed the halfway point in his sentence he started to feel his spirits sink a little lower with every passing day. At the start of his sentence it had seemed as if he would be locked up forever. The future was not a thing worth thinking about. Before there was any future there were months and months of time to serve. But once he was half way through the future was suddenly a lot nearer. Clearer. Nagging. Real.

As he lay awake night after night staring at the mattress above him he tried to find some kind of hopeful view of the future, but it was hard. On the day of his release they would give him a liberation grant which would be enough for a train ticket back to Dumfries and a few quid in his pocket. He would get off the train and report to his Criminal Justice Social Worker who would fix him up with a place in one of the hostels. And then what? There would be some sort of a course to try and help him brush up on skills so that he could get a job. But he had tried getting a job before and that was before he had a record for dealing drugs and giving a stationmaster a kicking. And nicking legs of frozen lamb. There had been no chance of a job when he had no record. Now it would be a complete impossibility. It all meant that the prospect of life outside the fences of the prison offered little to make him want to count down the hours to his release.

Autumn slipped into winter and the endless wet grey skies seemed to match the growing mood of depression that was wrapped about him like a mouldy overcoat. Every night when the warder locked the cell door for the night, Danny would sit on his bunk and listen to the sound effects of Rico cooking up on the bunk above him. He would hear the rustle of a piece of tin foil being unfolded. Then there was the click of the lighter as the Heroin was heated into smoke. And then there was the soft sound of sucking as Rico drew in the smoke as it drifted away from the foil and towards the ceiling. Then he would hear Rico sink back into his pillow and sigh with satisfaction. When they talked he envied the calm tranquillity that always settled onto Rico once the Heroin had made its way up into his brain. Nothing fazed him. The future was even less of a problem than the present and the present wasn't a problem at all. Nothing in the whole wide world was a problem and it was obvious from the bottomless contentment in Rico's eyes that nothing ever would be problem. Every night he bought a ticket to a sunny place far away from the stale smell of the cell and the distant sounds of the prison.

To start with it had interested Danny to watch the instant transformation in his cell mate. But as the weeks moulded themselves into months and the summer moved into Autumn, he started to become intrigued. What exactly was it like? This place where Rico travelled to every night. A place that put a small smile on his face. A place that was never disappointing. A place far away from all the bad stuff and tedium. And with every passing day, he was more and more tempted to join him there.

It was on a cold frosty night in November that he could stand it no more. Nothing out of the ordinary had happened that day. The routine had been just the same as it always was. What was different was that the calendar told Danny that he now only had 99 more days until they gave him back his stuff and opened up the gates to the outside world. It wasn't three figures any more. It was two figures. Only just over three months. And the prospect of endless days killing time on the streets of Dumfries was suddenly alarmingly close. All day he tried to find something positive in the idea of going back home. Some decent food. Proper fresh air rather than rationed time in the prison yard. A fish supper. A takeaway pizza. And . . .

No more 'and'. Nothing to even begin to compensate for the miserable prospect of a room in a hostel and days full of nothing.

"Rico."

"Yeah."

"I'll have a bit."

"Have what?"

"You know. A smoke. Some smack."

Rico eased his legs over the side of the bunk and dropped to the floor. Then he cleared some folded clothes of the chair by the small desk and looked mildly troubled.

"You sure about this man, I mean you're only a few weeks from getting out."

Danny nodded. "Dead sure."

"It's a big step. Once you cross the line . . . well you know . . ."

"I know. And I've thought about it. And stuff it. Show me what to do."

Rico looked for a moment as if he was going to argue some more and then shrugged and pulled down the foil from his bunk. He spoke as he measured out a small pile of light brown powder on the centre of the foil.

"Don't get your hopes up too high for the first time. Well. At least the first few minutes. What will probably happen is that you'll chuck your guts up. Most people do. You'll feel sick as a dog for a few minutes. Just go with it, OK. Don't battle it. If you're sick, then you're sick. After a little while you'll get an idea of what it's all about. Only an idea, mind. You will only really know after about the second or third time. So. That's me. I'll hold the foil and the lighter. You need to stick this in your mouth. As soon as the kit starts to smoke you suck it in. Follow the smoke. Get as much as you can until it's all gone. You're dead sure are you?"

"Yeah man. I'm sure. Let's do it."

He had barely finished chasing and sucking the smoke when an overwhelming urge to puke took him just like Rico had predicted. He just made it to the toilet before losing the mince and tatties he had eaten a couple of hours earlier. He closed his eyes and tried to grab hold of the gale force rush, but it was beyond him. He was sick again. And then again. But he kept his eyes closed and bided his time. And very slowly a sense of well being started to pass through him. It was like a gentle warm summer breeze and he was aware that his mouth was easing into a smile. The feeling was all through him now. All over him. Every inch. Every cell. He tried to get his brain to work out exactly what the feeling was. But there were no words for it. At least no words that he had available to him. Maybe if he had listened better in English he might have had the words. But it didn't really matter. Because nothing mattered. Not a single thing in the whole wide world. Being in prison didn't matter. Being disowned by his dad didn't matter. His mum going to Australia didn't matter. Sally disappearing off to England didn't matter. Blowing his chances of making it as a footballer didn't matter. Having nothing but a million years of emptiness to return to when he got back to Dumfries didn't matter . . .

"You OK man?"

"Yeah . . ."

He heard his own voice as if it belonged to somebody else. A different Danny. A Danny who was lying on a hard bed in a narrow-walled cell in a bleak prison in the midst of a dark Scottish winter's night. He wasn't that Danny. Not with his eyes closed. He was a new Danny. A better Danny. And he had found a special place that was far, far away from all the bad stuff in his life. It was like a secret meadow with the sound of birdsong and long warm grass and a big blue sky above. A place where nobody was ever going to hassle him. Tell him what to do. Threaten him. Tell him he was substituted. Send him to prison. Not any of it. Or them. Or anything. He was washed away. He was on a magic carpet. He was soaring like a buzzard. He was complete.

And nothing would ever be the same again. Heroin became the fourth great influence on his life. At times when he lay in the quiet of the night, relishing the warmth and security of it, he would reflect that all the great influences in his life were tied together. From the moment his mother had left him, he had started on the road that took him to becoming 'that' Danny McCann. If his mother had stayed, then the social workers and policemen would never have come to take him away to Stranraer. But Stranraer had introduced him to football, the second great influence that had dominated every waking hour for over six years. And would Sally Stamper have noticed him but for football? No chance. Not in a million years. Without football he was nothing. Just an ordinary boy from Sunnybank. Football made him special. It made him feel worth something. It made all his failures go away. And Sally had made him feel special. Sally and the Ecstasy and the dope and the fast rides in the 206 through tunnels of pine trees. But Sally and the pills and the smoke had taken away the football. And in the end the pills and the smoke had taken away Sally. And then he was left with nothing again. The wheel had turned a full circle and he was right back to the place where he had started after his mum had left and the police and social workers had come to take him away. Out of the nothingness he had re-emerged as 'that' Danny McCann. A Danny McCann who stole legs of frozen lamb for the price of a couple of pills and a share in a bottle of White Lightning cider to kill the boredom. A Danny McCann who rode the closes of Sunnybank on a stolen bike selling Valium to any youngster with a pound in their pocket. A Danny McCann who had been so eaten up by paranoia that he had attacked a station master for no other reason than he had reached into his pocket for a mobile phone.

It was all logical. One thing always led to another. When his mum left he went mad. When he found football and Sally he found himself again. Then when he lost football and Sally, he went mad again. And now he had found his fourth great influence. Not only the fourth, but the greatest of them all.

Heroin.

Heroin AKA smack, kit, gear, brown, 'H'.

Heroin of many names.

Heroin that turned the long empty nights from a time of grinding boredom into a time of perfect calm. Heroin that made him feel complete in his special place. Heroin that made nothing else matter. Nothing was a problem. Nothing was a threat. His life was in good hands. The routine of the prison took away any need to make any decisions. All he had to do was to follow the arrows. And with a smoke before the cell door was unlocked in the morning and a smoke when it banged shut again at night nothing could have been easier. The days floated by like clouds in a summer sky. Nothing altered or changed. Nothing was urgent. Nothing was a threat or a worry. It was as if he was on a luxury cruise liner that was chugging its way around the world and once it completed a circuit it would simply start all over again.

Then one day something different did happen. He was on his way from eating his lunch to an English class when one of the warders beckoned him over.

"Come with me McCann. You've got a visitor."

For a moment the shock of the man's words rooted him to the ground where he stood. A visitor! It had to be his dad. There was nobody else. There was no way that any of the lads from Sunnybank would have ever got it together to catch the bus north. He followed the warder with a tight nervous feeling in his stomach. What was his dad going to say to him? Probably he had come to make it absolutely clear that there was no way that he was having Danny home again and so there was no point in planning anything different. Or maybe he had thought about things and had a change of heart. Danny was determined not to get his hopes up. Bitter experience had taught him that every time he allowed a glimmer of hope into his life, things always went completely bad on him. He just focused on following the warder to the visitors suite. Each game as it comes, Danny.

Once inside he scanned the area for the familiar figure of his dad. It was a large room with plastic tables and chairs in bright colours. Most of the tables were occupied. Families sat together in small tight groups. There were parents and grand parents and brothers and sisters sitting round pale faced prisoners in their prison issue sweatshirts. Some were crying. Others were trying to brave it out. Others merely stared down at cartons of juice on the scratched plastic tops of the tables. No sign of his dad. So who? Then he recognised a familiar figure sitting at a table in the far corner.

Jimmy Doyle.

He rose to his feet and gave a guarded smile as Danny crossed the room to join him.

"Hello Danny."

Danny was so surprised that he found it hard to think of anything to say. In the end he settled on a simple. "Jimmy."

"I got you these." Jimmy slid over a carton of orange juice, a KitKat and a bag of crisps.

"Cheers."

Danny opened the crisps whilst his old coach took in his surroundings.

"So. How is it?"

"It's OK. I'm keeping my head down. Being a good lad. I'll be out just after Christmas."

"Playing any football?"

Danny smiled. Jimmy's priorities hadn't changed. "Aye. In the exercise yard."

"Any good?"

"Nae referees. There's plenty of tasty tackles like. But, aye. Not bad. It's OK. What about you? Still at Gretna?"

"Yeah. Still there. I'm on my way up to Alloa actually. We're playing there this afternoon. Seemed a shame not to drop in since the motorway more or less runs past the gates."

Danny finished the crisps and folded the packet into a square. "They're doing pretty good. Top of the league. Think they'll go up?"

"We should do. Lots of the teams in the division are part time. We tend to have a big edge on fitness. It will be a different story next season."

"But you're not coaching the first team."

This made Jimmy laugh to himself. "Hell no. That's the Gaffer. Rowan Alexander. He's one of the best young managers in the country. You watch out for his name Danny. He'll manage Scotland one day."

"So what are you doing then?"

Jimmy took a sip at his coffee and wrinkled his nose. They obviously didn't consider good coffee any kind of priority in young offenders institutes.

"We have a big community scheme. I'm part of a team of five coaches. We do all sorts. It mainly involves going into schools and running football workshops."

"What. And they pay you like?"

"They do."

"That's all right then. And there's five of you?"

"Yeah. I reckon there'll be more soon."

"So it's your job to watch out for young kids that might make it then?"

"No. Not really. I mean if I ever did see a lad who looked like he had what it takes I'd certainly get the lads from the Academy to come and have a look. But it's not my job. My job is just give kids a chance to play football."

Danny speared the lid of his orange juice carton with a plastic straw and took a drink.

"So why do they do it then?"

"Who? The schools?"

"No. Gretna. What's the point?"

Jimmy considered another sip of coffee but couldn't face it. He pushed the cup away to the centre of the table.

"It's all down to the owner. Brooks Mileson. Have you not heard about him?"

"Not really. Only that he's dead rich."

"Well he was brought up in Sunderland. On an estate not much different to Sunnybank. He saw how easy it is for lads to go off down the wrong tracks. To wind up in a place like this. I figure you know that well enough Danny."

Danny stared down and fiddled with the crisp packet.

"Aye. I know that."

"Brooks reckons the best way to keep kids out of bother is to give them something to do. And there's nothing better than football. I seem to remember that you did alright for a while when you were into your football."

Danny nodded, still staring down.

"And then when you packed up playing it all went to hell. Am I right, or am I right?"

"There's no need to take the Mick, Jimmy."

"I'm not taking the Mick, I'm just telling like it is."

Danny felt an edge of anger. He didn't need this. "Look Jimmy, it's good of you to come and see me and all, but I can do without a lecture. Why don't you just go and watch the match and leave me be."

Jimmy sat back and pushed his hands into the pockets of his jacket.

"I didn't come to give you a lecture Danny so cool down. I came to tell you a couple of things, that's all."

"Go on then."

"OK. One. I've talked a lot with your dad but there's no give. You know what he's like."

"I know what he's like."

"But nothing has to be forever. Get back to town. Get a place to stay. Keep your nose clean. Get a job and I reckon he'll come round. You hear me?"

"Aye. I hear you."

"Good. Number two. I've spent a bit of time around the training ground these last few months. I like watching the coaches. I've learnt a lot. You wouldn't believe the difference between what goes on now and what went on in my day. Anyway. We've got a good team. Obviously we have. We're ten points clear at the top. But I still reckon you could get in it. Seriously. It would take a tonne of work and there's no guarantees, but there's a chance. All you need to do is to keep out of bother and get as fit as you've ever been in your life and I'll take you down for a try out. Remember that last game? The Rotary Cup Final?"

Danny gave a rueful smile. "Hardly likely to forget it, am I?"

"No. I don't suppose you are. Well Brooks was there that morning. It was when he offered me a job. He saw you Danny."

Now Danny groaned. "Well that's me stuffed then. I was like a complete nutter."

"Aye. That you were. But you were a complete nutter who got a hat trick in five minutes. He remembers that you know. Asks about you from time to time. He's not the kind of bloke who will write you off because you've been a stupid little pratt. Like I said. He knows the score. If you come for a trial it will be a hundred percent down to Rowan, but I reckon Brooks will back me up in getting you the trial. You hear me Danny?"

Danny heard him well enough. He heard him only too well. For months and months and months he had assumed that he had totally and utterly messed up his chances of making anything of his football career. He had been given his chance and blown it. It was one of the main reasons that the depression had grown and grown inside him like a kind of cancer as the day of his release drew nearer. If there had been even a one percent chance that there might still have been some hope of pursuing his football dreams that would have been enough. But things had seemed absolutely hopeless and he had felt the loss of his football dream as badly as he felt all the other losses in his life. His mother. Sally. And finally his father. And it had only been when the despair had reached its lowest point that he had succumbed to the temptation that he felt every night when Rico got out the foil. But now at a plastic table with crisps and orange juice and a Kitkat everything had suddenly been turned on its head. All of a sudden his football career wasn't doomed after all. In fact it was the opposite. Everything about getting picked for the Scotland Under 16s had been about getting a chance with a club. And now he had a chance with a pro club. And it wasn't just any pro club. It was Gretna who was rising up the leagues like lava up the spout of a volcano. It should have been the best bit of news he had ever heard in his life.

But it wasn't.

Because his life wasn't his own to control any more. Just a few weeks before he would have been in a position to jump at the chance. But Danny McCann was no longer in charge of Danny McCann's destiny. He had a new master now who was calling all the shots. Heroin was in charge of things now and he could only take Jimmy Doyle up on his offer if the Heroin allowed him to. But of course the most important thing was that his new relationship with this new master was still a secret. A big secret which had to be treasured. So he went through the motions. He jammed a smile onto his face.

"That's brilliant Jimmy. Absolutely brilliant."

"So you'll spend a few weeks getting yourself fit?"

"Aye. That I will."

Jimmy nodded, but there was something about him that wasn't completely convinced. "Good. I won't say anything yet. As soon as you get out we'll do some fitness stuff and when I reckon your ready, I'll get it sorted. That sound good to you Danny?"

"Aye. Magic."

Jimmy took a look at his watch. "Well. I best be along. Don't want to miss kick off. I'll see you in a few weeks then."

Jimmy headed off to the match and a warder returned Danny to the wing. All afternoon his mind was locked in overdrive. He needed a plan. A real plan that he could stick to. There was no doubt whatsoever what he really should do. He should knock it on the head straight away. The sooner he stopped, the better it would be when he got out. The trouble was that he knew that he would never manage it, no matter how hard he tried. A fortnight earlier there had been a problem with a delivery from Rico's dad and the two of them had been without supplies for five days. It had been Danny's introduction to the rattle. The first day hadn't been too bad. He had been a bit twitchy, hot and sweaty, irritable, edgy and there had been no chance of sleeping a wink. By the time they had unlocked the cell doors, he was beginning to feel rough and it was all he could do to eat a piece of toast. By mid-morning he felt sick as a dog and threw up the toast a little after eleven. By the time they locked the door for the night, both cell mates were balled up on their bunks and doomed to a whole night of agony and vomit. It had felt like a night that would never end. Each hour felt like a year. Each minute trailed by like a long slow train loaded with coal. And Danny kept trying to convince himself that there was no way it could get any worse, but it did. His limbs were a burning agony. His arms. His legs. All of him. No matter how he tossed and turned there was no escape. On and on and on, until the pale light of a wet, rainy morning lit the small barred window.

Things started to get a little better at lunchtime and slowly but surely he returned to something close to normal. That night he had been able to snatch a couple of hours of sleep, but Rico was even worse than he had been the night before. Through gritted teeth he explained that day three was the worst. The longest. The most brutal. The day when the world of pain closed in and crushed and squeezed. He explained that he was suffering more than Danny because his body was way more dependent on the drug. Because for Rico it had been years not weeks. And all that night Danny listened in to the torment on the bunk above his head.

The memory of the pain was still crystal clear in Danny's head. It had been a terrible two days. A long, lingering nightmare that had left him shattered and shaken. He had dealt with it for the simple reason that there had been absolutely no choice. He was locked up in prison and the only way to find a fix would have been to escape and that wasn't ever going to happen. So he had gritted his teeth and fought his way through it. He realised that what had made it just about bearable was the knowledge that it would only be a mater of time before another fix came along.

Now things were very different. Was there any serious chance that he could endure the agony whilst Rico took his fix just a few inches above his head? Not even a chance in a million and there was no point in pretending otherwise. It was immediately clear that there was no way he was going to get himself clean in prison and it was a complete waste of time even thinking about it.

Which meant that it would have to be done on the out, and that was a great deal more manageable. The out would mean some sort of a room in a hostel and barely a penny in his pockets. That would be the time. He would spend whatever was left of his liberation grant after the train ticket on fruit juice and biscuits and he would barricade himself away. And one way or another he would get himself through it. Of course it would be a nightmare. But it would be worth it because once he had put the nightmare days behind him, a whole new life would open up. A better life. A brilliant life. The life that he had dreamed about before he had messed everything up.

In the meantime, he decided that he would make sure he made the most of the last few weeks with his new master. He would treasure every visit to the special place of ultimate peace. And then in the day he would work hard in the gym and give all he had in the wild football games in the exercise yard.

He had his plan. All he needed to do was to stick with it and his life would be back on the tracks again.

He hadn't thought the pain would start on the train. He had taken his last fix before the cells had been unlocked for breakfast. Then he had packed up his few belongings and said his goodbyes to Rico. They promised to stay in touch. Danny had said he would take a ride up to Kilmarnock once Rico was released. Then it had been paperwork and one door and gate after another being unlocked until he found himself standing outside the prison on a bright winter morning. They had given him directions to the station and told him where to wait for a bus. He had asked how far it was to walk and they had said it was about three miles. After nine months under lock and key, the idea of a long walk in the cold sunshine seemed pretty good. He took in the air in great gulps and felt like he floated into the small town. He treated himself to two bacon rolls and a steaming mug of hot chocolate and started to focus himself for the rattle that was waiting for him in Dumfries.

A passenger had left a paper on the seat opposite him on the train and there was a long article on the Gretna story and how the little club was on the fast track to the SPL. Danny read it twice and then stared out at the bright countryside outside the window as it glided by. That could soon be his world. All he needed to do was get through a couple of days of pain and the road would be wide open. No problem. Piece of cake.

He changed trains in Glasgow and bought a couple of Mars bars for the last leg of the journey down the Nith Valley. By the time the train drew into New Cumnock, the bright optimism of the first leg of the journey was starting to fade. Outside the day had clouded, and the valley the railway track followed seemed dark and threatening. Old slag heaps told the story of places where there had once been coal mines. Lorries trundled along the road that at times ran alongside the train. Clusters of sheep in grey fields of dead looking grass. A fed up heron on the banks of the river. Kirkconnel. Sanquhar. And the Mars bars were sitting badly in his guts. And he could feel the first sheen of sweat on his face. And his legs were already aching. He had thought that it wouldn't start until the evening when he was safe in a room somewhere. No chance. By the time the train drew into Dumfries the pain was already rolling through him.

CHAPTER THREE

The sight of the platform was a shock. This was where it had all happened. He pictured the twisted, terrified face of the stationmaster. And the shocked expressions of the lads. And the slamming sound of the policemen's boots as they came to knock him to the floor. It was still fresh. Vivid. This was the history he was returning to. And the need was getting sharper by the minute. And this was only the start. The first few yards of a marathon that would last for days. Forever.

He fought to keep his spirits up and to hang onto the soaring optimism he had felt as he walked away from the prison in the glittering morning sunshine. But the sun was long gone. The sky above was a bleak grey and an ice cold rain was cascading down. He pulled up his collar and started to walk. By the time he reached the offices of the Criminal Justice Department, he was soaked through and freezing. The lady behind the reception window checked her paperwork and told him to wait. Whatever she was doing took time. The minutes drifted along on the clock high up on the wall. Five minutes. Quarter of an hour. Twenty-five minutes. And all the while the biting pain was starting to crawl up the inside of his legs. And the sickness was growing in his gut. The rainwater had dried from his face to be replaced by a thin sheen of cold sweat. After his time in the prison he knew that this was only the start. It was nothing. The real hard part would swell and grow until by the empty hours of the night it would be a raging misery. In the days leading up to his release he had tried to focus his mind on the task he now faced. The key was to be strong. One hundred percent committed. Sure, the pain would be bad but the pain would pass. It was only a couple of days. Maybe three. Nothing. A mere drop in ocean of the rest of his life. And worth it. Easily worth it because once the Heroin was driven from his system he could start to get fit again and then Jimmy Doyle would help him back onto the tracks. He clenched his eyes shut and tried to find the focus he needed.

"Danny!!"

The woman's voice was annoyed. He opened his eyes to find that she was back behind the counter.

"Oh. You're back with us then are you?"

"Sorry about that. I was in dreamland."

"I should say so." She took a long look at him as he returned to the counter. Her eyes took in the sweat on his face and sheet white paleness of his skin.

"Are you feeling OK Danny?"

"Aye. Fine. I'm just tired, that's all. I never slept last night. Too excited."

She didn't look all that convinced, but started back with the paperwork. After a couple more sheets she turned the paper to face him and offered a pen. "Right. All done. I'll need an autograph please."

He signed as directed. Then he listened to the rules of the hostel where they were going to send him and about how important it was that he stick by them. Then she gave him directions but he knew where the place was anyway. He patiently listened about how this was now his chance to put everything in the past behind him. It was time for a new start. And there was all the time in the world for a new start. He nodded his way through the little lecture and felt a huge relief when she let him go. Outside the rain had picked up and a sharp wind was keeping the pavements clear of pedestrians. The only people who were out and about were those who had no choice. His legs felt terrible. He wanted to stride out and get to the hostel before he felt even worse, but his body wasn't in the mood. By the time he arrived the wet had seeped all the way through his clothes and his spirits were on their way down to rock bottom.

The manager was nice enough and she told him that the heating was on full in his room and he could have a bath if he wanted one. She showed him his room which wasn't much bigger than the cell he had lived in for nine months, but at least the lock was on the inside this time. Then she ran him through the same rules that the lady at the criminal justice department had already told him about. She explained that there was a support worker allocated to him but it would be next morning before they would make contact.

Finally he was alone. He took in the small room that was his new home. A single bed. A small wardrobe. A table under a window that looked down into a courtyard. A kettle and a mug. A sink.

He thought about what the manager had said. She had suggested a bath. Maybe that wasn't a bad idea. Maybe the hot water might ease the growing agony in his legs. And arms. And more or less every inch of his body. He decided that it could do no harm and made his way down the corridor outside to the bathroom. The hot water in fact did little to relieve his aching bones, but at least it warmed him up on the outside. He had brought in some dry clothes to change into and felt a little better when he closed the bathroom door to return to his room. He was in the process of unlocking when he heard a familiar voice.

"Christ Danny. It is you."

He turned to find that Chewit had emerged from the room two down from his. He recognised his friend but only because he had spoken his name. Had they passed on the pavement there would have been no way that he would have given him a second glance. Chewit was shrunken. It was as if somebody had pushed a super powerful vacuum down his throat and sucked him dry. His skin seemed to be stretched so tight across the bones of his face that it looked like it might tear like paper left out in the sun.

"What are you doing here Chewit?"

The other boy gave a shrug. Danny half-expected to hear his bones rattle.

"Mum and dad chucked me out like. Ended up here, didn't I."

Danny hovered for a moment and then waved his old friend over. "Come on in. It's cold out here."

Chewit sat on the chair whilst Danny rubbed at his wet hair.

"How come they threw you out?"

Chewit kicked at the faded pattern on the thin carpet.

"Nicking."

"Nicking? How do you mean, nicking?"

"Money and stuff. Then I took the tele. That was it. Last straw."

The words seemed to burn his lips. Miserable words that obviously haunted him.

"Hang on a second Chewit. Why the hell did you nick the tele?"

Chewit mumbled a reply which the carpet might have just about heard but Danny certainly didn't.

"Sorry mate. Missed that."

This time Chewit spoke a little louder. More words that were hard to say. More words that were the cause of shame.

"Started using haven't I?"

This was not what Danny had been expecting. Chewit had always been a bit daft but not that daft.

"Smack you mean?"

"Aye."

"What about the others? Deano and Nokey?"

Chewit's head shot up. There was a fear in his eyes that Danny couldn't begin to understand. "You never heard?"

"Course I never heard. I was banged up wasn't I? And I haven't exactly been overdone with visitors."

"Nokey's dead Danny."

Danny felt a lump of ice in his chest.

"You what?"

Chewit nodded. "Took an overdose. Ages ago now. Back in the summer. We'd only been using for a few weeks. It was the first time we jagged it like. He went first and . . ."

His eyes seemed huge in the pale, bony face and the memory of what had happened burned as sharp as if it had only been the day before.

". . . we were all laughing like . . . I mean we thought he was having us on . . . Then his lips went blue and the bloke we were with started to flip out . . . Said there was no way anyone was having an OD at his place . . . so he just lobbed us out . . . we called an ambulance and waited out on the pavement . . .

Again his head went down. "He just went really still. And cold like. Even though it was a really warm night. Cold. The ambulance men could'nae do nothing. They tried. But nothing. That was it. The police took me and Deano in and gave us the third degree. It was like they thought it was us that did it. They rang my dad, but he said that he was finished with me. Deano's parents came and they were blazing. They sent him to stay with that uncle of his. You ken the one. He's in Canada. I don't know how he's getting on."

Danny felt like he had been hit by a truck.

"I don't know what to say. How are his mum and dad?"

Chewit's face seemed to fall a notch. "They hate me. Told everyone. Said it was all down to me and Deano. Said there was no way their lad would have ever used smack. Said we must have forced them. I never go anywhere near Sunnybank now. It's a nightmare. People swear. Spit at me. Call me a murdering little junkie. It gets me down Danny. They don't understand he was my best mate. They don't know what it was like to watch him die."

Danny looked at the wrecked face of the boy he had grown up with. The saucer eyes were brimming with tears now. Chewit was desperate for everyone to understand why he was using Heroin. Why he needed it. Why he would do almost anything to get it. Heroin was the only thing that could take away the terrible memory of watching a friend die in front of his eyes. In the beginning it would have been a laugh. A dare. Three lads with nothing better to do. Ticking drugs off their lists like train spotters. Dope. Tick, done that. Eckies. Tick. Phets. Tick. Coke. Tick. Vallies. Tick, tick, tick, tick all the way till the pen slips off the edge of the page. Until there was just the one left. The big one. The one that they had always promised themselves that they would never touch in a million years. But they had touched it. Messed about. Dabbled. Convinced that they were fine because they were only having a smoke now and then so there was no way they could be like proper junkies because proper junkies injected. But that of course had merely added one more adventure to complete. Smack, chased the dragon. Tick. Smack. Jagged. Not ticked. What would it be like? Would it be as good as people said? And of course there had only been one way to find out. And for Nokey it had been the very last adventure. A tenner's worth of blackness.

Permanent blackness.

But Danny knew that in a way Nokey had been the lucky one. It was over for him. Deano had been lucky too. He had been flown far away to a place where he had no history. It was Chewit who was taking the rap. Carrying the can. He had to bear the looks of complete hate on the faces of strangers who knew him as the boy who had been there when another boy had died. And he had to bear it all on his own. No mum. No dad. No brothers and sisters and Nana and Grandpa. And every night when he was so tired that he would have given anything for a proper night's sleep, he would still fight to stay awake. Because every time he closed his eyes he was back on the pavement on a warm, sticky summer night looking down at a dead friend with blue lips and very still eyes that seemed to stare all the way out past the stars.

Unless he had a fix.

And if he had a fix it would all go away. The loneliness. The loss. The guilt. The nightmares. All of it. And Danny knew that he would find the same warm and safe place that he had visited so many times in the prison. And if he had to lie and cheat and steal to find the place he would do it. And if he had to make do without food and decent clothes to find the place then so be it. Because in Chewit's life, absolutely nothing else was important. Without the comfort of Heroin the world was a dark place where everyone seemed to hate his guts.

But there was a problem. As Danny had allowed his brain to understand his friend's need of the escape a hit gave him, it also allowed in the little voice that he had been trying to ignore for hours. It wasn't a little voice any more. It was a huge voice and it was screaming into his ears from about an inch away. Chewit is using. Chewit will know where to score. You have £20 left from your liberation grant. Forget the fruit juice. Forget the biscuits and the sweets. Forget locking the door and sweating it out. Forget ringing Jimmy Doyle and getting fit. Forget the lectures from the woman at Criminal Justice and the manager of the hostel. Forget everything. Name. Family. What one and one adds up to. Everything. All of it. Only one thing mattered.

Chewit was using.

Chewit would know where to score.

£20 in the pocket.

"Who do you buy off then?"

Chewit looked up sharply, surprised at the question.

"Baz."

Danny gave a small, annoyed shake of the head.

"Don't be daft. Baz doesn't knock out smack. No way. His dad would kill him."

"Aye, well his dad's not about any more is he? Got lifted. Massive it was. Vans, dogs, the lot. He's on remand and the word is he's going to get a ten."

Danny shook his head to try and make his thoughts get into some kind of order. It seemed inconceivable. Ever since he was a little boy Les Stamper had ruled the roost on Sunnybank. The idea of him being locked up seemed almost impossible to get his head around. He would have been less stunned if he had taken a glance out of the window and seen a Martian spaceship getting ready to land.

"I thought you said you never went to Sunnybank."

"I don't. I call him on his mobile. He meets me in the town so he does. Never takes longer than ten minutes."

Ten minutes. Nothing. The time it would take to get his shoes on and get out of the hostel. Ten minutes and all the pain would be driven away. No more burning bones. No more sick stomach. No more crashing headache. And he had £20 in his pocket.

"Call him."

"Who?"

"Who do you think? Baz."

Chewit frowned. "What for?"

Danny sighed. What was the point in pretending? "I'm using as well."

"Smack?"

Danny nodded. "Started in the jail. Got a habit. And right now I'm clucking. So call him, OK?"

There was a question that beamed out of Chewit's huge eyes like a search light.

"Yeah, yeah. We'll share it, OK. Just call him will you."

PART FOUR

Danny hugged his arms around himself to try and get some warmth into his limbs. Technically, Spring was supposed to be somewhere around the corner, but it didn't feel that way. All winter he had been promising himself that one way or another he was going to find the cash to get himself a decent coat. It didn't have to be something that would cost getting on for a hundred quid in one of the sports shops. Sure, that would have been nice, but it wasn't an option. He was thinking more along the lines of a fiver in one of the town's many charity shops. It didn't matter if it looked naff. All that mattered was that he could be half way warm for once. The crazy thing was that on three occasions he had actually got his act together and managed to nick really good warm jackets which would have done the job. But each time had been the same old story. He had gone into the shops with every intention of stealing a coat to wear. For personal use. But once he had successfully completed the thefts he had quickly realised that each coat was easily worth a tenner. So he had sold them within minutes of acquiring them. Because when it came down to it, the need for the next tenner bag of gear was always 500 million times more important than staying warm for the winter.

In a way the lack of a decent coat had become like a symbol of his life. For most of humanity, the concept of being able to stay warm and wrapped up on a winter's day was a simple one. It was a priority. A simple need, that would always be high up on the list of things to sort out. But Danny had joined the ranks of those who put all such basic needs second. Those who worshipped the God of Heroin put everything second. Coats, somewhere decent to live, friends, family, food, a belief in right or wrong. Everything. All that ever mattered was getting the next hit and they would do whatever it took to achieve the goal.

It had been a year since Danny had returned to Dumfries with a plan to do his rattle quickly and then focus on getting fit and waiting for Jimmy Doyle to get in touch. That plan had crashed and burned within a couple of hours of his arrival at the hostel. It had collapsed the very minute he learned that Baz was dealing and could be with him within five minutes of a phone call. And it had been five minutes. Baz was back on four wheels again, a Fiesta this time. At first his face had cracked into a wide grin at the sight of Danny. How had it been? What were the screws like? How did he manage all the Glasgow boys? Then his forehead had furrowed when he realised that it wasn't just Chewit who was in the market for gear. He had told Danny that he was stupid. Told him that he should knock it on the head before he got too far in. But when the £20 had come out he had merely shrugged and passed over the two, cling film wraps. Because business was business in the end. And if Danny McCann had made up his mind to be a smackhead, there was nothing he could do about it. He said they should catch up and have a pint or two. Maybe even take a ride out of town like they had done in the old days. Danny had asked after Sally. Baz had shrugged and said he never heard from her any more. She was at college in Reading.

The pint and drive never materialised. It wasn't the way things were. Danny and Baz now had a new relationship. Danny had become one of the desperate ones who would beg and plead for a bit of credit. Just till Thursday Baz. Honest. I get paid on Thursday. Only a tenner's worth Baz. Come on, be a pal will you? OK. A fiver's worth then. Christ Baz, I'm dying here. We're mates, aren't we? Baz heard these stories all day, every day. They were all his mates. They all had cash coming on Thursday. They were all dying. But he didn't do credit. Those who allowed their customers to get up to the eyeballs in debt then had the problem of collecting it. Not that it was a huge problem. They would lay some cash on a hard man and sent him round to do the business. It had to be done. Once word got around that a dealer hadn't collected a debt he was seen as a mug and every man and his dog would be at him for gear on the never, never. To Baz, it always seemed like lousy business. You ended up paying £20 to pick up a debt of £50. Stupid. And there was always a chance that the hard man you had paid to do the dirty would get lifted and grass you up to the law. He had learned that they were all as hard as nails when they were out and about on the streets. Once they were lifted and left to rattle in the cells for 24 hours, most of them were crying for their mothers and pleading with the cops for the chance to grass up everyone they could think of. It had been a so-called hard man who had grassed up his dad. He hadn't even lasted a full day when he had started blubbing in his cell. The other prisoners had heard it all. The crying. The begging. And then the cell door being opened and footsteps in the corridor. And then he wasn't returned to the cell to wait to see the Sheriff on Monday morning. He was let out through the night. And a fortnight later every copper in Dumfries and Galloway was crashing through his dad's door. His dad had sorted it of course. The grass had both of his legs broken and now walked the town like leper on crutches.

So Baz had watched and learned and made his mind up. No credit. Not ever. Not for Danny. Not for Elvis Presley. Not for George Bush. He was strictly cash and carry. Simple rules for a simple business. Danny had long given up trying the begging, pleading routine. It was completely humiliating which would have been OK if it had ever worked, but it never did work.

He knew that he had gone downhill in the year that he had been back in town. It had become a habit to avoid mirrors. He had always had a lean frame which had once been an advantage on the football pitch as it was a frame that his legs could carry up and down the park for a full ninety minutes without slacking. Now he had gone well beyond lean. All his trousers were hanging off him and his shirts and sweatshirts felt like tents. When he was forced to look in the mirror as he shaved, he had to admit that his skin was stretched almost as tightly across the bones as Chewit. His eyes seemed to have retreated almost all the way back into the sockets and they were ringed with grey. There was also no escaping the look in his eyes. Desperate. Hungry. Yearning. A look that from dawn till dusk said 'I need'.

The only thing that made him feel mildly good about himself was that he was in a hundred times better nick than Chewit. If he had seen himself go down hill, Chewit had fallen off a cliff. His veins were calling it a day one by one and now the only place he could find to inject himself was his groin. A few months ago his GP had told him that the reason his leg was so sore was that he had a blood clot. Deep vein thrombosis. It was something that the doctor said that was supposed to affect overweight businessmen in their fifties. Chewit was seventeen and at least two stones underweight. There were pills he had to take every day to keep his blood thin enough to get about his body, but he still hobbled round like a man of eighty.

From the very beginning the life had been hard. Danny's liberation grant had disappeared before the clock struck twelve on the evening of his release. Neither of them had any money. Both of their families had completely disowned them and the only way they could buy enough Heroin to keep the demons at bay was to steal. And steal. And steal.

Danny soon discovered why all the other users referred to shoplifting as grafting. They were simply stating the obvious. It was exactly that. Graft. Hard, hard graft. For several years the Heroin tide had been flowing through Dumfries at higher and higher levels. It sometimes seemed to Danny as if everyone between the ages of sixteen and thirty was on the kit. He knew this was stupid. The ones who weren't using simply lived in a different world. They were at college or they had jobs or they had moved out of town. All he saw were the ones who haunted the High Street day after day like walking ghosts. They would gather in small groups of three or four to exchange intelligence. Who had the best kit? How much was it? Were the bags a decent size? A new security man down the way that didn't know the score. So and so took an overdose yesterday. So and so got lifted. So and so got chucked out by his mum and dad. They would swap news in quick, breathless sentences then split up into groups of two or three to try to nick enough to make the price of the next bag. The sheer number of them was a problem. The black market for stolen goods was awash. The fences moaned that they were getting so much stuff that they couldn't move it on. By the time Christmas came and went, the going rate was down to a pound in ten. It meant that they had to commit a hundred pounds of crime for every tenner bag they bought.

After six months Danny was up to using two bags a day, which required an average of two hundred pounds a day worth of crime once his dole money was all gone. And even two bags weren't enough. The fantastic, magical place he had discovered on the bottom bunk of his cell was a place that he never got to see much any more. His dependency had become a treadmill with no upsides. If he could manage to get hold of two bags a day, he was able to feel normal. Not great. Not good. Just normal. If he only got one bag, then he would be quite ill. If he didn't get anything, he would be really ill. These were the worst of times because the more ill he felt, the less able he was to get out and graft. And if he couldn't graft, he couldn't score, which meant he would get even more ill and even less able to graft. The clock was always ticking. He was never longer than a few hours from starting yet another rattle. From the very minute he used he was already on the hunt for the cash to look after the next fix.

In the months leading up to Christmas he had found it harder and harder to ever get past the quite ill stage. Two bags a day just wasn't enough. Baz saw it and gave some advice. The big problem was that he was still smoking. Chasing the dragon. That was all very nice for someone with a big fat wedge of cash in the bank, but for the likes of Danny it was a luxury they just couldn't afford. Baz advised him to start jagging. When you shot the Heroin into the veins care of a needle you didn't waste any. It was more efficient. It offered maximum value for money and only the very foolish would waste something that was so expensive. Danny fought the advice for as long as he could, but in the end he saw it was pointless. The constant achy, sick feeling wore him down. He knew jagging was a stupid idea. And he was by no means stupid. He would have had to be stupid beyond belief not to realise injecting was a lousy idea. Every day he saw a limping, breathing example of the downside of injecting Heroin for a pastime, in the shrinking shape of Chewit. But cold, sensible logic only carried him so far. In the end the pure economics of his situation broke down the barriers. Like Baz said. He was too poor to smoke it. End of.

For a while jagging had relieved the situation. For a while he could more or less manage on a bag a day and still not feel sick all the time. This meant a hundred pounds worth of graft instead of two hundred and it almost felt like being on holiday. But it didn't last long. Baz hadn't mentioned the part about jagging giving nothing more than a honeymoon period. Soon it was back to two bags a day and it wasn't all that long before two bags a day, were barely enough to avoid feeling lousy. He was back to square one.

By the time his habit had reached the two injected bags a day stage, his grafting career was also getting tougher with every day that passed. He had been arrested twice for shoplifting since his return to the town and the stakes were getting steadily higher. The first offence led to eighty hours of community service and a dire warning from the Sheriff. The second offence looked like it would mean a return to prison, but thankfully it was a different Sheriff who must have got out of the right side of his bed and leniently doled out a further hundred hours of community service. The biggest problem was that his photo was now on the shoplifter's hall of fame that was circulated to the security guards of most of the High Street stores. Before even thinking of stealing anything, he had to find a way of getting into a shop at all. Increasingly the only places where he could make it through the front door were the shops that sold cheap rubbish that nobody really wanted.

Two weeks earlier he had allowed himself the dangerous thought: that things really couldn't get a lot worse. Big mistake. This careless thought had been based on the fact that he was finding it almost impossible to manage twenty pounds a day of crime, let alone two hundred. Every security man in the town seemed to know him and Chewit better than their own family. No matter how many hours they seemed to put in, they seldom got a result. It meant that they rattled miserably through the cold days of winter, counting down the endless crawling hours until they were able to cash in their Giros and find the blessed relief of the needle.

What neither of them saw coming was a time when having the money would not be enough. It had never occurred to Danny that the police would ever be successful enough to take Heroin off the streets. That was an idea that was so far fetched as to be a fairytale. A Disney film. There were always at least thirty faces knocking out kit, although Danny rarely used anyone but Baz. Of all the street dealers, Baz was far and away the most reliable. He took care when he cut the gear and by and large he sold a reasonably clean product. By this stage Danny knew well enough what could go wrong if you bought gear from one of the more cavalier dealers. They would give a sales pitch about how big their bags were. What they failed to mention was the only reason that the bags seemed so big was that they were loaded with anything that could be ground into powder and wrapped up. At best it meant buying a bunch of crushed aspirin mixed with something to colour it brown. At worst there would be something that would not dissolve once it was injected into the vein. This would lead to blockages, abscesses, infections, all kinds of nightmares. So Danny stuck with Baz. Baz was the devil he knew.

He knew all about Operation Roundup of course. They all did. It was like a huge shadow that hung over them every day of their lives. The police had announced the start of their Operation Roundup a couple of years earlier. The idea was to steadily work their way up the chain of the local supply network. They warned the public that at the early stages of the Operation it would seem like they were only focusing on the smaller fish in the pond. They asked for the public to show patience and promised that the real impact of their efforts would become clear in the fullness of time. Now, after three years, the impact was becoming as clear as crystal. The dawn raid that had sent the doors flying off the hinges in several houses in the Stamper Empire had been Operation Roundup's first real red-letter day. This had led to the worst Heroin drought the town had ever known. But Danny had been immune to it. He had been warm and cosy in his cell enjoying a fix every morning and night compliments of Rico. Once he had become part of the underworld of users, he had heard many stories of the great drought but they hadn't meant much to him. They were like stories of the Irish Famine that he vaguely remembered from history lessons at school or the pieces on the news from places in Africa where children had huge bellies and flies in their eyes.

But Roundup had not finished with the lifting of the untouchable Les Stamper. Far from it. And as the cold winds of winter at last began to lose their icy bite, the men of the Dumfries and Galloway police struck again and they struck hard. Within a crazy forty-eight hour period, two more major suppliers were removed from their Sunnybank fortresses in handcuffs and placed on remand wings to wait for long lumps of time. And suddenly the well was almost dry. All over the town users chased up the last remaining dealers, but it seemed like nobody had a thing to sell. The only dealers left were ones who bought their kit wholesale from the big three suppliers who were now under lock and key. Nobody had any direct contacts with the big wholesalers in Liverpool and Glasgow and what Heroin that was for sale was so heavily cut that it was almost useless.

STOPPAGE TIME

As Danny sat on a bench on the High Street and waited for Chewit, he was almost beyond hope. It had now been four days since he had used and the constant misery of the rattle had him all but beaten. He was past the throwing up stage now, but the pain in his bones seemed to keep growing inside him. He hadn't eaten. He hadn't slept. He felt as if he was barely alive. And it was cold. Even with a coat it would have been cold. But he didn't have a coat. And he had no food in his system. And he had no Heroin in his system. And all around him early morning shoppers were moving about briskly in the pure clear morning light and not one of them seemed to have the first idea of the kind of pain he was locked into. They didn't know and they didn't care. He was now used to being the lowest of the low. He had thought it bad enough all those years ago when the people of Sunnybank had closed their doors in his face. Then he had been known as a wee troublemaker. A toe rag. A pain in the neck. But now he knew that it had been nothing to the way he was regarded now.

The people of Dumfries had developed a burning hatred for Junkies. Maybe if there had been more people from Africa and Asia in the town, it might have been different. Or maybe if there had been more asylum seekers. But there were no other minorities in the community to attract hatred. Only the Junkies. And the Junkies were duly blamed for everything. It was their fault that the town centre was full of charity shops and boarded-up windows. It was their fault that the tourists didn't want to visit any more. It was their fault that the Council tax kept on going up. It was their fault that parents couldn't let their kids go and play on the swings because there were always needles left lying around. As soon as a person became known as a junkie, it was like they stopped being human. Everything that person had been in the past was completely forgotten. The slate was wiped clean. Before, they might have been known as a nice kid who was polite and from a good family who did well at school. But the very minute the word got out that they were using Heroin everything changed. All of a sudden they became lepers. Complete scum. Filth. Men in pubs would say that if they had their way they would put all the Junkies on a boat and sail it out to sea and sink it. Women queuing in the post office would yearn for a government that would send them all off to an island far away never to come home. Danny had learned that Dumfries was a place where you stopped being a human being the very minute that the word was out. Then you were treated like an animal. Worse. You were the lowest of the low. A figure to be hated. Loathed. He saw it every day of his life in the eyes of the shoppers on the High Street. If an eighteen-year-old lad was killed in a car accident on the by-pass the community would be united in its grief. What a terrible tragedy. How awful for the family. What an appalling waste of a young life. But if an eighteen-year-old turned blue with an overdose in some squalid Sunnybank flat, they would be unmourned. There would be talk of it serving them right. And after a few drinks people would feel brave enough to say that the only good junkie is a dead junkie, while yet another family would be left to the torture of grief with barely a word of sympathy. So Danny didn't expect a shred of sympathy in the eyes of the shoppers who glanced at him as they walked by. If they knew the pain he was in they would be pleased. Delighted. Made up. Because in their book, it served him right. The more pain the better. Nasty little junkie. Thieving little junkie. Junkie scum.

He took in a clock on the church tower and wondered what was keeping Chewit. He had said he was only going to be ten minutes or so and it had already been over half an hour. Not that it particularly mattered. There wasn't exactly much in the way of pressing business to attend to. At some stage they would have to put their minds into gear and get some grafting done. The thing was that unless Chewit had any promising news there wasn't a whole lot of point. Even if he had a pocket bulging with ten grand's worth of used tenners, it wouldn't have done him much good. There still would be nothing to buy. Someone had left a read newspaper on the bench beside him and he picked it up and automatically turned to the back pages. Straight away he knew this was a mistake.

All week the back pages of every paper he had looked at had been filled with the fairytale story of Gretna's journey to a Tennants Cup semifinal with Dundee up at Hampden Park. The game was the talk of the town and the whole of the football world was buying into the story of the village team who were defying all the odds. For millions of football fans all over the world Gretna's refusal to stick to the script was a cause for celebration. With Chelsea once again running away with the Premiership care of £300 million pounds worth of dubious Siberian cash, it seemed that the game was to be forever doomed to be dominated by those with the biggest chequebooks. League tables all over Europe told the same story every year. It was always the same clubs who won all the silverware and as they did so they got richer and richer whilst their competitors fell ever further behind. And then out of the blue a crazy little club from a village that straddled the border between England and Scotland had stepped out of nowhere and done the unthinkable. Without the might of Celtic and Rangers, the Cup had suddenly rediscovered its magic and the football world was lapping it up like a stray cat given the chance at a bowl of fresh cream.

The story might have been the cause of joy to football fans all over the planet, but it was the very opposite for Danny McCann. For Danny McCann every word he read was like a punch in the guts. This was something that he could have been a part of: should have been a part of. Jimmy had made the effort to dig him out in the prison and he had offered him a chance of picking up his dream from the gutter. His dream. Like the Gretna dream. Livin' the dream. That was what it said on all the T-shirts that celebrated the journey up to Hampden. Danny had been offered the chance. It had been handed to him on a plate and all he had to do was to pick it up. Instead he had kicked it away and chosen two tenner bags of smack from Baz in its place.

Stupid.

Stupid. Stupid. Stupid!

He tossed the paper aside and tried to clear his head of all thoughts of the semifinal. All it would do is fire up the flames of the self-hatred that would take hold of him whenever he was deprived of the comforting cloak of Heroin. Without the Heroin he could see his life for what it was. A waste. A miserable, endless, day in, day out failure. And no matter which way he looked at it there was no getting away from the fact that it was all his own fault. He had been given his chance and completely blown it and all he wanted now was to ram a needle into his arm and forget the whole thing for a while. And to stop feeling so completely ill. And cold. And to get away from the contempt he saw on the face of every person who walked by.

Finally he spotted the familiar hobbling figure of Chewit making his way towards him. It only took a single glance at his friend's face for Danny to know with wonderful certainty that good news was on its way. By the time he reached the bench, Chewit was wheezing like a man in his seventies but his eyes were alight with the news that he was bringing.

"We're on."

"How?"

Chewit sucked in quick gulps of air, impatient with the need to breathe at all.

"I just got hold of Baz. He's in the car. On his way back from Glasgow."

Seldom could the single word 'Glasgow' have had such an instant and magical effect. The word sent Danny's aching brain into overdrive. If Baz had been up to Glasgow it could only have been for one thing. He wouldn't have made the trip up the road to go and catch the latest play at the theatre or to pick up some bits for his room in the Celtic shop. Not a chance. If Baz had taken the ride to Glasgow, it would have been for an altogether different kind of shopping. Baz must have found a source for smack, and like every other user in Dumfries, Danny had seen the evening news. The Strathclyde police had issued a warning that the Heroin on sale in the Greater Glasgow area was double the normal strength, which had led to a spate of overdoses and deaths. The piece was intended as a warning to users. A wake-up call. An alarm bell. But on the Heroin free streets of Dumfries it had an altogether different effect. It was like being in the middle of the Sahara and watching an advert for Volvic mineral water when you hadn't had a drink in three days. It was like a hunger striker being forced to watch a Kentucky Fried Chicken ad. It was borderline torture. The idea of regular, miserable watered down Dumfries Heroin was good enough. Regulation Glasgow strength Heroin was close to perfection. But double normal strength Glasgow Heroin was straight out of fantasy land. And suddenly it wasn't such a fantasy. In fact it was a matter of hours from being reality. Maybe not even hours. Maybe even minutes.

"Where was he? I mean when you talked?"

"Not far. Just by Kilmarnock."

"And you reserved some yeah? For both of us?"

"Course I did. He said to call about noon."

Danny closed his eyes for a moment and allowed his brain to anticipate the moment of release from the hours of pain that seemed to have been with him for the best part of a thousand years. Then he forced himself to snap out of it. Cold hard facts needed to be addressed. As soon as the word was out that Baz had double pure Wegie kit to sell he would be inundated. The demand would make Auld Firm tickets look easy to come by. As regular customers, they would have a first chance to buy the gear. But that chance would not be there for all that long. Baz would keep stuff for them for an hour or two but no more than that. This of course meant that they had to come up with cash in the next hour no matter what it took. The idea of having empty pockets while Baz unloaded his whole shipment was just about unbearable. Having thought the situation through for a moment or two he gave his verdict on how the land lay.

"We're just going to have go for it. No choice. Take a complete maddy."

"How do you mean?"

"You ken that new jeans shop. Opened last week, yeah?"

"Aye."

"Well they have a rail just in through the front door. What we do is just dive in, grab an' armful of jeans and leg it. Nothing fancy. We'll just get right in their faces and completely go for it."

Chewit's jaw seemed to slip off its hinges as he took on board the bones of the idea.

"Just grab stuff like."

"That's it. Just grab it. We pull our hoods up so the CCTV gets nothing."

"But they'll see us."

"Course they'll see us, but it's not going to matter. They're not ready for anyone just grabbing stuff like that. They expect people to go in and sneak about. We take them by surprise. It's like taking a free kick whilst the keeper is still organising the wall."

Chewit really didn't have any colour in his wrecked face to lose, but what little there was drained away leaving him as white as a sheet.

"I don't know Danny like . . ."

"Glasgow kit Chewit. Uncut, double whammy. Think of it. Just think of it."

And Chewit thought and it was probably the best thought he had ever had in his short and disasterous life. For Chewit it wasn't only the pain of rattling that was the problem. Once the comforting fog of Heroin was taken away, his brain became suddenly clear and crisp. This wasn't at all a pleasant state of affairs. In fact it was complete nightmare. The clarity exposed the dreadful mess that he was in. His family had disowned him. Almost all of his old friends refused to even acknowledge him. And his health was falling apart at an ever-increasing speed. When his brain was working properly he had to face up to the chilling fact that at the rate he was going he would be lucky to see twenty. And deep inside he wanted to see twenty. Like he wanted to see his mum and his dad and his two younger sisters. Like he wanted a girlfriend and his own flat and a car and a job and a holiday every now and then. Instead he eked out a living in a hostel and seemed to lose a vein a week. Only a month earlier he had found out that he had tested positive for Hepatitis C. It was just another illness to add to a list that was already reaching the end of the page. Without Heroin, when he looked in the mirror, he saw a dead man walking. And it scared him. Really, really scared him. So suddenly the idea of jagging-up half a bag of double-pure kit was the only thing in life that mattered.

"OK. I'm up for it."

Danny reached out and patted his bony shoulder.

"Top man. Let's not think about it. We'll just do it. Right now. Yeah?"

Chewit took a gulp of air and nodded.

The shop was less than a hundred yards away. Danny walked fast along the street. He focused himself and concentrated on taking in slow, deep breaths. Once upon a time it was what he had done as he waited to take a penalty. He cleared his brain of everything other than the simple task in hand. He pictured the rail like he had once pictured the corner of the net. He decided to grab from the right hand side of the rail and once he had made up his mind, he wouldn't change it. It had been the same with penalties. Ignore the goalie. Pick a corner and stick with it. Put all the focus on watching the ball and getting a clean strike on it. This would be the same. Ignore the security man and focus on the rail. Just a few yards now. His hood was already up and the world was closed down to a small view ahead. The shop had a wide-open frontage and music was drifting out into the street. Not many customers in. The security guard was a few yards inside chatting with one of the assistants. Probably trying to chat her up. Perfect. Ideal.

He never varied his stride. Smooth. Relaxed. Like those few steps toward the ball waiting on the spot. Don't rush. Don't dawdle. Glide.

There now. He hooked his arm around ten pairs of jeans, lifted them clear of the rail and then turned and ran.

He completely ignored the faces of the pedestrians as he moved away fast. Some carried looks of surprise. Others who had realised what was going down looked disgusted. Danny blanked them. A hundred yards down the street he ducked down an alley. Thirty yards further and he pushed open an old metal gate that led into a small yard full of weeds and old junk. He reached behind an old smashed up desk and pulled out a bundle of bin liners that they kept ready to bag up any stuff they managed to pinch. He cocked his ear and heard the familiar sound of Chewit's limping run approaching. Only one set of footsteps crunching along the layer of broken glass that was a permanent carpet in the alley.

"Bloody hell Danny, we did it . . ."

Chewit was all ready for a high fives routine but Danny was having none of it.

"Later. Here. Get the stuff packed away. And fold them, yeah? Don't just stuff them in anyhow."

He tossed over a bin liner and both of them focused on folding and bagging the stolen jeans.

"Ten. How about you?"

Chewit grinned. "Eight. How much are they Danny?"

Danny flipped a price label and grinned back "£29.99. Nice. Thirty quid times eighteen. Over five hundred. We should get fifty. Five bags. Come on. Let's get out of town."

They had a well-practised route away from the town centre which avoided the busier streets and most of the cameras and twenty five minutes after leaving the yard they arrived at the door of their favoured fence. The fast walk had driven the cold from Danny's bones and all the depression he had felt whilst shivering on the High Street bench was long gone. After ten minutes of haggling they sold the jeans for the hoped for £50 and Chewit called up Baz from a phone box. He was just through Thornhill and his estimated time of arrival in Sunnybank was twenty minutes. They agreed a rendezvous. The waiting time was almost over.

Danny felt as if every vein in his body was tingling with the expectation of the release that was now so close. He remembered how he had once looked forward to birthdays and Christmas. Or big games for Sunnybank. Times when he would lie awake in his bed unable to get to sleep because of the excitement. Now those times seemed like nothing. There had been no excitement in his life that even came close to the feeling he now had at the prospect of his first hit in four days. This was ten out of ten excitement. Eleven. Everything else barely made it past five.

They reached the rendezvous point with ten minutes in hand and time seemed to grind to a halt as they waited to see the Fiesta. But at last it came. And at last Baz was with them looking like a man who was on top of the world. Fifty pounds was duly exchanged for five tiny cling film wraps of Glasgow gear.

"Just take care OK boys. This is the best kit you'll have ever tasted, ken?"

"Aye. Nae bother Baz. Got plenty have you?"

Baz gave a shrug. "I've got a bit. Don't know how long it's going to last. Bell me, OK?"

"Will do man."

The Fiesta went one way and they went another. It was only a matter of minutes to the disused pavilion which offered a discreet, sheltered spot to cook-up and use. Danny had to force himself to take each step of the ritual carefully and steadily. The temptation was to get the brown powder cooked-up and sucked into the needle as quick as it would go, but he knew that such undue haste would only put the fix at risk and there was no way he was about to do that. He had waited four endless, lousy stinking days for this moment and it would be plain stupid to ruin it for the sake of a few seconds of care. It seemed like it took longer than a Spielberg movie, but at last the job was done and the needle was ready to send pure relief into his body. Chewit gave him a rather jealous look as he easily brought a fat vein to readiness.

Then he eased the needle through his skin and slowly pressed home the liquid perfection that had become the only thing that mattered in his life. It was only a matter of seconds until it was completely clear that this was without a shadow of a doubt the best hit of gear he had ever known. Every single problem was suddenly dissolving like so many sugar lumps under a tap of boiling water. He closed his eyes and smiled a dreamy smile. He sensed his tensed up muscles opening and relaxing. Slowly he allowed his body to collapse backwards until it met the wall of the pavilion. He wondered whether it was worth opening his eyes. No. It wasn't. No point. Nothing worth seeing. Just the tired familiar grey walls of Sunnybank. It was so much better to keep his eyelids closed on the world outside. A world that mattered nothing. A bad place. A place where everything always went wrong. Not like the place he was headed for now. He could feel his soul on an escalator now. Slow. Lazy. Going smoothly up and away from all the endless dreariness of his life. Up and up. Out and clear. Already he was high enough to get the same view as one of the buzzards that soared the fields at the edge of the town. Soon he would be up through the clouds and he would arrive at the soft place where everything was all right. Not long. Up and up. He was warm all over now. The pain and suffering and anger he had felt on the bench on the High St were emotions from another lifetime. The cold that had settled into his bones was all gone. And there was no more feeling ill. The pain had vanished the very second that the needle entered his vein. Instead of feeling lousy and anxious, he was instantly wrapped in layer after layer of complete wellbeing.

Now it wasn't a matter of whether opening his eyes was worth it or not. It was no longer a choice. The muscles in his eyelids had called it a day. Every muscle in his body was on Bank Holiday. He tried to remember where his body actually was. No chance. It had become irrelevant. The Darkness was good. It was good and it went on forever and forever like a huge warm, silent ocean in a tropical night. Mile after mile after mile of smooth glassy water. Millions of miles. Trillions of miles. Zillions. Still. Smooth. Unthreatening. Not judging. Not moving. Not caring. Not bothered. Happy. Really, really happy. Happy all the way to the sand on the ocean floor many miles below.

As Danny entered his world of serene comfort, Chewit's world had suddenly become frightening and uncomfortable. Like Danny, every cell of his body was yearning for the release that would come with the needle. They had flipped a coin for who would go first and Danny had called heads and heads it had been. A voice in Chewit's head had howled in frustration and it had continued to howl as Danny had carefully cooked up and prepared his fix. And now the voice was wailing louder than ever. Everything was ready and waiting: spoon, lighter, needle, filter, citric acid, and most important of all, four bags of double pure Wegie kit. Waiting for Chewit. Right there in front of him.

CHAPTER FOUR

The problem was that the second that Danny had pressed home the needle he had lolled back into the wall like a sack of coal. The needle still stuck out from his arm. His eyes were closed and the merest trace of a smile curled his lips. Otherwise he was as still as a rock dumped on the ground by a glacier thousands of years in the past. Chewit reached out and shook his shoulder.

"Hey, Danny man. How is it like?"

Nothing. It was like shaking a sack of coal. And all the colour had drained from Danny's face leaving it like marble. And there was the beginnings of blue in his lips. Chewit had been a part of his world for long enough to know what he was seeing. Danny was checking out. Just like Nokey had checked out. Overdosing. And Baz's words of warning jumped into his head like a paratrooper. Just be careful lads. Proper gear this is lads. The business. Best you'll ever taste. And now there was no escaping the fact that Danny's lips were indeed blue and his chest was barely moving at all. Again he shook at the shoulder and again there was nothing. By now real panic was starting to get hold of him. He looked about the empty grass around the pavilion. Nothing. Not a thing. Not a soul.

Oh God. Oh Jesus.

No. No. No.

He was about to run for a phone when he remembered the poster on the wall in the hostel and quickly manoeuvred the inert body onto its side. He tucked an arm in and pulled the other out to ensure that a spasm would not roll Danny onto his back where he could choke to death on his own vomit.

Then he ran. The clot in his leg was a torture, but he ignored it. Around a corner he saw a figure walking towards him. It was a lad not much older than himself with headphones in his ears. His face broke into shock as Chewit stopped him and shook at his sleeve.

"I need a phone. Have you got a phone man?"

"Get lost will you . . ."

"It's my pal. He's dying. I need to ring for an ambulance . . . Please man . . ."

The walker weighed things up. If the wild-eyed character was planning on trying to leg it off with his mobile then there was no chance. He looked like the walking dead. No way he would make it thirty yards before he caught him. He came to a decision and passed over the phone.

Chewit hit 999 and immediately started gabbling and the voice at the other end urged him to slow down and be clearer. Having registered the words 'overdose' and 'pavilion', the owner of the phone grabbed it back and gave the operator clear instructions as to the location where they were calling from. When he was done, he snapped the phone shut and gave Chewit a look of disgust before walking away down the pavement, headphones once again in place in his ears.

Chewit hobbled back to where Danny still lay in the recovery position on the dusty floor. He felt worse than useless and couldn't think of a thing to do other than to wait for the sound of a siren. It seemed like an awful lot longer than the fifteen minutes it actually took for the call to summon the emergency team from the casualty department. As soon as it was clear that the wailing sound was indeed getting closer, Chewit scuttled away to a small clump of trees and watched. It was better that he was not at the scene because maybe the police might come as well and if they did they would want him to empty his pockets and if he did that it would mean a night in the cells and more rattling. Already his brain was re-planning how things would need to go. He would cook up no more than a third of a bag once it was time for him to take his fix. Maybe just a quarter. The gear was obviously right out of the top drawer and it was to be treated with respect. The voice in his head was telling him not to bother waiting on the ambulance. What was the point? He had done his bit. He'd made the call. Now it was his turn. Danny would be fine, and even if he wasn't fine, what else could Chewit do about it? But even though the voice was nagging and angry, he still waited until the ambulance bumped over the grass and the green suited medics jumped out and started to attend to Danny. For a moment one of them looked about to see if the person who had made sure that the body was in recovery position was anywhere to be seen. Chewit ducked in tight behind a tree and waited a few seconds until daring to take a peep. The ambulance man was now crouched down alongside his colleague.

They took a pulse and found the merest flicker of life. The massive tidal wave of opiates had all but frozen Danny's lungs. His heartbeat was down to under ten beats a minute and his hold on life was light as a feather. The medics talked in low, focused tones.

"They said it was Heroin on the call did they?"

CHAPTER FOUR

"Aye."

A nod. "Certainly looks that way. Narcan?"

Nod. A syringe was prepared and a vein was found. Neither realised how much easier their job was as a result of Danny having won the coin toss and gone first. He still had veins and finding one was no great difficulty. If Chewit had gone first, it would have been a much more complicated task. The needle was pushed home just a few centimetres from the one they had pulled out when they had arrived at the scene.

Somewhere deep inside Danny's fading brain things started to happen. No longer was the blackness quite so black. An almost imperceptible glimmer of light started to shimmer on the inky black waters of the mirror like ocean. Then, with a jolt, the elevator that was taking him far away into the warmth of emptiness juddered to a halt. Nothing for a second or so. Then it reversed and started to carry him the other way. But why? And suddenly the elevator wasn't so smooth any more. It was going faster and faster like a fairground ride. And as it hurtled him away from the black tranquillity of the warm night, he started to feel an awful fear as he flew backwards faster and faster and faster. Until a breathless messenger arrived in the command centre in his brain with the news that the muscles in his eyelids were working again . . .

Snap.

Eyes open. No warmth. No black ocean. No silence. Just two men in green clothes. And the flaking paint on the walls of the pavilion. And the cold grey sky over the cold grey walls of Sunnybank. And the white of a parked ambulance. Little by little his brain was firing back into activity and putting together what was going on. The men in green were medics. The ambulance was for him. Chewit was nowhere to be seen. He was lying on his back on the floor. The faces looking down at him showed relief.

Facts.

Medics. Ambulance. A police car now. No more warm nothingness. Awake. Wide awake and it was like he had never had a hit at all. Narcan. Had to be. Rico had told him about it one night in the cell when Danny had asked what they did when someone took an OD. Narcan was an antagonist. It basically gave the smack a complete kicking and totally wiped the effect. One minute you would be away in the gouch of your life. The next minute you were back in the world and wondering what the hell had happened. And Danny was very much back in the world, and it seemed as bad a place as ever.

There was a policemen there now, talking with one of the medics.

"All right is he?"

"Aye. He's fine. Touch and go mind. I reckon if we had been another two or three minutes there would have been no chance. He was down to eight beats a minute."

The policeman shook his head with a kind of resignation. He had been there on the morning they had knocked in the front door of Les Stamper's house and for a few days he had felt like they had done something to make things better. But nothing much was changing. For a while they would take the Heroin off the streets, but it always came back. It was just like the dandelions on his lawn at home. No matter how many times he chopped them down to size with his mower it never made a difference. Every year there would be more and there always would be. He had learned that there was a cycle that always followed the work of the police. Whenever they took out one of the big players, the levels of desperation on the street would escalate. The price of what Heroin was in the town would go up and, in turn, so would levels of petty crime. Then after a while, someone would manage to open up a new supply line from Glasgow or Liverpool and the overdoses would start up because whilst there was a drought, all the users would have lost their tolerance levels. Many times he had thought how lucky it was that Dumfries didn't have the kind of traffic that Glasgow or Edinburgh had to put up with. It would only have taken one queue and the lad on the floor would have been a goner. How old? Not very. Not even twenty. He was somebody's son and very nearly he had been nobody's son. He had very nearly made the change from being a young lad with a lifetime ahead of him to becoming a statistic. A number on a page in a government report.

The lad was sitting up now and trying to come to terms with what had happened. The policeman decided not to search him. Maybe, just maybe, he might just have learned a lesson. It wasn't very likely, but sometimes an overdose worked as a wake-up call. The chances of there being any drugs on his person were minimal. The drugs would be in his system. Inert now. Zapped by the Narcan.

"Are you lads taking him then?"

CHAPTER FOUR

"Aye. We'll get him looked over. You OK to come with us son?" The ambulance man's voice made it clear that he didn't think it all that likely. Usually his patients were up and running away as soon as their eyes were open. Lots of times they would wake up and get mega-stroppy and threaten violence. They would have a right go because in their book they had had their hit ruined. It was one of the main reasons that the police attended the scene whenever possible. Nice work if you could get it. You drive like a madman through the town to make it in time to save someone's life, and all they want to do is kick your head in because they reckon you've ripped them off a tenner. The lads in the pub could never believe it.

The boy on the dusty wooden floor didn't look like he was about to kick off. He was rubbing his face and watching the policeman nervously.

"You mean go in the ambulance?"

"That's it. It's nothing to worry about. I'm sure you're fine, but it never does any harm for one of the doctors to give you a quick once over. You'll be out in an hour or so. OK?"

"Aye. That's OK."

They lifted Danny to his feet and he was able to walk to the Ambulance and climb into the back. The policeman got into his car and drove away.

"Have you any idea how close that was son?"

Danny dropped his head and shook it.

"Two minutes. Maybe less. Two minutes more and you'd have gone. That close." The medic emphasised his point by holding his thumb and forefinger a few millimetres apart. "That close. So you need to think about it. Yeah?"

Danny nodded and stared down at the floor. It was more than his brain could come to terms with. Two minutes from being dead the man had said. Dead as in dead. As in no more life. Not ever. It was inconceivable. Impossible to grasp. How could he have been so close to dying? All because of some brown powder wrapped in cling film and bought for a tenner. Thankfully the man had said his piece and they completed the journey across town to the hospital in silence.

Jimmy felt like a complete burke. He had been coaching at one of the small village primary schools a few miles up in the hills and it had gone well. It always went well. Every day he thanked his stars that he had said yes to Brooks Mileson's offer. Spending his days running coaching classes was as good a job as he could ever have dreamed of. Getting paid for it was mind-boggling. There was certainly no shortage of work. When he had been down at the ground the day before, they had said that there were now over one-hundred-and-twenty schools using the community programme. The club was taking off. A BBC team were making a documentary of a year in the life of the club, and they must have felt that all their Christmases had come early. When they had started filming the August before, they had planned on an hour long programme about Gretna's challenge for promotion to the Scottish First Division. Now as the first hint of Spring warmed the air, the story had become a fairytale. The team were miles clear at the top of the league and about to head up to Hampden Park for the semifinal of the Cup. Every time he was at the ground there seemed to be reporters from all over the country wanting a piece of the story. The website was being hit from all corners of the football planet and shirts were being airmailed out to all points north, east, south and west.

Spending his days working in the schools across the region had drained every last drop of the poison that had been with him since his career was ended at Park Head all those years before. He had hated football for so very long. Hated it for dangling a dream in front of his eyes and then snatching it away. Now he could see how completely selfish he had been. He hadn't been able to see beyond the end of his nose. Now he saw football for what it really was. The miracle game that was the only thing that unified the planet. The only thing that seemed able to put war and terrorism and starvation and disease on hold for an hour-and-a-half. When the likes of Bush or Blair appeared on TV, there were some who agreed with them whilst others plotted to blow them up. Same with the Pope or the Mullahs from the mosques. But when Ronaldino left a defender kicking at fresh air, it was something that was cheered from the frozen wastes of Russia to the burning heat of Arabia to the humid jungles of the Congo. It was a game that had the power to do so much good in the world but sadly hardly ever did. Instead it had been hijacked by big businesses who put ticket prices out of the reach of millions and turned players into pop stars.

CHAPTER FOUR

And then there was Gretna. A crazy little club with a chain-smoking, ponytailed, jean-wearing Wearsider at the helm, which was doing all the things that football fans all over the world wanted their own clubs to do. Jimmy had spent most of his life watching the community of Sunnybank sink down into the mire. He had watched his players at Sunnybank Rovers slip off the straight and narrow and get themselves into all kinds of bother. And once they were in it, it seemed almost impossible for them to get out again. There were hardly any jobs for them and just about nothing to do. It was little wonder so many wound up drinking and taking drugs. Now at last, here was a football club that was willing to accept some responsibility for trying to make things better and he still had to pinch himself more or less every day at the realisation that he was a part of it all.

However it didn't look like he was going to be part of it all this afternoon. He had tripped up while carrying his bag of footballs back to his car and his middle finger didn't look anything like it should look. He had made a call to the school he was due to visit next and told them that he wouldn't be able to make it and then he had managed to drive himself to the hospital cursing the pain that was shooting up his forearm. He had announced himself at the desk and been waved over to the waiting area. A nurse had come out and checked the damaged finger and asked what had happened.

"I fell over in the playground."

"Mmm. Bit old for that kind of thing aren't we sir?" Her eyes were twinkling with amusement and Jimmy realised that he could have put it rather better.

"Aye miss. Could you call my mum please?"

She headed off to organise a doctor and Jimmy picked up a magazine that was almost a year old and discarded it when he realised that flicking through the pages was too much like painful hard work. He sat back and watched the comings and goings through the main door to the casualty department. Two medics in green uniforms came in with a young lad. Jimmy stiffened. Not just any young lad. It was Danny. The sight of him was a shock. He had lost at least a stone since the day Jimmy had last seen him in the prison visiting area. His face was as pale as a sheet and his hair was limp and greasy. Danny was staring down at the floor as he shuffled along and he didn't notice his old coach's stare.

He strained his ears to hear what was being said. The older of the two medics was guiding Danny over to the waiting area.

"You just take a seat over here for a minute or two son. I'll go and let the doctor know you're here. OK?"

Danny nodded and slumped into one of the plastic seats. Jimmy got up and went over.

"Hi Danny."

Danny's head came up very slowly and his eyes registered a dull sort of shock. When he spoke his voice was dry and quiet.

"Jimmy."

"Are you OK Danny? What's happened?"

The head went down again. Low. The voice was little more than a mumble.

"Took an overdose. They want me to see a doctor. To check me out like."

Jimmy could hardly believe what he was hearing.

"What do you mean an overdose? What kind of overdose?"

Now Danny raised his head and his eyes were like those of a young soldier who had seen far too much. The dead, beaten expression sent ice into Jimmy's chest. He remembered once reading a book about the teenage soldiers who fought in the jungles of Vietnam. The writer had described the look in their eyes as the thousand-yard stare. Now Danny's eyes looked out on the world in the same way. When he spoke, he spat his words out as if they were something foul.

"I'm on the smack Jimmy. Been on it for ages. I went over. Big time over. The guys on the ambulance said I was two minutes away from dying. Now they want the doctor to check me out. Just routine, so they say. I'll be away in half-an-hour."

Jimmy was completely lost for words. The thought of it was inconceivable. He was still reaching around for something to say when the medic came back over and told Danny that the doctor was ready for him. The boy got to his feet like an old man and shuffled away.

Jimmy made his way back to his chair. It seemed unbelievable. All of it. Danny had been within seconds of dying and yet in a few minutes he would simply walk out of the door and back onto the streets. Then what? He had no home to go to. He knew that Bill McCann still refused to talk to his son and he had made it very clear to Jimmy that it wasn't a subject he was willing to discuss. So it would be back to some hostel or another and no doubt he would be hunting out the next fix. His spirits started to drain away like dirty cold water from a bath. It was all such a miserable waste. It had only been two years ago that Danny had bashed his front door and brought the news that he had been picked for the Scotland Under 16s. He had been a lad with the world at his feet. And now he had been within two minutes of leaving the world altogether and it didn't seem like there was a thing that anybody could do about it.

He would walk out of the door just the same as Jimmy would walk out of the door. The difference was the world that they would walk out into. Jimmy's life was better than he had ever known it. He had a job that he loved. A home. A family. Everything. And what did Danny have? Nothing. No home. No family. A criminal record. A gnawing Heroin habit and the burden of carrying round a rucksack loaded full of broken dreams. Would this be a wake up call? Maybe. But what would he do then? If he stopped using, would his dad speak to him again? Maybe one day, but Jimmy knew his old friend well enough to know that it wouldn't be any time soon. Would he get a job? Not a chance. One look at his criminal record and most employers would run a mile. Would the community open up its arms and welcome him in? They would be more likely run up flags of the cross of St. George and support England in the World Cup.

Not a prayer.

As far as the community was concerned, Danny McCann was a thieving little junkie who deserved everything he got. So when Danny walked through the door it would be to return to the cold misery of his life on the streets. And maybe next time the medics might not get there in time. Maybe next time the ambulance might be held up in some road works and a few days later Jimmy would be watching Danny McCann's coffin being lowered into the ground.

He was so lost in his thoughts that he didn't notice the nurse had returned.

"Hello. Anybody home?"

"Oh. Sorry about that. I was miles away."

"The doctor can see you now."

He started to get to his feet but then stopped half way up.

"No."

She frowned. "What do you mean, no?"

"Right. Sorry. But I can't. I need to wait for someone. I can't miss them you see."

"I don't see, actually."

"No. I don't suppose you do. It's a lad I know. They just brought him in. I want to catch him. Before he leaves. So I'll just wait here. So I don't miss him."

The nurse rolled her eyes. "Look sir, you have a broken finger, you are in a casualty department, and a highly-trained doctor is waiting to fix the problem. Don't you think this is all just a teensy-weensy bit silly?"

"I know. It's plain stupid but I'm waiting right here. Sorry, but there you go."

"OK. Fine. I can assure you that all of us here in the NHS have quite enough to keep ourselves busy without trying to persuade very foolish men to have their broken fingers mended. No doubt you'll be along later."

Jimmy tried a grateful smile which didn't seem to have a lot of success. "Maybe I will."

Once the nurse had departed, he sat back down and watched for the curtains to open and Danny to emerge from his once over from the doctor. Just like Danny had said, it didn't take long. The doctor gave Danny a pat on the shoulder and then moved along to the next bay. Danny looked about for a moment and then started for the door.

"Danny!"

The boy turned and his face registered surprise as he saw Jimmy marching towards him. Then the surprise was replaced by a look of worry.

"Still here Jimmy?"

"You want a lift?"

A shrug. "S'ppose."

"Come on then."

Outside the wind had quickened and it lanced through Danny's thin clothes. Suddenly he was very thankful to have been spared the long walk back into town. Once they were inside, Jimmy killed the radio and cranked the heater up to full.

"You ever see that film 'The Shawshank Redemption' Danny?"

"Aye. I did."

"There's a line in it. It was when they were in the exercise yard, talking about how to do their time. One of guys said there were basically two choices. 'Get busy living, or get busy dying.' You remember that line Danny?"

"Aye. So?"

"So which is it to be? Your choice. It's a simple question. Living or dying? What's it going to be?"

"I dunnae ken what you're on about Jimmy."

"Yes you do Danny. I'm on about you lying there two minutes away from being deader than dead. Two minutes Danny. One-hundred-and-twenty seconds. So what is it to be? Make your mind up."

Danny hunched down in his seat. If it hadn't been so damned cold outside, he would have opened the door and legged it. But it was cold. And where was there to leg it to? But he really didn't need the third degree.

"How do you mean make my mind up? I dunnae understand."

Jimmy turned in his seat so he could look the boy right in the eye. "I'll make it really, really simple. This is a one time offer. If you tell me right now that you're ready to knock all this on the head, then I'll help you. Not next week or next month. I mean right now. Today. I'm blowing the whistle and it's time to kick off. So what is it to be? Living or dying?"

Danny was getting wound up. "It's not that easy Jimmy. It's all very well you just saying . . ."

"I never said anything about it being easy. I said I would help you. And we'll sort it."

"How?"

"I haven't got a clue. You say yes and I'll find out. Living or dying Danny?"

"But . . ."

"NO BUTS! Just make your bloody mind up. Tell me yes or get out of the car and walk. My bloody finger's killing me and I'm not going to sit about all day."

Danny pushed his hands as far as they would go into his pockets and chewed on his lip. So cold outside. And nowhere to go. Nowhere and nobody. Nothing.

"All right then. Yes. Living. Why's your finger hurting?"

"Because I broke it. That's why I was in casualty."

"You're not going to get it seen to?"

"It can wait."

Jimmy pulled his mobile phone out of his pocket and punched speed dial.

"Hi it's Jimmy. Listen. Remember that guy from the Drugs place in Dumfries who was in a few weeks ago. That's it. The First Base Agency. Whereabouts are they? Buccleuch Street. OK. No, it's just someone who needs some advice. Cheers."

He dropped the phone back into his pocket and engaged first gear.

"So where are we going then Jimmy?"

"A place on Buccleuch Street. They do all the drugs awareness stuff in the schools where me and the lads do the coaching. Seems like a good place to start. You know it?"

"Aye. They do food parcels. I've been in a few times. They're good people. They don't judge you in there. And there are these ladies from some churches who bake cakes and that for the food parcels. The cakes are dead good."

"Right." Jimmy wasn't quite sure what to make of that. His plans to sort out Danny were as yet not all that well-formed and dead good cakes didn't seem to be the ideal way to start. His footballer's instincts took over and he decided to follow the tried and trusted policy of taking each game as it comes. Danny looked on anxiously as Jimmy awkwardly drove through town more-or-less one-handed.

"When are you going to get that finger fixed Jimmy?"

"Later."

They parked and walked along Buccleuch Street to The First Base Agency. As they approached the door, Jimmy suddenly started to feel out of his depth. What would it be like in there? He had never in his life been inside a drugs agency. What would the people be like? Would they think he was some kind of nut? No point worrying. Each game as it comes.

Danny opened the door which rattled with a wind chime. There was a lady behind the counter who recognised him and smiled.

"Hi Danny."

"Hello Yvonne."

"How can I help you?"

"I've come in with Jimmy. He wanted to talk to you."

"I see." Not that she did but she was well enough used to going with the flow.

Jimmy stepped forward for an unfamiliar handshake with his undamaged left hand.

"I'm Danny's coach. Well I was. I'm at Gretna now. You're working with Gretna aren't you?"

"That's right. We go into the schools they are working with and do drug and alcohol awareness classes."

Jimmy nodded and struggled to think of how to kick things off. "I just do football. Coaching and that."

"Right." Yvonne carried on going with the flow. Things would come clear in time. They almost always did.

Jimmy looked about the room hoping for some inspiration.

Yvonne tried to help him out. "And you have some questions?"

"Aye. That's right. Questions . . ."

Yvonne smiled. She could see he was struggling. "Why don't we all go upstairs for a cup of tea?"

Jimmy nodded. "Aye. Cup of tea. Champion. Come on Danny."

The little voice suddenly appeared from nowhere. If he left now he could be back on the High Street in two minutes. He could go for the same plan again. It had worked once, so why not again? In and out. Get a few quid together. And maybe Baz would still have gear to sell. An hour and he could be cooking up. Maybe even less if he got really lucky. The voice in his head wasn't playing it cool. It was just yelling. Go. Go. Go. Go.

"Shawshank Redemption Danny. Think."

Jimmy had sensed the moment. His voice was very quiet. Not threatening. Only stating the facts. The options. You get busy living or you get busy dying. Danny closed his eyes and tried to drive the voice away. Then he slowly nodded and commanded his legs to take him towards the staircase and away from the door. Away from the High Street. Away from Baz and his double pure Glasgow smack. Away from being two minutes away from being dead.

Suddenly the voice wasn't quite as loud. There was a shrillness to it now. It was only such a very small thing, but the voice knew that this was a crisis point. It was the first time since leaving prison that Danny McCann had said any kind of no. The first time since he had become a disciple to the great god of Heroin that he had not jumped when his master had clicked his fingers. The first time that he had put anything ahead of the chance of a hit.

They went upstairs to a large, airy, colourful room that didn't look anything like he would have expected a drugs place to look like. Yvonne gestured to a couch and two armchairs.

"Tea or coffee?"

"Coffee please. Black with two."

"Danny?"

"Could I have one of those fruit juices you have in the food parcels please?"

As Yvonne made the drinks, Jimmy took in the walls. There were lots of newspaper articles and letters. A4 sheets said 'CONFIDENTIALITY' and 'PRIVACY'. As he read, Jimmy could see that these things were a big deal in First Base. Then his eyes were drawn to a king sized cheque for £20,000 from Gretna Football Club.

Yvonne brought over the drinks and a plate with cakes. So these are the famous cakes thought Jimmy.

"So. You have some questions Jimmy?"

He stirred his coffee. "It's about Danny really. He . . . well he's got a problem. Heroin."

Yvonne nodded, clearly completely unsurprised by this piece of information. Jimmy ploughed on.

"Do you know he used to be a hell of a player? Football I mean."

"No. I didn't know that."

"I mean seriously good. He got into the Scotland Under 16's, so he did. I was his coach back then. Sunnybank Rovers. We won the Rotary Cup. Then it all . . . well you know . . . things just went wrong for Danny."

Danny's head was down again. He hated it when anyone mentioned what he had once been. It was a thing that he spent his life trying not to think about.

"Well. I fell over this morning and busted my finger. Stupid. I was carrying a bag of footballs across the playground and I tripped. Anyway. That's by the by. The thing is that I went to the casualty department and I saw Danny. He came in with these two medics. So I asked him what was happening. He told me he had overdosed. A bad one he said. He said that if they had got there two minutes later then . . ."

His voice trailed away and he gave his coffee another unnecessary stir. Danny's head was so low now that it was almost between his knees. Yvonne broke the silence.

"I'm afraid there have been more overdoses than usual recently. There has been a big shortage of Heroin since the last round of arrests. When the Heroin goes short, everyone loses their tolerance levels. And then when new supplies do arrive in the town, people find it far too strong and they can't handle it. Are you OK now Danny?"

The bowed head gave an almost imperceptible nod. Jimmy picked up the thread of his thoughts.

"I waited. And when Danny came out from seeing the doctor, I collared him. I mean it's like he has a straight choice the way I see it. He can carry on and probably die. Or he can knock it on the head and have a life. I said that if he wants to knock it on the head then I'll help him."

"And did you agree Danny?"

This time he looked up. "Aye. I did."

"Do you mean it?"

"They said I was nearly dead. Two minutes. I'm scared."

Yvonne nodded. Surviving a near fatal overdose was one of the triggers that was sometimes enough to persuade Heroin users to give up. Jimmy was relaxing now. It wasn't as hard as he thought it would be.

"The thing is, I haven't got a clue about any of this. That's why I'm here. How do I help him to stop?"

This made Yvonne smile. It was a question that everyone at First Base was very familiar with. Every day mums and dads and grandparents asked the very same question. How do we get them to stop? And the First Base team would explain that the real question needed to be 'What can we do to help them to stop?' She focused on Danny.

"How much have you been using Danny?"

He shrugged. "Two bags a day. Sometimes more if I can afford it."

"Smoking or injecting?"

"Jagging, but only for a few months."

"But you won't have used much in the last couple of weeks."

He shook his head. "Hardly anything. There's nothing about. I had couple of bags last week but they were rubbish. I don't think there was even any kit in them. Then nothing since Friday. Well. Until just now."

"That's good news then isn't it?"

"How do you make that out?" Danny really couldn't see how the miserable two week long drought could possibly be seen as good news. Yvonne was unfazed.

"Because you've more or less done your rattle already. Think about it. If you had been using two bags a day all the way up to today then it would be loads harder to come off. Well. Wouldn't it?"

"S'ppose so." The logic was indeed hard to argue with.

"So what does this mean?" Jimmy wasn't really with them.

"Normally a rattle goes something like this. Day one isn't too bad because there is still Heroin in the system. Day two is worse, but there is still a little Heroin still active. Day three is by far the worst because that is when the body has to live with having no Heroin at all. From day four onwards it gets a little easier every day. Usually after a week almost all the physical symptoms are over. In Danny's case I think it will probably be a lot less. I wouldn't be surprised if you were feeling not so bad by the weekend. Like I said, you've got the worst of it out of the way already."

To Jimmy this seemed like far better news than he was expecting. "And then that's it? After a week Danny can be clean."

Yvonne gave a rueful smile. "Not really. Not at all in fact. These are only the physical symptoms. People tend to think the cold turkey is the hardest part. I'm not saying it's easy, but many of our clients tell us that coming off Heroin really isn't nearly as impossible as people think. Staying off is a far bigger problem."

"Why is that?"

"Let me guess a few things about how life has been these last few months. You tell me if I'm wrong Danny. You are living in a hostel, I know that much because of the referral slips they have given you for food parcels. I guess every hour of every day is taken up with trying to come up with the money for your two bags. Not only that, but you will have been spending all that time with other people in the same boat. All you will ever talk about is Heroin. How to get the money? Who is selling the biggest bags? Who has been arrested? Who has got ill? Who has been sent to prison? It will have been the only thing in your life from the second you wake up to the time you fall asleep. Am I right Danny?"

He nodded. She continued.

"So. The questions that you need to ask yourself are these. If you stop, where are you going to stay? If you stay in the hostel, you will still be in contact with people who are still using every day. Still talking about using every day. Temptation. And if you don't fill every minute of your day in the pursuit of Heroin, what will you do instead? Think about it. There will be an awful lot of empty hours to fill. You will have to avoid all your mates because all they will be talking about is Heroin. So who will you see? Have you any friends who don't use drugs? Well?"

Danny shook his head. "Not any more."

"Family?"

"There's only my dad and he won't talk to me."

Yvonne turned back to Jimmy. "Can you see now? The big problem is staying clean. Danny will need a really good plan of action. Ideally he needs to move somewhere where there isn't Heroin in his face all the time. And I would recommend that he seriously considers Naltrexone."

"What's that?"

"It's a medication. A pill you take every day. So long as you have Naltrexone in your system, there is no point in using Heroin. The Naltrexone completely annuls all the effect of the Heroin. In fact you've probably had some today. Did the medics give you a Narcan injection?"

"I don't know. They gave me a jag of something."

"That will have been Narcan. When you came round did you feel any effects at all from your hit?"

"No. Nothing. It was like I hadn't used at all."

"There you go then. If you take Naltrexone, that's just how it would be if you had a relapse. Nothing. So there's no point. As long as you keep taking the pills you can't get a buzz for at least three days. They even do implants now, though our treatment centre doesn't have the funding to supply them."

"Implants? What do you mean implants?" Jimmy had visions of Invasion of the Body Snatchers.

"It is a small capsule of Naltrexone that is implanted under the skin. On the arm usually. Every day it releases a small amount. They can last anything up to a year."

This widened Jimmy's eyes. "You mean if somebody gets one of these implants put in there is no way they can use Heroin for a whole year?"

"That's right. Well. They can use of course, but it will have no effect. The only way out of it would be to remove it."

Jimmy winced at the thought, but now his brain was in overdrive.

"So where do you get one of these implants?"

"Sheffield. There is a doctor who specialises in the procedure."

"Does he charge?"

"I'm afraid so. A three months implant costs about £1500 and for a year it is nearly £2000. I have a brochure if you want."

"Yes. Please. And can you go onto this Naltrexone stuff straight away."

"No. If you take it while there is still any Heroin in your system you can get quite ill. You need to wait at least seven days."

"So next Tuesday then?"

"Theoretically, yes. Assuming they aren't booked up. Are you thinking of helping Danny to pay for one?"

Jimmy chuckled. "Not me. Two grand is out of my range. But I know a man who might. Look Yvonne. That's brilliant. Perfect. I know what I'm doing now."

"Please. Wait a second. Like I said. There are many issues. The most important thing is to have a proper plan. We call it an action plan. A plan that covers everything that will be needed to help Danny to free himself of his dependency. So before you go chasing off Jimmy I am going to make a few notes. OK?"

Danny couldn't help but smirk at the look on Jimmy's face. Yvonne picked up her pad and started making notes.

"The first thing is that someone needs to be in charge of the plan. Is that going to be you Jimmy?"

"Aye. It is."

"And Danny, are you quite happy to have Jimmy doing this for you?"

Danny nodded.

"Good. OK. Number one. Danny needs somewhere to stay where he is well away from people using drugs. A safe and caring environment."

"Sorted."

"Number two. The next step is the Detox. There will need to be support. People around. Is that possible?"

"It is."

Yvonne nodded. "Number three. How will he fill his days? There will need to be some kind of structure. Activities. Every hour needs to be filled."

"Sorted."

"And how will he meet people. New people. People not using?"

"Sorted."

"Number four. The Naltrexone. When will you know if you will be able to arrange the finance for the implant Jimmy?"

"Hopefully by the end of the afternoon."

"That's excellent. I suggest that you both come back tomorrow and we will make arrangements for an appointment in Sheffield for you. Danny will need to go and see his GP to have some blood tests to make sure his is OK to take the medication. There isn't usually a problem. Now. If there is a problem with the finance then all is not lost. We can arrange an appointment up at the local treatment centre and you can go onto the pills. Your GP will be able to arrange that for you."

Now her voice hardened a notch. "And is this really what Danny wants to do?" She stared at Danny until he at last raised his head and looked at her.

"Aye. It is Yvonne. Honest."

Jimmy felt that he needed to justify himself

"Look, I'm sorry if it seems like I'm acting the bully here. It's just . . . well I'm a football coach not a counsellor. It's the only way I know. Besides, this one always did need a proper kick up the backside and I'm not changing that now just because he's using Heroin. That right Danny?"

"Aye Jimmy. It's right enough."

Jimmy got to his feet. "Well that's all sorted then. Brilliant. Thanks for all the help Yvonne. Spot on. We best be off now."

Yvonne was worried that things were going rather too fast. "Please. Wait a minute. Just sit for a minute or two."

Jimmy was a ball of energy. A man on a mission. But he did as he was asked and sat. "Sorry."

"No need. But it really is very important that you realise that coming off Heroin is never simple. You need to know that there is much, much more than simply getting the chemical out of the system. Assuming Danny gets his implant next week I think it is very important that you both come back in to see us. There will be some reasons why Danny has been using. There almost always are. It will be important that he talks these things through. Gets them out of his system if you like. We can help find someone for Danny to talk to. I would also ask you to seriously think about some kind of relapse prevention therapy. Maybe even Narcotics Anonymous. I know these things might sound a little alien to you, but they really are very important."

Jimmy grinned. "Twenty years ago I would have wondered, but not any more. The shrinks are almost as important as the fitness trainers in the pro game today."

"Not shrinks Jimmy. People to talk to."

"Aye. I ken where you're coming from. Look, as soon as Danny has this implant thing in place we'll be back. That's a promise. You can take it to the bank. And we'll go and see whatever people you reckon he needs to see."

"It has to be Danny's choice Jimmy. All of it. It is the only way this will work."

Danny could see that Jimmy was becoming increasingly uncomfortable. It seemed like it was time to help out.

"Honest Yvonne. It is my choice. I've had enough. Really. I just want my life back."

"I'm glad Danny. Really. Now there is one last thing. You said that your dad doesn't speak to you any more."

"No. Not for ages now."

"We might be able to help. You know we run a family mediation service. It means that we try to help families to start communicating again. Properly communicating. Not shouting and yelling at each other. It is very successful. As soon as you get your implant in place we will see if we can make contact with your dad. We can write to him and see if he might be willing to come and meet you here at the Agency. Would you like us to do that Danny?"

"Aye. That I would."

Jimmy chipped in. "I'll deliver it if you like. Save the price of a stamp."

She could se that Jimmy was itching to get up and crack on with whatever plan he had in mind.

"Well you best be off then."

Jimmy jumped up from his seat.

"Would your left foot have been any use if me and your dad hadn't made your life a misery by getting you to kick a ball against a wall for two hours every day?"

Danny grimaced at the memory. "No Jimmy. My left foot wouldn't have been any use if you and my dad hadn't made me kick a ball against a wall for two hours a day."

They went back down the stairs and Yvonne gave them both a carrier bag full of information leaflets covering Detox and recovery. She watched them march out onto the street and thought that it had been by far the strangest interview she had ever had in the Agency. All kinds of issues came up when the topic of Heroin dependency was discussed, but never before had kicking a ball against a wall with the left foot come into the equation.

Once they were back in the car Danny started up with questions.

"You said I wouldn't go back to the hostel. What did you mean?"

"You can come and stay with us. Jamie's away at college. You can have his room. It won't be forever. Once we get this implant thing sorted I'll get to work on your dad."

"There's no chance there Jimmy."

"Just leave him to me. I'll sort him out."

"And you said that filling my time was sorted. And meeting people away from the gear. What was that all about?"

"Wait and see. Now, shut it for a minute. I need to make a call."

He pulled a number from the memory and dialled.

"Hi it's Jimmy. Is Brooks about?"

Brooks was about and came to the phone a minute or so later.

"You OK Jimmy?"

"Yeah. Good as gold. Look Brooks, I'm on my way in. Will you have ten minutes to spare?"

"As long as it can be spent smoking in the car park. This smoking ban's killing me man."

Jimmy chuckled. "The car park will do fine. See you in half an hour or so."

The journey from Dumfries to Gretna was just over twenty miles and Danny gave up trying to find out what was going on before they were half way. He relaxed back into the unfamiliar comfort of the car seat and enjoyed the feel of the warm air blowing down onto his feet. It seemed like the further they drove from Dumfries, the quieter the voice in his head was getting. It was if the voice which had been right up close and shouting in his ear in the First Base Agency, was now a long way away. Somewhere over a couple of fields and the wind was making it harder and harder to pick out the words. He thought about what Yvonne had said about how he had already done the hard part of his rattle and he had to admit that he really didn't feel so bad at all. It was different in the town. Every minute was spent plotting and scheming how to get hold of the next bag. It was all anyone ever talked about. Who was selling? Was it any good? How much had they got? It was because he spent all day, every day thinking and talking about it that he was convinced he was rattling right down to his toenails. But now it was different. There was no way in a million years that he was about to get hold of a bag at the football ground in Gretna and so the nagging voice was becoming quieter and quieter and quieter.

In the space that was left there was something new.

Hope.

Only very, very faint, but there all the same. For months he had been resigned to the fact that he had blown his life beyond repair. There was no way that his dad would ever want to know him again. His mum was long gone. All his grandparents were dead. The only friends he had were fellow users who would gladly stab him in the back if it meant an extra bag. He had no home, hardly any clothes, no money, no hope of a job. Nothing. And the looks on the faces of those who passed him on the street said it all.

Junkie. Horrible, thieving junkie.

Scum.

Filth.

He could now begin to see that he had completely given up. What point was there in trying? Everybody hated him. And they always would. If he stopped using, he would just have to avoid what few mates he had. Then what? He would just stay in his room all day watching daytime TV. Worse than prison. At least in prison there was stuff going on and a game of football in the exercise yard and three decent meals a day.

But now, completely out of the blue, things were starting to change. Jimmy Doyle was obviously bothered. He had even said that Danny could stay with him and his wife. And Yvonne had been bothered. And now they were about to meet Brooks Mileson and maybe he would be bothered as well. It began to dawn on Danny that everything might not be lost after all. Maybe there still might be some kind of way forward. Some kind of future. Some kind of hope.

It had been a long, long time since he had known the faintest glimmer of hope and he found it hard to trust it. But as each green road sign showed them getting closer and closer to Gretna, Danny McCann felt his spirits lift higher and higher.

As they pulled into the car park, Jimmy spoke for the first time in a few minutes. "OK. One last time. I need to know that you are completely serious about this. Because if you're not, then you're probably going to make a mug out of me. So?"

By this time the voice in his head was silent. Dumfries was a mere twenty-three miles back down the road but it seemed like a million miles. Suddenly Danny was back at a football ground for the first time in two years. He had no idea what Jimmy had in mind, but he was certain that it was about to involve football in some shape or form. And no matter how hard he had tried to kill the memories of his football dream with bag after bag of Heroin, those dreams had never died. Now they were sparking back to life and this time he would let nothing in the whole wide world interfere with them.

"I'll do anything Jimmy. Anything at all."

Jimmy weighed his words and they sounded good enough as far as he was concerned. "All right. Come on then, let's see what we can do."

The offices were two Portacabins bolted together and inside there was an atmosphere of barely controlled frenzy. Phones were ringing more or less constantly. A small group of fans were choosing shirts from a merchandise area. A radio reporter was locked into conversation with a man in a tracksuit. In the corner of the room under a portrait of Napoleon there was a large table holding piles of tickets. Two fans were paying up whilst those sitting round the table were obviously handling telephone sales. Danny felt a small shiver as he saw that two of those selling the tickets were wearing a T-shirt that read 'Livin' the dream'. It was almost spooky. It made him even more convinced that this was the moment when his life was at last about to turn after the terrible years of prison and addiction.

Danny recognised Brooks Mileson easily enough. The man had become a fixture on the back pages of the discarded papers that he picked out of bins on the High Street to read. He looked the same in real life as he did in the papers and that was basically not at all like a man who owned a football club. He spotted Jimmy and jumped to his feet, pulling on an anorak at the same time.

"That's us over five thousand Jimmy. Brilliant isn't it? Double the population of the village. It's the same as Celtic taking about two million to a semifinal. Come on. Let's get out quick. If I don't get a fag down my neck I'm going to keel over."

The radio reporter had half turned with his mic and was looking hopeful. Brooks gave him a grin.

"In a bit, OK. I'm gagging."

He had a Marlboro lit the minute he was out of the door and as he pulled in the smoke he looked like a man having his first glass of water after walking from Cairo to Cape Town.

"OK Jimmy. I'm all yours. What's the problem?"

"No problem. Do you remember this lad, Brooks? Danny McCann?"

Brooks heaved in another mighty lung full of smoke and held out a hand that Danny shook. There was definitely something familiar about the lad.

"I'll help you out. Sunnybank Rovers. The Rotary Cup Final. The day you offered me a job."

Now Brooks was with the programme. "Yeah, I remember. You're the lad who got a hat trick in about ten minutes. Then you made a bit of a spectacular exit."

Danny blushed at the memory but forced himself not to look down. Jimmy took a deep breath and started his pitch.

"It wasn't just a spectacular exit from the match. Danny pretty well made an exit from everything. That was basically the last proper game he played. Over the last two years he has gone clean off the rails. Drugs. Prison. Homeless. The lot. I found him a couple of hours ago down at the casualty department. He had overdosed and they had got him back with two minutes to spare."

Brooks's face became sombre. It was the kind of story he was only too familiar with. The story of Danny McCann was the same as so many lads from the estate where he had grown up back in Sunderland. It was why the Gretna Community Programme was so important to him.

CHAPTER FOUR

"Sounds like you're a lucky lad Danny."

"Aye. I am. Dead lucky."

"Actually, I think it is 'alive lucky'. So what can I do?"

Jimmy swallowed and went for it. "A deal Brooks. In my opinion this lad has it in him to be one of the top players in Scotland. I know he has gone to the dogs for a while but he's still only eighteen. Danny has convinced me that he wants away from the Heroin. I've said he can come to my place to do his cold turkey. If he can stay clean for seven days, he can get a Naltrexone implant. Basically this is a kind of slow release medication that makes it pointless using Heroin for a year. We went into The First Base Agency and they gave some pretty good advice. The first thing is to get off the stuff. That shouldn't be too bad. There has been virtually no Heroin on sale in the town since the last big drugs bust a couple of weeks ago. Basically it means that Danny has already done the hard part of a Detox. I'll see him through the rest. The bigger part of the job is staying off. The implant can sort out part of the problem. The biggest hurdle is to find something to do to get clear of the whole life he has been leading. Well. I've got a plan."

Brooks's fired up another cigarette. "Go on then."

"It's a contract with a difference. Danny signs on for Gretna. The club pays for the implant which is £2000. The contract is for minimum wage for one year. He gets no cash until all the money for the treatment has been paid back. For the next few months he's a dogs-body. He sweeps the terraces after games, helps the ground staff, makes hotdogs, anything. Whatever needs doing. In that time, I'll get him fitter than he's ever been in his life. Then he has a run out with the first team squad for three days when they start pre-season training. If he makes it, he makes it. If he doesn't, he doesn't. Simple as that. In my judgement, this is an opportunity to sign a player who might one day be worth a million plus for a one year contract at minimum wage."

He hadn't really known what Brooks's reaction would be. He had hoped that his boss remembered Danny's barnstorming ten minute cameo in the cup final. He had certainly not anticipated the look of concern on Brooks's face as he smoked furiously.

"I don't know Jimmy. I mean the implant bit, fine. No problem. And the helping out round the ground. No problem. It's the trial part that's the problem. I mean I can't say anything about that. That's for the Gaffer. He'd kill me if I made a promise like that. But I know what you're saying. I remember watching you well enough Danny." He rubbed at his hair and grappled with the problem.

Then he came to a decision and pulled a mobile phone from his pocket and dialled.

"Gaffer . . . it's Brooks . . . Have you got a minute . . . Top man . . . no, I'm in the car park . . . Yeah, yeah, having a fag. Having three in fact. See you in a sec."

He snapped the phone shut. "Right. He's coming. I'm sorry Danny, but I just can't say anything about you getting a trial. The rest, sure, no problem. And don't take any notice of any of this stuff Jimmy's on about. You go and get the implant and then we can talk about things. If you want to come and help out then great. But you won't owe me a thing. OK?"

"Thank you Mr Mileson."

"It's Brooks."

The manager, Rowan Alexander appeared a few minutes later and Danny thought that shaking his hand was much the same as sticking it in one of the vices that he had once used in the woodwork classroom. He was about to give Jimmy the same treatment but Jimmy had shaken hands with the Gaffer before and there was no way he was going there with his busted finger.

"Finger's knackered. I'll pass."

"What have you done to it?" Asked Brooks.

"I tripped at one of the schools and broke it. That was why I was at the casualty department."

"Did you get it fixed?"

"No. Didn't have time."

"What do you mean you didn't have time?"

"I just wanted to get hold of Danny before he headed back into the town."

Brooks nodded. He could see the sense in that. "Well. You're lucky. Fiona's here at the moment. You best go and see her and get fixed up. But fill in the Gaffer first." Fiona was the club doctor.

Jimmy repeated his proposal, feeling a little more confident now that he knew that the implant was a definite. Rowan took the story in with a concentrated expression. Once Jimmy was done, he started with his questions.

"Why the first team Jimmy? Why not the Academy?"

CHAPTER FOUR

"The way I see it, the main job of the Academy is to sort out lads who are hard enough for the pro game. Well you can take it from me that Danny here is hard enough. He always was. I figure now he's harder still after the life he's led for the last couple of years. So I don't think character's the issue."

Rowan nodded. It was something that he was very familiar with. There were thousands and thousands of kids who shared exceptional technical football skills. But mere skill was only a small part of the package that any manager was always searching for. In many ways, skill was the easiest element to find. Next came athleticism. Fitness and stamina which would work not only on a warm afternoon in May, but also on a freezing night in February when the rain was horizontal on the wind. Then there were those all so important few inches between a player's ears. Did he have a football brain? Did he have a positive attitude? Ambition? Determination? Dedication? And then, last but probably most important of all was that almost indefinable asset called bottle. A will to win. A determination never, ever to give up. The sheer guts to play on when every muscle in the body was screaming in pain. The ability to find the peak of a performance when the pressure was at its highest.

Rowan knew that it often took a fellow pro to be able to spot bottle and Jimmy Doyle knew the game well enough. Not only was he recommending the lad for a trial, but he was saying that he had the bottle. He knew Jimmy well enough to realise that this was not a thing he would do unless he was a hundred and ten percent certain of his man. He turned to look Danny full in the face.

"I knew about you of course."

Danny was surprised by this. "Did you?"

"Well of course I did. There aren't many from round here who get into the Scotland Under 16's. I wouldn't be much of a manager if I didn't know about you would I? And then Brooks came to see me a while back jumping up and down about this lad he had watched. So, yes. I was going to have a look at you. But I never got the chance did I?"

Danny was itching to look down but his instincts told him not to. It was time he stopped looking down and staring at the floor. "No sir."

"No. Because when I asked about, it turned out you were banged up for beating up a station master."

Danny's eyes widened with surprise that the manager knew so much. "Like I said Danny. I believe in being thorough. It's why your man here pays me my salary. And if I stop being thorough, your man here will stop paying my salary and fire me. OK. Now I find out that having served your time you've come out of prison and become a Heroin addict. Nice one Danny. Great rehabilitation."

Brooks was itching to say something but he lit another cigarette instead. Sure the gaffer was being hard, but he knew his manager well enough to realise that everything always had a purpose. Jimmy merely watched with a serene smile. If Rowan wanted to go in hard, it was OK by him. The silly sod deserved all he got.

"Well?"

"What can I say sir?" Danny was almost cramping his neck muscles to stop himself from looking away from the fierce eyes.

"Well you better say something, because Jimmy here is suggesting that I break all the rules and fast track you for a trial. And the idea is that this football club digs into its pockets to pay up for an implant to keep you off the poison. So you really need to say something Danny McCann. And it better be a pretty convincing something because I really, really don't like breaking the rules and especially not for a Heroin addict that beats up station masters. Talk. Or walk."

He folded his arms and glowered. Danny realised that once again he had reached one of those moments when his life could go one way or another. Every time it had ever happened before, he had always made the wrong choice. Somehow this time he had to get it right. But what was it that Rowan expected him to say? What words could he possibly find that would work? And then he realised that all the man wanted was the plain truth. No lies. No excuses. Nothing but the simple truth. And if that wasn't good enough, then so be it.

"Sir, football has been the best thing in my life by a mile. I loved it. I lived for it. And then I forgot how much I loved it for a while because I was stupid. By the time I remembered, I had blown it. I never thought I would get another chance. Then Jimmy turns up. It was like a miracle. I nearly die, and Jimmy turns up. You might not believe me, but I now know what football means to me Mr Alexander. It's everything. I might not be the best player you'll ever have, but I swear I will be the one who tries the hardest. I'll do anything to make it. The only way I can ever live with all the stuff I've done is if I use it to make me remember how important football is. And if I manage it, then maybe my dad will speak to me again. So you might say I'm not good enough, Mr Alexander. But you will never, ever say I didn't try hard enough. I can swear on that."

It seemed to Danny that Rowan's face didn't move for about thirty-six hours. He was like a statue. Not a flicker of movement. Then, very slowly, he nodded. Just once.

"Three days is a waste of space. You know that as well as me Jimmy. All that is going to happen for three days is that the other lads will try and kick him into next week. I'll give you three months, starting July first. You better make sure you turn up fitter than you ever dreamed of or you won't stand a chance. If you can cut it, then you're in. If you don't, then you're out. Simple as that. It's called football. And hear this Danny. You can thank your lucky stars that Jimmy here has stuck his neck out for you. If you let him down, I'm not going to come down on you like a tonne of bricks. I'm going hit you like a cruise missile. You hear me?"

"I hear you sir."

"Good." He held out his hand and once again Danny felt his fingers crunch. "That's us done then. Not that it is down to me. This is the man who pays the wages. I'll go a year at minimum wage Brooks. Your call now."

He didn't wait to hear Brooks's judgement. He knew that his decision would be backed. "Come on Jimmy, I'll take you to see Fiona with that finger. Brooks will dot the 'i's and cross the 't's."

"Fair enough. I'll see you back at the office in a bit Danny."

Danny was too elated to speak. He just nodded. As Rowan and Jimmy walked away Brooks spoke in a quiet voice.

"When I was a little lad I fell and injured myself. I couldn't walk at all. The doctors said I would probably never walk again. I hate that. You know, when people tell you what you can and cannot do. So I thought stuff them. I decided to prove them wrong. I taught myself to walk. Then I taught myself to run. I must have done all right because I got picked to run for England at cross-country. I'm not telling you this to show off or anything. It's just I can remember you that morning when you lost your rag and got sent off. I remember how angry you were. And I could understand that anger because it was the way I had felt when those doctors tried to tell me

I'd never walk again. All your anger has got you nowhere because you haven't learnt how to use it properly. Now's your chance to change all that. Jimmy and Rowan are good people. Really good. The best. Listen to them. Trust them. Follow their instructions. And they'll help you use that anger properly. I want to see the lad who got the hat trick. I don't think any of us want to see the lad who got sent off. It's a great chance Rowan and Jimmy have given you. Make sure you take it."

"I will. Honest. I really will."

Brooks outed his cigarette under a work boot. "Champion. Come on then, we best get back to it."

There had been a steady stream of fans making their way by them on the car park and heading into the offices. Once inside, they saw a small queue at the table waiting to buy tickets and a father with two young sons was looking through the merchandise. Brooks took Danny into the small office by the front door.

"Danny, this is my son Craig."

Craig Mileson stood and shook hands. His eyes held a quizzical expression. He had no clue who Danny was or what his father expected him to do with him. It would come clear soon enough. Things generally did.

"You all right Danny?"

"Aye. Great."

Brooks clapped him on the back. "Danny's on board. He'll be having a go with the team in July but until then we're going to keep him busy. I'll leave that with you."

Craig was about to ask his father exactly what kind of thing he wanted Danny to be kept busy with, but already Brooks was marching over to the table to sell some more tickets. He gave a shrug and asked. "Do you have any experience in retail Danny?"

"A bit." Danny felt it best not to mention that his retail experience was selling vallies at a pound a go for Baz Stamper.

"Good lad. Come on then. We have some punters looking to buy some merchandise. You might as well get stuck in."

He took Danny over to the father and his two sons.

"Afternoon lads. This here is Danny and he is going to help you find what you want. All yours Danny. "

And with a smile he dropped Danny in at the deep end.

CHAPTER FOUR

So Danny's first achievement as a pro footballer was to sell two scarves, two hats, one flag and two T-shirts to a father and his two sons for £27.50. As he folded the T-shirts and put them into carrier bags he couldn't help but smile.

Because on the T-shirts it said 'Livin' the dream.'

PART FIVE

It was August. It was really hot outside. And it was a complete and utter disaster.

Sitting across the table from Brooks were his manager and his club doctor. Both wore expressions that were a mirror of his own. In the age old language of football, all three looked as sick as parrots.

"Tell me again Fiona please. I'm not sure that I took it all in first time."

Doctor Fiona Vernon wished there was any way she could make it any better. But there wasn't. "I'm afraid that it has been confirmed. It is flu, and it is one of the nastier varieties. I have called everyone I can think of and they all have the same opinion. The players who are ill will be out for at least a week. I have to recommend in the strongest terms that none of them take the trip to Poland. It is essential that we isolate them from the players who are unaffected. All they can do is to go home, rest up, take the medication and they should be fine to play in a week to ten days."

Brooks couldn't stand it any more and jumped to his feet and paced. "How many is it?"

"Six. There are two who I can't be certain about yet. But I think you need to assume that it will be eight."

"Look, I'm going to have to go out."

The doctor's face took on a stern expression. "Brooks, you really . . ."

He held up a pleading hand. "I know Fiona. I know. Give a break. Just this once. Special circumstances and all that."

She swallowed down the usual telling off and shrugged. "Fine. We'll go and stand out on the car park and you can smoke yourself to death. Why listen to me anyway? I'm only a doctor after all."

Brooks couldn't get out quickly enough. No way was he about to give his club doctor the chance to change her mind. Secretly Fiona didn't begrudge him a cigarette at all. The whole thing was just such downright bad luck that it was sickening. The football world had gasped in astonishment as Gretna had taken Hearts all the way to a penalty shootout in one of the most exciting Scottish Cup Finals that anyone could remember. Their reward had been a place in the UEFA Cup which was uncharted waters for a club newly-promoted from the Scottish Second Division. The draw in July had pitted them against the Polish side Wisla Krakow, and the first leg had been played at Fir Park, Motherwell as Raydale Park was not up to required UEFA standards. The same experts who had confidently predicted that the Cup Final would be a stroll in the park for Hearts had told the world that there was no chance that a small team like Gretna would be able to adapt to the demands of European football. They predicted that the dream would crash and burn. Enough was enough. The romance of the cup was one thing. This was all about the grinding harsh reality of Europe and the minnows would be taught a lesson.

And yet again they had all been proved wrong. Gretna had played a high tempo game and never once allowed the Poles to be comfortable on the ball and keep possession. They hounded and harried them and it was only because the Krakow keeper had the game of his life that the final score was only one – nil thanks to a second-half header from Kenny Deuchar.

It had been like the cup run had never ended. All of a sudden everything seemed possible. One – nil was a long way from any kind of certainty, but it certainly meant that the men from Raydale stood a chance. They hadn't conceded an away goal to a team that included three players who had represented their country at the World Cup in Germany. The Poles had undoubtedly played the slicker passing football, but they had been clearly rattled by the in your face passion of the Scots. Once again, Gretna was attracting the attention of the football media who were hungry for a story to fill the void between the end of the World Cup and the start of the Premiership.

CHAPTER FIVE

It had seemed as if everything was set up for a second leg classic. And now the club doctor felt like she had brought the dream crashing down to the floor by breaking the news that up to eight first team players would be unable to travel because they had flu.

By the time she caught up with Brooks, he was already drawing hard on his cigarette.

"You can't believe it, can you? I mean flu . . ." He threw up his arms to take in the expanse of deep blue sky that stretched all the way from horizon to horizon. "It's August. It's eighty degrees. And we've got the flu."

Fiona wondered whether it was worth explaining that the flu bug had nothing to do with cold weather, in fact it actually thrived in hot temperatures, but she decided that it wouldn't really be a worthwhile contribution.

"OK Fiona. The lads can't travel and that's all there is to it. Are they home already?"

"They are."

"Is there anything else?"

"It might be an idea to avoid any areas where the virus might be lurking. Changing rooms, that kind of thing."

"OK."

"Otherwise, there really isn't anything else that I can tell you." It occurred to the doctor how very differently the two men at the helm of the club were reacting to the crisis. Brooks as ever was a picture of constant motion as he kicked at a stone angrily. Rowan on the other hand stood stock-still and seemed lost in thought as he stared at a small copse of trees.

A car parked up and Graeme Muir the Chief Executive climbed out and joined them with a nervous, questioning expression. Rowan answered it with a shake of the head.

"Not good. There's eight can't travel. It's flu. Not a thing we can do about it."

Graeme rolled his eyes whilst Brooks kicked another stone.

"Have you decided who is going yet?" All the travel arrangements were down to Graeme and it was clear that there were going to have to be a lot of last minute changes. Rowan reached into his pocket and pulled out a folded piece of A4.

"All here." He gave a wry grin. "Last of the Mohicans."

Brooks intercepted the sheet before it made it to Graeme. He quickly took in the names and then looked up sharply.

"You're taking Danny then?"

His manager grinned. "Aye boss, I'm taking Danny. Maybe we'll see how good you are as a talent spotter. Only the bench mind."

Brooks looked happier than he had since walking into the office that morning to be met with wall to wall disaster.

"He's doing all right then is he?"

"Aye. He's doing well. He's that fit it's frightening. It makes me shudder to think what Jimmy must have put him through to get him ready. He's a talent. No doubting that. Keen as mustard and a heart of a lion. The first two days, all the boys kicked him all ends up. Know what he said?"

"Go on."

"He told them they were pathetic. Nothing compared to the hard men in the Glasgow v. Edinburgh games in the jail. Every time someone clattered him, he would just jump up and tell him to keep working on it and maybe they'd make the grade. All the boys have taken to him. You never know, we might just have landed ourselves the bargain of the decade."

Suddenly the flu epidemic didn't seem all that bad any more. Brooks had taken to Danny McCann from the very first time he had seen him for ten crazy minutes in the Rotary Cup final. Jimmy had been keeping him up-to-date on the lad's rehabilitation from the heroin and it seemed like all was going well. He had been itching to ask Rowan how things were going with the trial, but he didn't want to seem like he was interfering. Now he had his answer. And the fact that young Danny McCann would be sitting on the subs bench in Krakow suddenly filled him with hope. Only a few months earlier the boy had been two minutes away from dying. He had landed in the very bottom of the gutter and all must have seemed completely lost. And yet here he was with a fighting chance of making his debut as a pro footballer in the UEFA Cup in Poland. It was yet another Gretna fairytale.

"He must have been chuffed to bits when you told him."

Rowan chuckled again. "I thought he was going to explode."

Graeme however being a Chief Executive was much more concerned with the practicalities.

"Has he got a passport?"

Rowan shook his head. "No, but it shouldn't be a problem. Jimmy's taken him up to Glasgow to get one on the express service."

"Well I best get busy with changing the flights and everything."

Rowan headed back to his office whilst Brooks lit up another and made a couple of calls. He needed to rearrange a few things.

There was someone he had to go and see.

Three days later Danny had finally given up pinching himself and accepted that what was happening was indeed really true. He had barely been able to take in the news that he had been selected for the squad to travel to Poland before Jimmy had him in the car and heading north for the passport office in Glasgow. He had never had a passport before. It was the first of lots of brand new experiences that came one after another. The next morning he was taken to be kitted-out in a suit for the flight and the transfer to the hotel.

It was the first time he had ever worn a suit.

Then he made his first journey on a team bus as they travelled up to Prestwick Airport.

Then when they arrived at the airport he had an experience that wasn't new at all, but it seemed like it was. As he looked around the waiting area in the Departures area a familiar figure got up from his seat and came over to him.

His dad.

"Hello Danny."

Danny was almost too shocked to speak. "Dad."

For a moment the two of them just looked at each other. Much to his own surprise, it was Danny who broke the silence. They had met up at The First Base Agency on a few occasions and slowly but surely they had been getting their relationship back on track. But Danny had felt that they were still a million miles away from his Dad catching a plane to Poland.

"So Jimmy managed to persuade you then?"

Bill McCann shook his head and smiled. "No. It wasn't actually. Though it hasn't been for lack of trying. He's been driving me absolutely mad for months. In fact it was your man over there." He nodded over to where Brooks was speaking away into a couple of microphones. "He came to see me Tuesday night. He's a persuasive lad."

"I'm glad you're here dad."

"Aye. Me too. It wouldn't do to miss seeing you make your European debut would it?"

"I'm only on the bench dad. I don't suppose I'll get on or anything."

"That's good enough for me. You look fit."

Danny laughed. "I should do. I think Jimmy must have been a trainer in the SAS at some stage. He's nearly killed me these last few months."

"Serves you right."

"That's what he says."

The next new experience was his first time on a plane. Then he looked out of the coach window in complete amazement as the coach took them to their hotel in Krakow. The road was like a farm track and full of potholes that the bus driver had to swerve to avoid. As they came to the edge of the city, he couldn't believe how poor everything was. They passed line after line of huge grey tower blocks that all looked so battered that they seemed ready to fall down. Pavements were little more than muddy tracks. And the sky was filled with towering pillars of smoke that were being thrown out of the chimneys of an enormous factory. It made Sunnybank look like Beverley Hills.

The flight had only been a couple of hours, but he felt like he was on the other side of the world. As they approached the city centre, it was different again. Suddenly all the buildings were magnificent. The streets were lined with fine-looking four-storey blocks and trams rattled around. More shops now. And a great towering castle that seemed to be sitting in the middle of the river. He took it all in with eyes like saucers.

The hotel was old and magnificent. Not that Danny was in much of a position to make many comparisons because it was the first time he had ever stayed in a hotel of any kind. After training the next day, he was able to spend the whole afternoon walking around the old city with his dad and slowly but surely they put the past behind them as they sat at tables on the pavement outside bars and cafes.

The night before the game, he had his first taste of being prepared for a match as a proper professional. Rowan took them through numerous DVDs which demonstrated the way Wisla Krakow went about their business. Danny was amazed at the detail. The strengths and weaknesses of every player in the squad were picked apart. Their set pieces were examined. The way the full backs liked to overlap. The way they liked to knock the ball around the back four. Patient. Relaxed. Easy and natural on the ball.

An early night had followed, but Danny found sleep to be an impossibility. He lay on his bed and listened to the sound of trams and scooters in the street outside until by two o'clock the city was almost silent. His mind wandered back to all the other sleepless nights he had spent in strange beds. The remand cell at the police station. Prison. Hostels. All those times he had been unable to sleep because of drugs or fear or shame or all three rolled into one. Now it was pure excitement.

He replayed the DVD's they had watched in his head, until by the time a clock outside chimed three he was focused on a single image. Rosinski. The Wisla Krakow sweeper. Tall and elegant. Forty-three caps and only injury had kept him out of the World Cup. He had played in the Bundesliga for three years for F.C.Cologne Whenever they worked their routine of rolling the ball around the back four, Rosinski was always the orchestrator. And when the ball came to him, he seemed to have all the time in the world to decide what to do. Mostly he would simply roll a pass to his right or his left. But sometimes he would look up and throw a forty-yard pass into the feet of one of the strikers. Every inch of the man spoke of complete confidence in what he was doing. And as Danny finally felt his eyes close, he wondered if the man with forty-three caps and four years with Cologne wasn't just a little bit too confident.

The day of the match had passed in a blur. Breakfast. The final training session. The coach ride to the stadium. The dressing-room. A walk out on the pitch to see the open stands which could hold over thirty thousand. The final warm-up session. A last team talk. And then he took his place on the bench with the other substitutes.

The ground was a little over half-full and all of them were made up to see a clutch of 500 flag waving fans who had made the trip from Scotland. It was easy to see how the game was going to go after the first few minutes. The Poles had latched onto the news of the flu outbreak and they started the game at a ferociously high tempo. They could smell blood. Weakness. And they were determined to exploit it.

The pressure on the Gretna goal was instant and enormous and Danny's ears rang with the bellowing noise all around him. It seemed impossible for such a comparatively few fans to produce such a baying barrage of sound. After ten minutes he could see no way that the injury-ravaged men in white shirts could possibly hold out.

But miraculously they did, primarily because the first choice keeper Alan Main had avoided the flu. For a full forty-five minutes he kept out everything that Wisla threw at his goal and as the teams walked off at half time the Poles had a slight anxiety about them.

The team talk at half time was about more of the same. All that was to be done was to keep the shape and give it everything. Five minutes into the second half Rowan got his subs off their seats and told them to take a run up and down the line. This took Danny down to the corner flag and a close up view of the desperate defending that was taking place in the box a few yards away.

Fifty minutes.

Sixty minutes.

Endless, unrelenting pressure. Increasingly desperate now. But still Main kept them out.

Seventy minutes. A double substitution. Two fresh midfielders for two midfielders on the brink of exhaustion. The sky had lost all its light now. The world beyond the harsh brightness of the floodlights was inky black. The sound all around him seemed to grow and grow.

Seventy-eight minutes. A slick Polish one – two on the edge of the box. The centre forward about to spring clear. A desperate lunge made with tired legs. Whistle. Free kick. Inches away from a penalty. A yellow card. Main yelling over the sound of the fans to get his wall into the right place. The number ten poised over the ball. Hardly any run up at all. A perfect connection and the ball looped up and over the wall and beyond the keeper's clawing fingers and into the top corner of the net.

The explosion of sound all around him made Danny feel like he was shrinking. It was terrifying. Almost overwhelming. He felt himself curl into his plastic seat. So very far from the muddy field in Sunnybank with the dog walkers and the dumped needles.

"Danny!"

Rowan had to lean down to make himself heard.

"Go on. Have another run. We might need you if this goes to extra time."

CHAPTER FIVE

It was good to get up. He sprinted up and down the touchline and focused on blocking out the sound. The score board now said eighty-three minutes. Maybe ten minutes to go including stoppage time. Then it would be extra time. Would he get on? Probably not. The manager still had the choice of four other subs, all of them much more experienced than he was.

A corner now. The twenty second Wisla corner in eighty-three minutes. It was high and to the back post and the Gretna centre half rose to head it clear. But the centre half's legs were all but gone by now and his jump barely lifted him clear from the turf. The ball flew two inches over his head to be met by the Wisla number 14 who crashed his header home.

2 – 0

2 – 1 on aggregate. And the Poles were mobbing the goal scorer. And the supporters were all going ballistic. Gretna had lived the dream but now it seemed like it was finally coming to an end.

They took ages to get the game started again and straight away they were piling on the pressure again. Another goal now would kill the game beyond all reach.

eighty-nine minutes. He saw the fourth official getting the board ready. And Rowan was waving him over. As he reached the bench, the board was lifted to show three minutes of stoppage time.

Rowan was the calmest man in the whole stadium.

"OK. On you go Danny. Nothing much to think about. Just get the ball, score and we go through on away goals. Easy as that. It's your moment Danny."

He dragged off his tracksuit in record time and was waved onto the pitch with the scoreboard clock showing two more minutes. By this stage, Wisla had eased off on the pressure. Instead they had decided to keep the ball safe and sound by passing it among themselves. The Gretna players had left everything they had on the pitch. Their legs had nothing left to chase down the ball as the Poles knocked it about between them.

But Danny McCann had watched the DVD. And he had replayed it in his head when it had been impossible to find sleep. So when the right-sided midfielder rolled the ball back to the right back he knew exactly where it would be going next. Suddenly a huge calmness came over him. All the noise from the stands faded to nothing. The game seemed to go into slow motion. The right back waited until a tired white shirt started to close the space on him and then he rolled the ball square to the waiting figure of Rosinski who was running the show. They were killing off the small, amount of time left in the game.

Danny instinctively knew that everything was down to timing. He started his run a fraction of a second before the right back made his pass. As the ball rolled over to Rosinski, Danny closed the space.

By the time the sweeper controlled the ball Danny was almost there. Rosinski looked up for his next pass. Relaxed. Almost casual. Completely assured. And as his eyes looked to pick out a team mate, Danny hit him at full speed.

He focused on going in with only one foot with no studs showing. He went through the sweeper like a combine harvester and left him flat on his back and wondering what on earth had happened. Then Danny was on his feet and bearing down on the goal. The keeper had a look of utter surprise on his face. In ninety-three minutes he hadn't had to make a single save and suddenly he was facing one-on-one. Danny was still wrapped in calm. He knew his legs must be running at full speed, but he felt like he was floating. His brain quietly reflected the words of his manager.

"Your moment Danny."

Over the years to come, when he became a regular in the Scotland side and had helped Gretna to the Scottish Premier League and more trips to Europe, pundits often spoke of his moment. That split second when it all started. The moment that the keeper went down early and Danny effortlessly chipped the ball over him and into the left hand corner of the net. The moment that his team mates had piled on top of him in a great celebrating heap. The moment that the sound of the unbridled joy of the five hundred travelling fans filled the Polish night.

It was the moment that Danny McCann arrived, a moment captured by the TV cameras and replayed many times down the years. And when reporters asked him about the moment, he would always smile and shrug.

What he never spoke about was that the real moment of his life came when an ambulance had made it to the old pavilion in Sunnybank with two minutes to spare. And that Jimmy Doyle had happened to fall down in a playground and broken his finger. And that

CHAPTER FIVE

Brooks Mileson and Rowan Alexander had been willing to give him a break when it seemed like the whole world despised him. These were all things for later. When he was retired and ready to write his autobiography. Then the football world could know how Danny McCann had gone down all the way to the gates of death.

But until that time came, he was quite happy for them to replay those few seconds in Krakow that launched him onto football's great stage.

And just like on the floor of the old pavilion, there had only been two minutes to go.

Stoppage time.

The End

Additional Information

**A FIRST BASE ARTICLE FROM
THE DUMFRIES STANDARD NOVEMBER 2005**

'THE FIRST BASE AGENCY AND GRETNA F.C.
TEAM UP TO GIVE THE DRUGS
INDUSTRY A RUN FOR ITS MONEY'

We hear an awful lot about 'The War on Drugs'. We've heard a lot for the last thirty-five years. As wars go, this has been one of the most prolonged and miserably unsuccessful. All over the world Governments have taken more and more cash from their tax payers and pumped it into the endless battle against a selection of chemicals, most of which come from plants. Last year the total stumped up by the tax payers of the planet was over 65 billion dollars. Yes. As in Billions of dollars. As in enough to stop every famine in the world. As in enough to inoculate every one of the twenty thousand kids who die needlessly every day from perfectly curable diseases. And what return have we all seen for our money? I'm sure you've already guessed the answer. Every year the problem gets bigger and bigger as it spreads like a plague to every corner of the planet.

Of course the idea of a 'War on Drugs' is a somewhat bizarre idea. With the best will in the world, it isn't easy to declare war on plants. F16 fighter jets are hot stuff when it comes to vaporising Iraqi armoured columns but they have a very limited effect when it comes to attacking fields of poppies or coca plants. Likewise the Abrams tank is a fearsome piece of kit when used to flatten buildings in Fallujah, but it struggles to make much of an impact against potted cannabis plants in someone's back bedroom.

Maybe I am being over-flippant in looking at the exact meaning of the words. In reality 'the War on Drugs' is more a war on those who sell drugs. Huge amounts of police and customs time is given over to surveillance and phone tapping and paying informants with a view to crashing down doors in dawn raids and locking up those who profit from selling these illegal chemicals. Prisons all over the world are stuffed to bursting point. And does it make any difference?

Not a jot. Every year we lock away more dealers and every year more drugs are sold.

The truth is that we are attempting to fight a war against a market. A very interesting voice to listen to on this topic is Richard Brunston, the Chief Constable of North Wales. His views are both radical and uncomfortable for the generals in charge of the 'War on Drugs'. He describes a period of his career when he was responsible for policing the Moss Side area on Manchester. During this time he oversaw an operation where a dawn strike put through umpteen front doors and resulted in a high percentage of local dealers being under lock and key by mid-morning. On the surface it was a hugely successful operation. Under the surface it turned out to be a disaster. Why? Basically, he soon realised that all his operation had achieved was to take out those supplying the market not the market itself. There were still hundreds and hundreds of addicts gagging on their next fix. His operation merely put the price up. Remember the supply and demand thing?

Less supply + same demand = up goes the price.

Like Maggie Thatcher said, you can't buck the market. In Moss Side the heroin price went through the roof and of course that meant a huge profit opportunity that others were very interested in. They were so interested in it that they were willing to fight it out. And so it was that Uzi machine guns appeared on the streets of Moss Side for the first time. Richard Brunston's message after this experience is very clear. The war on those who sell drugs is doomed to failure. The only war worth fighting is the war to try and somehow reduce demand. To reduce the market.

Before we even think of trying to reduce demand for illegal drugs it is vitally important that we have a proper understanding and respect for the industry that supplies the ever-growing demand. We like to think of those who deal drugs as the wild-eyed crazies that Hollywood loves to put on our screens. What we hate to admit is what a phenomenally successful operation the illegal drugs industry has become. It is right up there with Shell and Coca Cola and McDonalds. In fact only Microsoft comes close to being in the same league. Some statistics. The top of the league table of world trade. Number one: oil. Number two: weapons. Number three: illegal drugs. Not wheat. Not sugar. Not coffee or alcohol or cars or TVs or clothes. Every year the illegal drugs industry successfully markets $700 billion of its product. The wine industry manages $17 billion. Makes you think doesn't it? This is a blue chip, Rolls Royce of an industry and there is no point in pretending otherwise.

Is it possible to reduce a market? Actually it is. Here are a couple of examples where people weighed up how they were going to spend their money and decided to be more fussy with their shopping. Those of you from my generation will remember how it became more and more unacceptable to buy South African goods for as long as the Apartheid regime kept Nelson Mandela locked up. In the end the South African wine industry couldn't sell a bottle of red at any price and Barclays were losing current account holders hand over fist. The rest, of course, is history and the most famous prisoner in the world walked free and became President of his country. Next example. Genetically modified crops. These were being forced into Europe by the Monsanto Corporation of Arkansas. Now here was a mighty company that had bankrolled Bill Clinton all the way to the White House. Bill did his bit and twisted Tony Blair's arm up to his shoulder blades and Tony did his bit and forced measures through Parliament legalising Monsanto's products. But then it all went wrong. Punters all across Europe made it quite clear they didn't want to buy Frankenstein crops and supermarkets soon realised that GM groceries were a PR disaster. The result? The boats of GM corn and wheat never made it across the Atlantic and Mosanto is still licking its wounds.

So how do we start to eat away at the market of the third biggest industry in the world? Actually, it isn't rocket science. There are two ways. Number one, make it as easy as possible for the drugs industry's best customers to become ex-customers. These customers of course are those who spend £40 and £50 a day to feed their heroin and cocaine habits. Every heroin user we help clear of addiction takes £15,000 of the turnover from the drugs industry. This is why waiting lists of up to six months for treatment are such a disaster.

The second road we can take is by far the most important. We need to persuade the next generation of customers that buying illegal drugs isn't a good idea at all. As in that tired old chestnut, Drugs Education. This of course has been a topic that has been frantically debated for the last three-and-a-half decades. One thing is very clear – just about everything we have tried so far hasn't worked. If it had, the sales of illegal drugs would be falling by now. Again the task that faces us is by no means all that complex. How do we persuade more young people to think twice before they take the plunge and start spending their disposable income on drugs? This is essentially the kind of market analysis exercise that companies carry out all the time. Who are the opposition's customers? What products are they buying? How much are they spending? And absolutely most important of all, why are they buying these products?

So let's take a look at the local market. Dumfries and Galloway has become a Global Drugs Plc flagship when it comes to great marketing. With at least 7% of the 15 to 25 age group already using heroin, all sales targets are being exceeded by a country mile and no doubt the executives in charge are looking forward to a spectacular return on their share options. The question we need to ask is why? Why is Global Drugs Plc having such a bonanza in these parts. Well any marketing man will start at the beginning and ask the customer why they are choosing a particular product. We have given a lot of space on this page to this topic over recent months. Young people are telling us the answer loud and clear if we care to listen to them. They say that they are bored, they have nowhere to go, nothing much to do and they feel increasingly alienated and excluded. If we don't give them a place to take their minds and bodies like a youth club or a skate park, then Global Drugs Plc will give them new places to take their minds on an outing for under a fiver a trip. The whole situation was once put to me with great simplicity by a thirteen-year-old – "Why are there so many bowling clubs in Dumfries and no skate parks?" Why indeed.

It is probably also fair to say the Global Drugs Plc has had more than usual success at making its various products seem cool. In the cities most kids realise that being a heroin addict is anything but cool. It is something they have seen at first hand for years. Locally we haven't reached this stage yet. There are still plenty who are naïve enough to believe that 'smoking some brown' is pretty down and hip. So basically we need to start to try and turn this around and to do it quickly before yet another generation is swallowed up.

Our view at First Base on this is very straightforward. There is little point in standing up in front of young people and saying 'don't do this because it is really very, very naughty and you will be in trouble if you get caught'. It doesn't work. It never has. Ask any parent since the dawn of time. Instead, we try to explain the exact truth about the possible consequences of using illegal drugs. Tell a youngster that if they smoke cannabis they will get addicted and die and they will snigger at our stupidity. Of course they will because it is completely not true. Tell them that mental health wards all over Britain are filling up with teenagers with psychosis and schizophrenia as a result of smoking skunk, and they start to take an interest. Because it IS true. When we go into schools we promise to fill in the ten percent gap that youngsters have in their knowledge of drugs. Much of the ninety percent they know about comes from the drugs industry. This is the cool bit. We consider it our job to tell them about the 10% of nasty stuff that Global Drugs Plc likes to keep quiet. And you know what, they are really interested. Well of course they are. Kids are fascinated by drugs. Look at the DVDs they watch and the Playstation games they play and the music they listen to. Drugs, drugs and more drugs.

Take the example of a best selling American burger company whose name I won't mention because First Base is far too broke to be taken to court. Their adverts show images of lots of trendy people who are tanned and slim and having the absolute time of their lives and completely lovin' it. There is no mention of sky high levels of fat and sugar that lead to compulsive eating and obesity. Obviously there isn't. That is the 10% bit that the well known American burger company likes to keep under wraps

Our job is to publicise the 10% that Global Drugs Plc likes to keep under wraps. We are very well qualified to do this because parents bring in those whose lives are being ripped apart by the 10% bit through our doors every day of the week. It means we are up to date with how things are right here, right now.

So far trying to do this has meant ploughing a rather lonely furrow which at times has seemed pretty hard going. Telling the truth seldom gets much reward. We are the messenger and we seem to get shot on a daily basis! However, as of last week we now have a partner.

The Gretna FC phenomenon has been a story that has almost defied belief. The success of the team has caught the imagination of the football world, especially after Brooks Mileson decided to let the fans in to see last year's cup game with Dundee Utd. free of charge as a thankyou for their support. What is happening off the pitch is if anything even more spectacular. The Gretna philosophy is that a local football club should be actively involved in helping the community from where it draws its fans. This means that a team of Gretna coaches now provides free football coaching to nearly a hundred schools across the region. Now they want to expand and improve this involvement with a major new initiative to try to turn the local tide against Global Drugs Plc and they have signed on The First Base Agency to help with the job. This new initiative was released to the media last week and things will start to happen fast. Mark Frankland is writing a new book called 'Stoppage Time' which will tell the story of how a local 15-year-old footballing prodigy goes from having the world at his feet to seeing his life go into a freefall into the nemesis of addiction and crime before finding redemption through football. The story will be drawn from what is very real in Dumfries and Galloway right now and copies will be distributed free of charge to schools across the region in the spring. Then First Base will be taking our message into more schools alongside the whole of the Gretna team. So basically the furrow that we are ploughing isn't going to be so lonely any more. Now we will be ploughing alongside the fast growing community team of Gretna Football Club and we all believe that together we can be a force to be reckoned with. Our goal is to start giving Global Drugs Plc a run for its money. With luck it won't be very long before its executives start to take a few nervous glances over their shoulders much like those in the boardrooms of the SPL are already looking down the leagues and bracing themselves for the day that the Gretna Express pulls into the station!

A SPOTLIGHT ON CANNABIS: A FIRST BASE
AGENCY ARTICLE FROM THE DUMFRIES STANDARD, 2005

We can learn a lot about the way that society has come to feel about cannabis smoking from the way it is often presented to us. Take the case of T-shirts. It is a common sight on the High Street to see people of both sexes and most ages marching happily along in a T-shirt with a cannabis leaf on the front. Why? What message are they trying to give out about themselves? And what message are we expected to receive? Ever since Woodstock and Dylan and the long hair version Beatles, cannabis has had a Peace and Love and flower power image to it. The person in the T-shirt is saying look at me, I smoke dope which makes it pretty unlikely that I have a Stanley knife on me and I'm not the sort of guy to get in your face and scream "What d'yu think you're looking at pal?" with beery breath. Instead the image is one of a laid-back, thoughtful person who might well watch films with subtitles.

These T-shirts emphasise the fact that cannabis is a plant that has been grown for thousands of years and is very much a part of nature. Fair enough. And yet few other substances seem to able to make this link and get away with it. We see people in Jack Daniels and Budweiser T-shirts, but I am yet to see anyone with a picture of some ears of barley emblazoned over their chest. Similarly if our local hero-in users took to the High Street in T-shirts with pictures of nice colourful Afghan poppies I don't think it would be all that well received by the public at large. Maybe the poppy is after all a more wicked type of flora than the cannabis leaf.

If it is not a cannabis leaf that is on display, it is often a burning joint. Again the message is meant to be fairly cosy; the wearer of this T-shirt likes to smoke an illegal substance but that only goes to show he has a heart of gold. Again a picture of a needle poised over a vein or a nose hovering over a line of coke would not be T-shirt acceptable.

Of course the reason why dope smokers wear leaf pictures whilst lager drinkers wouldn't dream of adorning themselves in grain images is easy to find. Drinking lager is perfectly legal so long as you are over eighteen, which means that the drink itself isn't remotely cool. It is the label that can be cool which is why the drinks industry spends endless millions on trying to make their brands give out the right messages. There are no cannabis brands. Only the plant itself, so when the cannabis smoker wears the T-shirt, their message is that yes, I may not carry a knife but I'm not boring because I break the law on a regular basis.

Is this relevant? Scotland and Holland, compare and contrast. Both are North European countries with a population of about five million. In Holland, once you reach a certain age it is OK to go into a cannabis café and choose your dope from a menu. In Scotland dope smoking is illegal even if you are a hundred years old. The result? In Holland, 5% of the 15 to 30 age group regularly smoke cannabis. In Scotland the figure is double that. 10%. So the place where it is illegal under all circumstances has twice the number of regular smokers. Why? Maybe it is only the fact that cannabis is illegal that makes it cool. Dutch youngsters look through the doors of a cannabis café and see people like their parents inside. Nothing cool about that. I don't suppose you would make much of a fortune peddling cannabis T-shirts in Amsterdam.

The way we see dope smoking on television is also interesting. Those shown having a joint are generally characterised as mildly goofy figures, but good old boys at heart. It isn't all that different to the way that drunk people are portrayed. Somebody who is falling down drunk is fair game for comedy. Similarly, someone who is stoned and giggling is often seen as amusing. And yet when we see the needle being pressed home or the cocaine going up the nose it needs to be well after the watershed and we are warned that we are about to watch 'scenes of drug use'. The unmistakable conclusion that many young people draw from all of this is that cannabis really is pretty well OK and that is why the government has finally seen sense and downgraded it from a Class B drug to Class C. Surely over the next few years they will at last see sense and make it legal alongside the other legally available drugs, alcohol and tobacco.

On the surface, the arguments in favour of cannabis being acceptable are quite compelling, especially when it is compared with fags and booze. Here are the bare bones. Cigarettes. Smoked by fifteen million Brits. Fiercely addictive. Responsible for 100,000 deaths per year. Alcohol. Used by over fifty million Brits. Fiercely addictive. Responsible for 30,000 deaths a year and 75% of all violent crime. Cannabis. Used by between five and fifteen million Brits. Non-addictive. Responsible for no deaths per year. No link with violence. On the basis of this information, many feel that any sane Government would rush to legalise cannabis and ban booze and fags. In 2000 the Eindhoven Council was facing a rough couple of days. The small Dutch town was battening down the hatches and bracing itself for an invasion of thirty thousand English football fans and they feared it would be like a human version of hurricane Katrina. They dealt with the threat by offering short term licences for many of the town's bars to sell cannabis and the visiting fans all got well and truly stoned and went round hugging the locals rather than head butting them. The Council were so pleased with the result that they passed the information to the Council of the small Belgian town, Charlerloi, which was the next port of call for the travelling fans. The Belgians took no heed of the advice and the fans got drunk instead of stoned and the town was duly smashed to pieces. When we watch pictures of our Saturday night town centres on the TV, it is hard not to have some appreciation of the Eindhoven solution. The UN has recently voted Scotland the most violent country in the developed world and that is not a result of cannabis smoking.

I can sense that many reading this must now be getting hot under the collar and about to toss the paper across the room in anger. Are these First Base people using this space to extol the virtues of the weed?

Actually, we're not.

Honest.

The first part of this article has been an attempt to show just how much confusion now surrounds the whole issue of cannabis. On the one hand the Government says it really might not be so bad after all so we will downgrade it. On the other hand the police still have the power to lock us up for a decent period of time if they catch us with a lump in our pocket. In the middle of all this, it gets pretty difficult for parents in particular to know where to start when it comes to talking to our children. If we start to tell them things that are completely untrue they will simply switch off. This is where we tend to go wrong. If we say something along the lines of 'if you smoke cannabis you will get addicted and die' they will immediately switch off on us completely because they know full well that it simply isn't true. That is why it is important to talk in facts and not in myths and media hype. So here are a few facts which when added together make not smoking cannabis seem a pretty good idea.

1: The legal stuff. It is important to remember that all the news stories about it being OK to smoke a joint refer to England NOT Scotland. Being picked up with a lump of cannabis in your pocket in Dumfries means something very different to having the same thing happen in Carlisle. The police line here is very simple. If you get caught the cannabis will be confiscated, you will be charged, and the matter will be referred to the Procurator Fiscal. If the issue goes all the way to the Sheriff you will end up with a record for being caught in possession of drugs. With the best will in the world, this isn't the best thing to have on your CV. If you're expecting a copper to give you an avuncular wink and send you on your way, well don't hold your breath.

2: Exams. Even the most ardent cannabis fan wouldn't try to claim that smoking dope makes the brain work like a Rolls Royce. Basically cannabis and exams mix about as happily as Celtic and Rangers fans. You might have read about the school down in Kent where they have introduced random drugs testing amidst a blaze of publicity. The trial has now been running for a year and some results are starting to emerge. Last year, before the testing, 22% of pupils achieved five good GSEs or better. This year the figure has risen to over 40%. Same school, same teachers, same subjects. The difference? Cannabis stays in the system for up to thirty-five days so it looks like the kids in Kent decided to play it safe and stop the joints.

3: Avoiding brain damage. This is a secret that at last seems to be making its way out from under the carpet. For thousands of years human beings have smoked the cannabis plant without doing any great harm to ourselves. In fact these are the kinds of varieties that many would now like to see licensed for medicinal use. The problem we now face is that many of the varieties of cannabis bear no relationship to the stuff that Dylan and the Beatles took on board. Like many other plants, cannabis has fallen into the hands of the scientists who have done their stuff and genetically modified new superstrength varieties that are generally called 'skunk'. People smoke cannabis to alter their brains into a different shape where things seem funny and food tastes great. Skunk alters the brain a whole lot more than the regulation product which is why it commands a premium. Unfortunately we are now finding that skunk can alter a young brain all the way to psychosis and schizophrenia. Since the drug was reclassified a couple of years ago in England, we have seen cannabis related admissions to psychiatric units quadruple. I'll say that again. Quadruple. As in scary, scary. Research into this new phenomenon is in its infancy, but it appears that the developing brains of adolescents are horribly vulnerable to skunk. Think of a tree. If you have a swing at a hundred-year-old oak tree with an axe, you really won't do it much harm. But if you clobber the same tree when it is just a year old sapling you will probably kill it. The growing number of young people who now have serious mental health problems as a result of smoking skunk is a new nightmare that we will all come to know more and more about over the next few years.

4: Depression. It is important to remember that what cannabis does is enhance the way you already feel. So a mildly amusing joke suddenly becomes the funniest thing you've ever heard. A banana milkshake, which normally tastes pretty good, suddenly seems as if it has been beamed straight down from somewhere in heaven. What people forget to mention is that this swings both ways. So if you are feeling a bit down and you decide a joint might make the world a brighter place, then think again. All it will do is change feeling a bit gloomy into full on depression and the more you smoke the worse it will get. We see a lot of depressed youngsters who keep trying to smoke themselves happy and only make it worse.

5: The 'gateway drug'. Start smoking cannabis and you'll end up on heroin. We hear a lot of this and there is barely a shred of evidence to back it up. In Holland where smoking cannabis is acceptable they have about 8,000 heroin addicts. We have 65,000. A pretty compelling statistic. However there is plenty of evidence that shows that smoking cannabis is indeed a gateway to the number one killer drug of them all. Lots of young people successfully stay clear of smoking cigarettes. Then they start smoking joints and find that they need more and more. It takes a while for the penny to drop. It isn't the cannabis their body is craving. It is the nicotine which of course IS very addictive. So they start buying cigarettes instead.

Hopefully these are five reasons for youngsters to think long and hard before saying yes to a joint. Permanent brain damage really isn't very cool no matter how you try to dress it up. Skunk is very, very dangerous and the sooner we all wake up to the fact, the better..

A FIRST BASE ARTICLE FROM
THE DUMFRIES STANDARD NOVEMBER 2005

VALIUM — GOING ROUND THE BENZO WITH SCRAPPY DO

When it comes to grabbing most of the pages dedicated to the media's coverage of drugs, heroin and cocaine tend to rather hog the limelight. On occasions, other drugs can muscle in on the scene and enjoy fifteen minutes of fame for awhile.

Many of us will remember the media frenzy that accompanied the tragic death of Leah Betts ten years ago when she died as a result of taking an ecstasy tablet at her 16th birthday party. Over recent months, cannabis has enjoyed a star billing as numerous academic reports have firmed up the link between the world's oldest narcotic and the very new phenomenon of teenagers being admitted to acute psychiatric wards with cannabis induced schizophrenia and psychosis. And, if we all watch this space, it is a racing certainty that over the next year or two the tabloids will be getting themselves onto a bird fluesque state of excitement and horror as Methamphetamine starts its inevitable spread out of London and across the rest of Britain and starts to wreak its own very unique brand of havoc. However as time rolls on those two old favourites, heroin and cocaine, always nudge their way back to the front of the crowd and smile for the cameras.

We have spent many words in this column over the last year talking about the particular problem that Dumfries and Galloway has with heroin and I don't suppose that there are many in the community who don't know that our region has become one of the worst affected in Europe .

I suppose this is why there was such surprise in the room at a recent presentation I gave to a community group at the answer I gave to a particular question.

"Which do you think is the worst drug?"

"Everywhere or in Dumfries and Galloway?"

"Here. Dumfries and Galloway."

"And do you mean in terms of killing people or in terms of causing chaos and misery?"

"Both."

"OK. The worst killer drug is tobacco, but you know that. The worst for causing chaos and misery is booze, but I guess you know that as well. Anyway, they are both legal. I expect you are asking about illegal drugs, yes?"

A nod from the questioner.

"Valium. As is illegally sold street valium." And it caused looks of surprise and a general shaking of heads. Not heroin. Not cocaine. But valium. It is a statement that I am more than happy to stand by and since that meeting things have only got worse.

For me, mention of "blues" will always shovel up images from Quadrophenia — scooters and parkas and Mods and Rockers knocking ten bells out of each other on the beach at Brighton.I suppose that it just goes to show that "blues" ("blues" because 10mg valium pills area blue colour) have been part of British nightlife culture for getting on for half a century now. Valium has always played a part in what you could call a Grand old Duke of York-style of drug taking. With speed, and more recently ecstasy, he marches his men up to the top of the hill, and with blues, jellies and Moggies he marches them back down again.

Diazepam is still a drug more normally associated with the GP's surgery than the streets. It is prescribed by doctors to patients who are anxious, stressed out or depressed.How very strange then that this rather staid drug is causing such general mayhem on the streets of Dumfries and Galloway.

Blues, Yellows, Benzos, Vallies, Scoobies,Scrappy Dos, there are lots and lots of colourful names, but call it what you like, it seems to be on sale around every corner for a quid per pill. So why has this happened and why is it escalating so quickly?

STOPPAGE TIME

Up until relatively recently, the only way that valium could find its way onto the illegal drug market was if it was stolen from a pharmacy, hospital, or the medicine cupboard of someone with a prescription, or if someone sold on their prescription. All of this guaranteed that the volume of illegal pills up for sale was pretty well capped. Those days are long gone. Science has moved the world along in just the same way as it has moved it along in every other walk of life. Fake pills are manufactured by the thousand in small illegal laboratories, mainly in Pakistan.

I just tapped the word "valium" into the Googlesearch engine. Nought point two seconds later it proudly informed me that the page on view gave the first ten of 5,070,000 hits. C l i c k . . . Lo-and-behold, I'm on a website offering me 5010 mg Roche blue valium pills for $179.00 delivered by air mail in ten working day s .It's that easy. Remember this is a Class A drug that can get you some serious prison time for possessing it and seriously, serious prison time for dealing it. This works out at something like £2.30 a pill which is much higher that you would pay on the streets of Dumfries and Galloway. OK. So it's cheap and it's as easily available as a pint of milk at the corner shop. Probably more so. You can only get a pint of milk from a couple of 24 hour shops and garages at 3 a.m. but you'd find plenty who are open all hours to sell you 20 vallies .

But how widespread is it? I don't suppose anyone really knows, but I had a young lad into see me a few weeks ago who told me that his pal was making a clear £400 profit per day from selling va l i u m .Maybe this was a little exaggerated, but I got the strong impression that the story was true. It meant that one eightee n-year-old lad was selling eight hundred pills a day. Eight hundred! And that is just one lad. I guess you're getting the picture. We haven't just got a trickle of valium being sold. It's a flood.

So how much of aproblem is it? Surely valium is a drug designed to mellow people out when they are wrapped far too tight. Maybe youngsters might be better necking a few blues rather than a bottle of Buckfast. Sadly not. Valium is designed to help with short-term anxiety at a rate of about a couple of pills a day or so. It was never designed to be taken by the handful. It basically blocks off the receptors in the brain that register such emotions as fear and nervousness. However if you take enough of it, it blocks off a whole lot more than that. The brain basically starts to get into a complete muddle, especially when a few drinks are thrown into the mix. Normal situations get distorted. Is that bloke staring at me? What's his problem? He's talking about me now? What's he saying . . . that's why they call it Scrappy Do. Lots of fighting over nothing. Lots of smashed windows and doors. And faces.

The problem is made worse because many ofthe fake "pound a go" pills may look like the same thing but are entirely different. Some are 95 per cent diazepam, some are 65 percent, some have no diazepam at all. A tenner's worth one day gives the brain 95mg. The next day none whatsoever.

A few months ago there were lots of fakes kicking around the town with 'RIMA' stamped on them. They were a slightly darker blue, slightly more speckled, and slightly thicker than the prescribed version. They actually had no valium in them whatsoever. Instead they were made up of Nitrazepan and Promethezine — sleeping pills and travel sickness pills that pull the brain in all directions.

Take a few of these one day, a few regular blues the next day, and wash it all down with a few drinks and what is going to happen? Without getting too technical, you're likely go into the library and ask for a loaf of bread. The scientists haven't even started to do the research into what the consequences are of people taking such huge quantities of blues day in, day out. Something tells me that it won't be anything good.

There are several very important issues that we all need to be aware of. First, when the brain is pulled in all these different directions, acute paranoia and aggression tend to come to the fore. We have seen many clients who we have come to know as quiet, gentle people completely transformed by 20 valium a day.

It is a real Jekyll and Hyde drug and there are a growing number of Mr Hyde-like characters. The United Nations recently named Scotland as the most violent country in Europe and you can be pretty sure that millions of valium pills are playing a major part in this. If someone close to you is taking high levels, then you need to be careful. They may have always been a really kind and placid person who wouldn't harm a fly but a handful of vallies a day can soon change all that.Remember Jekyll and Hyde and tread carefully. Saying the wrong thing at the wrong moment can set the fists flying. And when their head clears the next day they won't remember a thingand they will be at a complete loss as to why they could possibly have behaved like that.

Secondly, valium at high levels is fiercely addictive.Physically addictive.You can't just stop and go "cold turkey". If you do, you run the risk of taking an epileptic fit. If anyone close to you is using lots of pills a day make sure you mug up on what to do if they start fitting.

Thirdly, a pound a pill is cheap enough to be affordable to children. Why would they try and go and buy a tube of glue or lighter fluid for £3 or £4 when the same amount of cash buys a handful of pills from someone who is never going to ask them for proof of their age. Those who sell the pills don't care much what age their customers are. All they are bothered about is the colour of their money. Sadly the flood of the illegally sold "pound a pill" valium is a very real problem and one that is growing every day and leading to more and more violence on the streets and in the home. It is a desperately dangerous drug when taken in high quantities and we all need to be aware of it.

As ever, if you want any more information or if you are worried about someone close to you, don't hesitate to call us on 01387 279 680.

GOOD GUYS AND BAD GUYS AND TRYING TO TELL THEM APART: A FIRST BASE AGENCY ARTICLE FROM 'DUMFRIES BY NIGHT', SEPTEMBER 2005

Think onion. And think layers. Down and down you go with your eyes filling up with tears as each layer comes off to reveal the one underneath. It is the same with the heroin story, only the tears are a different kind.

Layer one. User. This is generally someone who has had something or other really bad happen in their life and a helpful mate has suggested some medication that keeps all the nightmares away. And it costs a tenner a go. Smack. 'H'. Kit. Brown. Whatever. About one-fifth Diamorphine and four-fifths of whatever is kicking around in the dealer's kitchen that looks about right. Good guy or bad guy?

Layer two. The street dealer. This is usually the guy at layer one plus three or four years. By this time the medication is costing £40 a day and shoplifting is a big no-no. So how to make the £40 a day with no job? You deal to a few mates and cover your own habit out of the profits. Good guy or bad guy?

Layer Three. The guy who brings the stuff into town. In the eyes of the public this guy usually seems pretty stand up. Maybe he'll play golf. Maybe he'll have a shop or something. There will be a nice car and nice house and nice kids going to a nice school. And nice holidays and nice donations to nice charities given with a nice smile. (No. He won't have to wait for a NHS dentist) As a rule these guys wouldn't touch a bag of smack in a million years. They are business-men on the greatest gravy train since the Klondike gold rush. Good guy or bad guy?

Layer four. The nation-wide wholesaler. A couple of hundred years ago the British Empire sent raw materials from all over the world to the UK to be made into finished products in new-fangled buildings called factories. It was called the Industrial Revolution and one city more than any other built up expertise in importing and distributing. It's the one with Pier Head and the Liver Building and the newly crowned Champions of Europe. Liverpudlian importers learned their trade on sugar and slaves, then they moved on to cotton and bananas. Now they distribute most of the UK's heroin. Good guys or bad guys?

Layer Five. The shipper. As often as not this guy will be Turkish. Like his Liverpudlian colleague, he will be drawing on a long, long tradition. In his case the tradition goes back not hundreds of years, but thousands. The produce of the East was flowing through Turkish merchants when Alexander the Great was in his prime. Spices, silks, heroin. It's all the same. Commodities that we in the west want and those in the east produce.

Layer six. The feudal baron. This guy will be an Afghan. Almost all of the heroin that hits our streets starts in an Afghani poppy field. To get a handle on this guy, you need to think Robin Hood films and think Sheriff of Nottingham. He will have a bunch of lads around him all armed to the teeth and he will rule the roost over a couple of hundred square miles of countryside. Any poppy farmer who doesn't sell their crop to him gets a bullet in the back of the neck. It is called a closed market. These chaps had a torrid time of it in the nineties. That was because the Taliban took control of things in Afghanistan and they believed that growing poppies for heroin was against the Koran. So they started putting bullets through the back of the Feudal Barons' heads. But in 2001 it all came good again. Some crazy guys drove some planes into American buildings and the good and the great decided that the Taliban had to go. So the feudal barons were all signed up by the CIA to join the great crusade and their part of the bargain was that they got their old business back. The Taliban were duly kicked out and this year's poppy crop will break all records. One of these gallant friends of America, Tony Blair and the free world, now has 4,000 tonnes of pure heroin in his warehouse. It is enough to keep Great Britain going for the next forty-five years. It has a street value of two hundred billion pounds. Good guy or bad guy?

Layer seven. Grower. This guy will have a wife and a few kids and a pretty dour sort of a house. If he grows anything other than poppies he will get shot through the back of the head. So he grows poppies and if he is lucky he'll make enough for the family to eat. He works fifteen hours a day and he will probably have never watched a television in his life. Good guy or bad guy?

Answers. Who the hell knows? Maybe you're a bad guy unless you might be of use in the War on Terror?

Some Useful Numbers

CHILDLINE

Free counselling, information and advice to help children and young people to cope in very different situations.

> FREEPHONE   0800 1111
> 24 Hours a day, 7 days a week

The NSPCC's National Child Protection Helpline is aimed at those who are concerned that a young person is at risk. Children and Young People who need help can also call.

> FREEPHONE   0808 800 500
> TEXTPHONE   0800 056 0566
> 24 Hours a day, 7 days a week

PARENTLINE

For parents who need support
> FREEPHONE   0808 800 222

DRINKLINE

For confidential information and advice on alcohol

> FREEPHONE   0800 917 8282
> 9 a.m. – 11p.m. / 24 Hours at weekends

KNOW THE SCORE

Free confidential information and advice on drugs

> FREEPHONE   0800 587 5879

GAMCARE

Free confidential information and advice on gambling:

HELPLINE   0845 600013

EATING DISORDER ASSOCIATION

Callers are offered advice, guidance and support. Advisors can provide a signposting service to other agencies:

HELPLINE   01603 621414
             9 a..m. – 6 p.m.
YOUTHLINE   01603 765 0504
             4 p..m. – 6 p..m.

If you find yourself low, stressed or anxious about things, or even if you have a friend who may be feeling like this, them these websites may be able to help:

www.livinglifetothefull.com

www.streeandanxietyinteenagers.com

www.justlikeme.org.uk

www.thecalmzone.net

Other titles by Mark Frankland

**To order copies please
complete the order form
at the back of the book
or tel. 01387 270 861**

**All prices include P&P
to customers in the UK**

www.thecull.com

RED ZONE
MARK FRANKLAND

*6000 Asylum Seekers are housed in the giant
tower blocks of Sighthill in Glasgow. A vast
unexploded human bomb. The clock is ticking . . .*

**To order a copy complete
the order form at the back of the book
or tel. 01387 270 861**

£6.99 plus £1.00 P&P

Red Zone
by Mark Frankland

"An unrelenting pile driver of a read"

An asylum seeker goes berserk on the late night streets of Sighthill.

Three local teenagers are hacked to death. The worst riot Glasgow has seen in a generation rages through the night.

The Israeli Defence Forces stage a dawn raid on a house in Gaza City and capture one of the PLO's most senior fighters.

Two events that by pure accident happen within hours of each other. Two events that are in no way related. Two events in two cities thousands of miles apart.

But they become related, and the fifty year war between the Israelis and the Palestinians is brought to the towering blocks of Glasgow's Sighthill Estate.

"You watch pictures from Gaza and the West Bank and you think it could never come here. Then you read this book and you think again."

To order a copy complete
the order form at the back of the book
or tel. 01387 270 861

£6.99 plus £1.00 P&P

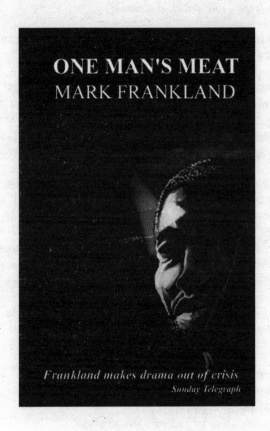

**To order a copy complete
the order form at the back of the book
or tel. 01387 270 861**

£5.99 plus £1.00 P&P

One Man's Meat
by Mark Frankland

*"Fast, furious and you never know
what is waiting around the next corner."*

Cornelius St John and Vincent Allenby run a very strange
business. They solve people's problems: for a price.
Sometimes the solution is to be found within the law.
Sometimes they break a rule or two.

They enjoy a certain discreet reputation within certain circles.

So when Sir Alistair McIntyre comes to call they are all ears.
McIntyre is one of the richest men in Britain and
he offers then their biggest ever problem to solve.
The job is huge. But then again, so is the prize.

As their work takes them from Argentina to Matebeleland
to the windswept Scottish hills, it soon becomes clear that
the stakes are rising higher and faster than anyone expected.

And what starts as a problem
to solve becomes a fight for survival.

*"A page-turner plus. You're well
and truly hacked off when it finishes."*

**To order a copy complete
the order form at the back of the book
or tel. 01387 270 861**

£5.99 plus £1.00 P&P

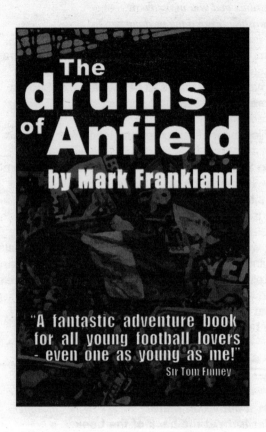

The
drums
of Anfield
by Mark Frankland

"A fantastic adventure book
for all young football lovers
- even one as young as me!"
Sir Tom Finney

**To order a copy complete
the order form at the back of the book
or tel. 01387 270 861**

£4.99 plus £1.00 P&P

The Drums of Anfield
by Mark Frankland

"A fantastic adventure book for all young
football lovers – even one as young as me!"
Sir Tom Finney

Once in every generation a great new star emerges
into the world of football. Out of the slums of Sao Paulo
came Pele. Out of the bullet-scarred streets of Belfast
came Georgie Best. Out of the shanty towns of Buenos Aires
came Maradona. When Liverpool's veteran captain,
Tony Hobbes, suffers a crippling injury and receives a long
ban for violent conduct, he decides to take his son to Africa.

He expects to find lions and elephants amidst the Dark
Continent's endless wild plains. Instead, far away in the East
of Uganda under the shadow of the Mountains of the Moon,
he finds a boy called Simon Matembo. He knows that the
boy's talent is so huge that he could become the greatest
of them all. He knows that this boy can take Liverpool back
to the great days. But first he has to find a way to take him
back, and to do this he must overcome many huge challenges
from the tribe, the club, and even the forces of nature.

"Anyone who loves football will love this book.
Football is about passion, unrelenting excitement
and, more than anything else, it is about dreams.
Exactly the same can be said about 'The Drums of Anfield".
Gerry Marsden, from 'Gerry and the Pacemakers'

"Genuinely hard to put down", **FourFourTwo Magazine**

**To order a copy complete
the order form at the back of the book
or tel. 01387 270 861**

£4.99 plus £1.00 P&P

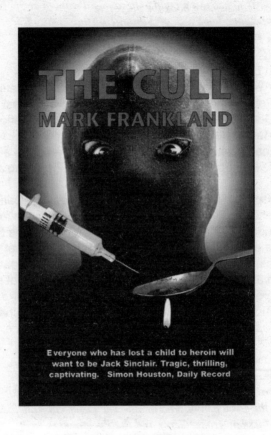

Everyone who has lost a child to heroin will
want to be Jack Sinclair. Tragic, thrilling,
captivating.   Simon Houston, Daily Record

**To order a copy complete
the order form at the back of the book
or tel. 01387 270 861**

£5.99 plus £1.00 P&P

The Cull
by Mark Frankland

'Everyone who has lost a child to heroin will want to be Jack Sinclair. Tragic, thrilling, captivating' **Simon Houston, Daily Record**

'Mark lifts the lid on Drug Town' **Sunday Post**

Will Sinclair is dead. It seems as if he will be just another statistic. Another young man dead before he reaches twenty. Another Scottish junkie unlucky enough to shoot up a bad bag of heroin. A few column inches in the local paper. Ten seconds on the radio news. And then he will be added to the long, long list. Just another dead junkie

But this time it is different. It is different because Jack Sinclair will not accept his son's loss with resigned grief. He refuses to forgive and forget. He was once Major Jack Sinclair of the Scots Guards. In three tours of Northern Ireland he learned all about fighting an unseen enemy. Then there were rules. Regulations. Restrictions. Red tape. His war against the drugs gangs who killed his son will be very different. This time the gloves are off. This time he has a free rein

As Jack Sinclair lights his small fire, the story sweeps from the empty wilderness of the Galloway Forest to the war-torn streets of West Belfast, from the mean council estates of South West Scotland to the Cabinet Room of 10 Downing Street. And the fire becomes an inferno.

To order a copy complete
the order form at the back of the book
or tel. 01387 270 861

£5.99 plus £1.00 P&P

**To order a copy complete
the order form at the back of the book
or tel. 01387 270 861**

£6.99 plus £1.00 P&P

Terrible Beauty by Mark Frankland

" Gripping and horribly realistic." **Glasgow Evening Times**

It is the story of the making of an outrage. An outrage which will be the greatest of them all. An outrage that will make Omagh and Enniskillen look like mere sideshows. An outrage that will blow the Good Friday Agreement into a million pieces.

It is the story of two men from West Belfast. It is the story of how their lives are swallowed up by the endless war of their peoples. Sean O'Neil travels the road of the IRA. For Davie Stanton it is the British Army and the UVF. Their journey carries them through thirty years of pain – Burntollet, the riots of 1969, the Battle of Ballymurphy, Internment, Bloody Sunday, Warrenpoint, The Hunger Strike, Loughgall.

Slowly their lives become intertwined. They become puppets in the dark game where their strings are pulled by the shadowy forces of the British Security Forces. And their destiny becomes one. In the end one man can no longer stand the Peace that he sees to be a lie. The Peace he sees a betrayal of his people. He plans an act so appalling that the fragile Peace will be shattered beyond repair. And there is only one man in the world who can stop him.

"A compelling read. Terrible Beauty is lovingly written, imbued with compassion, humanity, and great attention to detail. It will keep the reader entranced from the moment they pick it up." **An Phoblacht – Republican News**

"This book identifies the murky world of terrorism, it also shows how in more cases than not, an incident opens the path towards violence." **David Ervine – Leader of the Progressive Unionist Party**

"Frankland shows insight and authority about the perennial problems of the Province. It is also a rivetingly good read!" **Rt Hon Sir Robert Atkins MEP, Minister of State, Northern Ireland Office, 1992 – 1994**

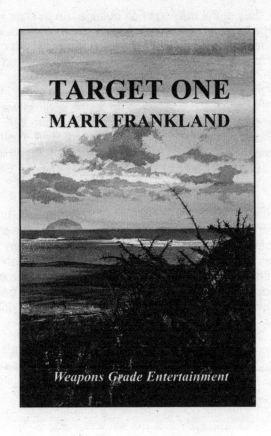

**To order a copy complete
the order form at the back of the book
or tel. 01387 270 861**

£6.99 plus £1.00 P&P

Target One by Mark Frankland

'A head-spinning "Day of the Jackal" for the Twenty-First century. The pages almost turn themselves'

Roland McMillan is 95 years old and his doctors see little chance of him making it to 96. In 1926 he fled the desperate misery of his life in the mining town of Kirkonnel and emigrated to America. Over 79 years he has built up a colossal family fortune. Now it is time to tidy up his affairs.

McMillan's greatest treasure is his gallery of paintings which is reputed to be the most valuable and extensive private collection in the world. He has always known that one day he will bequeath it to the nation. The question he needs to resolve is which nation – Should it be Scotland, the land that bore him? Or should it be America, the land that made him?

His solution is an old-fashioned one. The fate of the McMillan collection is to be decided by a game of golf played by modern day gladiators. America's number one golfer will challenge Scotland's number one over Turnberry's majestic Ailsa course for the greatest prize in the history of sport.

George Albright the Third is one of the greatest sportsmen America has ever produced. A world figure. A sporting icon. The undisputed Number One in the world with a fortune fit for a king to his name. to his name. Archie Banks is an unknown. A hard-smoking, hard-drinking nobody from ttorious Sunnybank estate in Dumfries who is only his country's number one as a result of a fluky streak of results.

The twenty-first century version of David and Goliath catches the imagination of the world and sends the lives of both players into chaos. It is an event that everyone wants a piece of. Even the American President will be there to watch.

As the eyes of the world are fixed on the event, unwanted guests plan a dramatic intervention. When the news of the President's intentions reaches Al Quaida, they put in place a plan to assassinate their TARGET ONE.

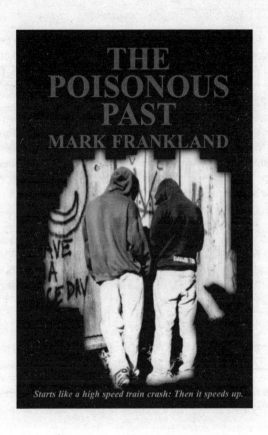

Starts like a high speed train crash: Then it speeds up.

**To order a copy complete
the order form at the back of the book
or tel. 01387 270 861**

£6.99 plus £1.00 P&P

The Poisonous Past by Mark Frankland

"This book is about why people take to the streets and throw stones. Like they did in the sixties. And the eighties. It's about how far some people will go when they get angry. And how far other people will go to stop them.'

South Yorkshire. 1984: Lenny Baxter and over 150 thousand coal miners take on the Conservative Govern-ment in a long awaited showdown. What starts as a strike is soon more like a war. Yorkshire becomes a near police state as the Government takes off the gloves and starts to fight dirty. And Lenny Baxter becomes the most hunted man in Britain.

Scotland. 2005: Once again Lenny goes to war. This time in a small Scottish town. And once again he finds the dark forces of the State deployed to meet him.

Lenny's journey spans the eras. From the burning sun of Orgreave to the killing fields of Iraq. From Reagan to Bush. From Thatcher to Blair. From the Cold War to the War on Terror.

From its shocking start to the nerve-shredding finale, The Poisonous Past takes the reader to the darkest corners of British life. It is a story from the places far away from the glossy image of Great Britain Plc. The sink estates, the baseball caps and hood-ies. Discarded needles and burnt out cars. And the faceless man in anonymous offices whose job is to make sure the lid stays on . . .

"Here is a book that challenges our assumptions. The assumption that young people don't rebel any more. The assumption that their only icon is the Nike tick. The assumption that the Multinationals and the politicians they pay for will always win"

**To order a copy complete
the order form at the back of the book
or tel. 01387 270 861**

£6.99 plus £1.00 P&P

THE LONG AND WINDING ROAD TO ISTANBUL

MARK FRANKLAND

A Mersey Gone With the Wind that races like a high speed bullet train all the way from Rome 1977 to Istanbul 2005.

**To order a copy complete
the order form at the back of the book
or tel. 01387 270 861**

£6.99 plus £1.00 P&P

The Long and Winding Road to Istanbul
by Mark Frankland

"Putting this book down would be like switching off the TV during the second half in Istanbul. It's just not an option."
Ian Callaghan. Liverpool FC legend

25 May 1977

On the day of Liverpool's first European Cup final in Rome, the destinies of two families become intertwined. The Tates and the McGuires; same neighbourhood, different sides of the track. The Tates are the notorious ones and twenty-year-old Eddie Tate is on the fast track to the top of the Merseyside underworld. At thirteen his youngest sister Lucy is beginning to realise what it means to have Tate as her second name. Frank McGuire is about to leave school for the growing dole queue and sees Eddie as his way out. So when Eddie needs a small lad to go through a chemist's window, Frank press gangs his little brother Mickey for the job. What starts off as a simple burglary sets of a chain of events that span twenty-eight years and five European Cup Finals.

25 May 2005

Eddie Tate has become the undisputed king of the Liverpool drugs trade and Frank McGuire is his feared enforcer. Lucy Tate has left her family and past far behind to become a BBC reporter. Mickey McGuire's life has been a story of endless decline and failure. He goes from underachieving pupil, to minor rock star, to drug addict, to prisoner to a hospital porter. Like his beloved Liverpool FC, it seems like he is all washed up. Then against all odds, he is offered one last chance to turn it all around. To take his chance he needs to make it to the Champions League Final in Turkey. To raise the cash he crosses Eddie Tate and as the great red crusade heads south, death waits round every corner on Mickey's road to Istanbul . . .

"A story of red blooded passion and Turkish delight."
John Keith – Writer and broadcaster

**To order a copy complete
the order form at the back of the book
or tel. 01387 270 861**

£6.99 plus £1.00 P&P

Order Form

Name ---------------------------------------

Address ---------------------------------------

Telephone ---------------------------------------

Email ---------------------------------------

Please send me ----------------- Copies of

Please send me ----------------- Copies of

I enclose a cheque for ---------------------------

Please make cheques payable to:
'Glenmill Publishing'

Return this form to:

Glenmill Publishing
Glenmill
Dumfries
DG2 8PX

Or Telephone   01387 270 861